D0015774

The DEATHWATCH BEETLE

Also by Kjell Eriksson

The Night of the Fire

Stone Coffin

Open Grave

Black Lies, Red Blood

The Hand That Trembles

The Demon of Dakar

The Cruel Stars of the Night

The Princess of Burundi

The DEATHWATCH BEETLE

A MYSTERY

Kjell Eriksson

Translated from the Swedish by Paul Norlen

MINOTAUR BOOKS
NEW YORK

This is a work of fiction. All of the characters, organizations, and events portrayed in this novel are either products of the author's imagination or are used fictitiously.

First published in the United States by Minotaur Books, an imprint of St. Martin's Publishing Group

THE DEATHWATCH BEETLE. Copyright © 2021 by Kjell Eriksson. Translation copyright © 2021 by Paul Norlen. All rights reserved. Printed in the United States of America. For information, address St. Martin's Publishing Group, 120 Broadway, New York, NY 10271.

www.minotaurbooks.com

Library of Congress Cataloging-in-Publication Data

Names: Eriksson, Kjell, 1953- author. | Norlén, Paul R., translator.
Title: The deathwatch beetle : a mystery / Kjell Eriksson ; translated from the Swedish by Paul Norlen.
Other titles: Dödsuret. English
Description: First U.S. edition. | New York : Minotaur Books, 2021. | Series: Ann Lindell mysteries ; 9 | "Originally published in Sweden by Ordfront förlag under the title Dödsuret"
Identifiers: LCCN 2021021936 | ISBN 9781250766168 (hardcover) | ISBN 9781250766175 (ebook)
Subjects: GSAFD: Mystery fiction. | LCGFT: Detective and mystery fiction. | Novels.
Classification: LCC PT9876.15.R5155 D6313 2021 | DDC 839.73/74—dc23
LC record available at https://lccn.loc.gov/2021021936

Our books may be purchased in bulk for promotional, educational, or business use. Please contact your local bookseller or the Macmillan Corporate and Premium Sales Department at 1-800-221-7945, extension 5442, or by email at MacmillanSpecialMarkets@macmillan.com.

Originally published in Sweden by Ordfront förlag under the title *Dödsuret*

First U.S. Edition: 2021

10 9 8 7 6 5 4 3 2 1

The DEATHWATCH BEETLE

You won't get away! The thought was dizzying. Both terror and power were present; the feeling of having absolute control over another person also involved fear. Like the executioner with his hands around the shaft of the ax raised to strike.

Traces of blood showed the way. Small but revealing dark drops over moss and leaves, still damply glistening, tender herbs trampled down in their spring luster, soiled.

Like a drunken dog with its scent out of whack he had staggered off, but the question was how long would his strength last? Ten minutes perhaps, fifteen minutes at most. The terrain was brushy and difficult. There was nowhere to go. If he made his way down to the shore he would be met by stones and thickets of sea buckthorn. If he decided to go out into the water he was inexorably lost.

Was he hoping for mercy? Maybe.

It took twenty-five minutes to find him, a surprisingly long time considering his injuries. Semi-recumbent against a crooked, wind-lashed pine.

His head was hanging, his hands were crossed over his belly, where the second stab wound was. It was a fine picture, where the late afternoon sun framed his figure. It could have been a painting by Oskar Bergman, if you removed the dying man. That would happen soon, and the work would be completed.

He lifted his head. It was as if all humanity had been erased from the expressionless face. His eyelids fluttered. There was nothing there, no terror, no hope for reconciliation or even mercy. He was dead, practically speaking, and knew it, and he knew why. For a moment you might be tempted to believe that he wanted it that way.

They had not exchanged many words during the crossing to the island. An island they both knew well, which did not require any comments; it was like an everyday trip along a subway line in Stockholm or by bus from Alunda to Öregrund, a trip that has to be made. It hadn't been a problem getting him into the boat, across the strait, misled to believe in forgetting the past and forgiveness. "Move on," he'd repeated and nodded. The idiot! It was only when the stab in the neck came and he twirled around, only to be met by a second attack, the decisive one, that he understood. This was about a knife. A knife meant a closeness that firearms never provided. A knife was soundless, produced no recoil. A knife was driven in, to stay for a moment or for good. The power was there, likewise the decisiveness, and not least the nerves.

Now he was sitting there. Blood bubbling from his mouth, bubbles that burst. The eyes that were suddenly wide open, the hands that fumbled in the dirt as if he was trying to get support to stand up. Did he feel death take hold, twist? Was it now that it happened, the transition?

It was not a pretty sight: The cheeks had lost all their sheen and the healthy suntan had paled, the beard stubble that he always thought was sexy appeared sparse and straggly, the now half-closed eyes stared in toward an eternal darkness and in his half-opened mouth his tongue lay like a disgusting injured animal. For a moment a shadow of what could be doubt passed by, but it was more like a breath of distaste, a ripple over the strait.

That thing about pissing on his body, a thought that had been there as a final degradation, was suddenly no longer important. Now it was crucial to be collected. Move on. He was dying, dead. So it would be.

"I'm not crazy!" The words sounded loud and clear, each syllable was forced out with a conviction that produced a smile. A smile like before. The sweetness of victory. Friends had said: Your smile can crush everything.

He opened his eyes, his lips were moving, perhaps he wanted to say something about that triumphant smile, which was the last thing he saw in life.

The work of getting him down to the shore and into the boat was heavy and difficult, but it was done mechanically, fueled by adrenaline.

Without any ado he was tipped overboard, like an old sack with rusty junk from a farmyard being dumped in the sea. An arm made a swing toward the vault of the sky, like a final, desperate greeting. Within a few seconds he was swallowed up by the dark water. The last thing that was visible was the white shirt.

It was a good day. A beautiful day. Now life could move on.

It had all started in Lisbon. Ann Lindell was struck sometimes by the thought of how random life seemed: A glass of wine at an outdoor café, a former colleague who unexpectedly made himself known and displayed several signs of fixation and confusion, and then you were stuck.

"Why?" Edvard had asked. Ann had laughed, yes, why? "Why did you come to my office at the homicide squad in Uppsala almost twenty years ago?"

"Because I'd found a body in the forest" was Edvard's given response. "That was murder, but a woman who disappeared from the island of Gräsö a few years ago, and who probably did so voluntarily, why should you worry about that?"

Edvard Risberg, who had been her great torment but also her great love. Now they were sitting across from each other at his kitchen table, middle-aged, marked by time, like a couple. She reached out her hand and placed it on top of his.

"Of course you're right, I should forget about it, but there are things that bother me, disappearances for example. Look at it as brain exercise. And then I have a reason to be on Gräsö. Your island, Cecilia Karlsson's island. The island you either disappear from or to."

Edvard looked at her for a moment before he looked out over the yard again. *Does he love me?* was the thought that passed through her head, and the old worry flared up. As an answer he turned his powerful hand and grasped her tender one. It was no declaration of love but more like a sign of confidence, of trust? She longed for a glass of wine but knew that was impossible.

She observed him in secret. Many things had to be done in secret, or not at all. Not in a bad way, instead it was consideration she'd learned, to occasionally reduce her own significance, take a step back. The benefit was obvious.

Should she tell him that she herself had done a "Cecilia"? It had been a year before she met Edvard, when she was roughly the same age as Cecilia, but it was not for several years in southern Europe. It was for two weeks in Copenhagen. That had to be enough, Ottosson, her boss at Homicide, thought, and sent a retired colleague down from Fraud who physically saw to it that she returned to Uppsala. Ottosson had covered up what happened, tried to limit the gossip and the harmful effects. He had to do that later on several occasions.

It was a black hole in her life, where a lot could have gone badly, not least her career at the police department. She got two weeks on the streets of Copenhagen, never before or since had she walked so much, but what was it that happened? What was it that made her go away, hide out? She was not completely clear about that.

Maybe Edvard wouldn't understand. *Yes,* she said to herself, *he left everything too and ran away here to Gräsö.* Maybe it was in some people's nature, to break away so as not to be broken down. Ann wanted to meet Cecilia, was it that simple?

One

"This is hers." The woman lingered in the doorway before she stepped to one side. She was "stylish," that was the word that came to Ann, but with an almost girlish way of moving. The bare shoulders testified to self-confidence and strength.

Her husband remained standing on the stairs with one hand on the railing, stopped in midstep, as if he had to catch his breath. Ann stepped into the room, which was surprisingly large, perhaps thirty square meters, and sparsely furnished. Along one wall was a bookcase, filled with a mixture of old works in half-bound leather, book club editions from the 1970s, and paperbacks. It was not a collection, but it struck her instead as a random hodgepodge from several sources. The opposite side was dominated by a large bed in the same massive style as the bookcase. A tidy desk, the only modern feature, was in front of the window.

"She's orderly, always has been," the mother said, and Ann understood that she was addressing Edvard. The two had immediately made a connection, perhaps because Edvard was a Gräsö resident. They'd run into each before; he had visited the farm together with Victor several times.

Ann went up to the window and from there she could see a little patch of the sea. An aggraded bay, and a boathouse, unusable for its original function, testified to the land uplift.

"She loves the view," explained her father, who had unobtrusively made his way into the room and was standing right behind Ann. "But let's go downstairs now, Gunilla. I understand that as a former police officer she'll want to be left in peace. To think."

Without further ado he left the room and took his wife with him to the ground floor. She no doubt would have liked to stay behind and tell about their daughter, her life and possessions. She was that type, someone who happily accounted for things; Ann had perceived that immediately. Edvard sat down on a stick-back chair.

"He's watched too many TV series," he said, but Ann was grateful that they'd left. The father had understood correctly, she really did want to be left in peace, look around without preconceived notions, without anyone telling her what to think.

Ever since she and Edvard met Folke Åhr in Lisbon she had thought about Cecilia Karlsson now and then, what had become of her. Missing for four years, as if swallowed up by the earth, as one of Edvard's neighbors had expressed it. Her disappearance had naturally aroused a great deal of attention on Gräsö. Her parents were well-known, Rune Karlsson had been a successful middle-distance runner and Cecilia's mother was a multiple champion in archery with international records.

Folke Åhr had a summer house on the island and after retirement from National Homicide became interested in Cecilia's fate. His engagement had not decreased since an old schoolmate of Cecilia maintained that on two occasions he had seen her in Lisbon. The first time he'd thought it was a doppelgänger he'd glimpsed in Estrela Park, but when he caught sight of the same woman again a few days later he was convinced that it was Cecilia. She had boarded a trolley, while he was sitting on a park bench.

He immediately leaped up and tried to follow, but that was hopeless. The trolley left the square and disappeared.

"It was her, quite certain," he'd firmly maintained when Ann called him. He had obviously not been sober but tried to pull himself together, Ann recognized the signs well. It was a problem, Åhr had also pointed out, Nils "Blixten" Lindberg was often intoxicated. Was he that way in Lisbon too?

"How can you be so sure?" Ann Lindell asked.

"Her ass," Lindberg said without hesitation, and she was forced to smile. "She has an amazing ass, always has had. The shapes." It could be taken as sexist, but he'd said it with such warmth in his voice that she understood there was a lot of love in what he said.

"She was the first girl in the class who had to wear a bra," he added, as if to make Ann truly understand Cecilia Karlsson's physical advantages.

"Why did she run away?" she'd asked, and the answer came after some hesitation. "That Casper." After that he was silent, didn't want to say one more word.

Ann recalled the conversation with "Blixten," as the witness was called on the island, as she studied some framed photos on the bookcase. She took them down one by one. They were traditional pictures from holidays and parties, and Ann could see that he was right. She was curvy, in a way that surely drew men's gazes to her. Was she beautiful? Both yes and no. Her face had pleasant proportions, the close-sitting eyebrows reinforced the impression of a strong will. She resembled a Mexican female artist whose name Ann Lindell could not recall.

The shelf with the photos and some nondescript decorative objects was dust-free. It occurred to Ann that she did not have a similar arrangement of photos of herself, her parents, or her son, Erik. Was that good or bad? A little of both, she thought. She remained standing in the middle of the room.

"Check behind the books," Edvard said.

Ann had a memory from the past. Then it was her old colleague Sammy Nilsson who would make similar comments and directions. She obeyed, reached a hesitant hand over the books arranged by height, and in that way searched through shelf after shelf. On the last one, behind volumes of yearbooks from the Swedish Tourist Association, her hand encountered something. She immediately suspected what it was.

"Letters," she said, coaxing out a thin collection, bound together with a red cord with a rosette, which gave a teenage impression. Edvard got up from the chair. "Shall I?" she asked, even though she knew the answer, and carefully pulled on a length of twine.

"No," said Edvard.

"What do you mean?"

"It's hers."

"But . . ."

"Leave it to the police," said Edvard, "or to her parents."

There was something to his objection. If Cecilia Karlsson were alive, or had died by her own hand, in principle it was an illegal act to open her mail. If she had been killed then it was a case for the police.

"The address is a post office box in Uppsala," said Ann. "Strange, didn't she live on the island, here in the house?" She turned up a tab of the topmost envelope and checked the rest; all were addressed to the same P.O. box. "There are four letters."

Their eyes met. Ann felt his resistance. "I have to check," she said.

He left the room and clumped down the stairs. She quickly undid the rosette, carefully opened one of the envelopes, and took out the letter, which in reality was a postcard in a somewhat thicker quality of paper, with crimped edges, handwritten in an open style with even, careful lines. She held it by one corner and read:

Dear!

Thanks for last time! It was pleasant as usual, and I only wish we'd had a little more time.

There was just one thing that puzzled me: what you said about the incident at Hasselbacken.

I don't think Rune really meant what he said, he'd probably had

quite a bit to drink. Don't pay any attention to that misadventure. Can
we meet next week? I'm going to Sundsvall. We can stay at Knaust, you
know the hotel with the stairs. Don't you have some relative up there in
the Lapp country that you can pretend to visit?

Hugs!

No signature, no date. She inspected the envelope; no legible postmark. Rune, her father, what had he said? "Misadventure," what kind of word was that?

From the ground floor came the clatter of porcelain. Cecilia's mother had insisted that they should have coffee. Ann hurriedly took out the remaining postcards, lined them up on the desk, and photographed them with her cell phone. Just as she replaced everything and tied the letters together again, steps sounded on the stairs. Ann dropped the letters behind the STA books.

"Shall we have a cup?"

"Let's do that," said Ann.

"Have you thought of anything?" The woman spoke quietly. There was a confidence in her voice that had not been there previously. "Rune gets depressed sometimes," she continued unprompted. "He rarely goes in here, I was surprised that he came along upstairs."

"Depressed because of Cecilia?"

"Yes, it's probably that, that she doesn't want to or isn't able to make herself known. We would really like to have her here."

"You believe that she's alive?"

Cecilia's mother looked at her, and without saying anything gave her an answer. Her otherwise soft facial features bore a sharpness that left no room for reservation. She was convinced that her daughter was alive.

"But now let's go down, otherwise Rune will start to wonder."

She hooked her arm under Ann's. "He wants to keep track of everything, like with the lap times when he competed, or like now when he stares at all those galas on TV." Ann recalled that the man had been a runner.

"No, I haven't thought of anything."

"Why are you here?"

"Perhaps out of curiosity," said Ann.

"That was an honest answer," said Gunilla Karlsson, who stopped for a moment on the stairs.

"I don't like mysteries," Ann continued.

The table was set in the kitchen. Rune sat half turned away by the window with his hands resting on either side of the coffee cup. His thin lips, almost nonexistent, were tightly compressed. He had a sturdy crease over the bridge of his nose and his gaze was far away, looking out over what had once been a bay. He gave an elderly impression, even though he couldn't be that old. A patriarch. Sixty-five? He still looked good, and when he was young on the running track he'd no doubt been an attractive sight. The most prominent feature was the sturdy nose.

His wife was considerably younger, she must be over fifty anyway considering Cecilia's age. Archery. Ann associated that with Olympic games. How successful had she been? That could be searched on the internet. A well-filled trophy case stood in the living room. Gunilla Karlsson had a peculiar way of pushing out her one hip. Perhaps it was a carryover from her days as an archer?

Edvard sat across from Rune. Soon he too would be there, in old age. She as well. It was hard to imagine. Would they grow old together? A feeling of discomfort gave her the impulse to say thank you, leave the house as well as the questions around Cecilia's disappearance. She actually had no business there! She didn't have time for other people's mysteries.

"I was born here," Rune Karlsson suddenly said. "My siblings and I. There were five brothers, one is gone."

"Martin?"

"I see, you knew him?"

"Yes, we were on the same job in Forsmark one time," said Edvard. "He was a skilled painter."

"The best," Rune said with a smile that at once made him fifteen years younger.

Edvard hummed a little, the way he did when without words he agreed or did not have anything to add.

"Then we could set out nets and in a flash fill the boat with herring. Now the trawlers vacuum up everything, they pick up a hundred times more herring than the local fishermen do. It all goes to hog feed in Denmark. Hog feed. And to hogs that live in hell, enclosed in cages."

Edvard nodded. This was his turf. Ann knew that he'd worked with hogs in his previous life.

"Yes, help yourselves!" said Gunilla, setting out yet another plate. Her strong hand, *archery*, Ann thought again, made an inviting gesture over the table.

"And then the pastures, the fences and the old drying barns, all that has disappeared almost completely. You wouldn't believe what orchid meadows there were at one time. There's a book, it's called *At Home in Poverty* and—"

"Now let's have coffee!" his wife interrupted. Ann suspected that Gunilla Karlsson knew that he would get carried away if he continued. Rune Karlsson sighed, gave Edvard a look but submitted and raised his coffee cup. Despite his obvious strength there was something extremely resigned about his figure.

A cautious conversation slowly started, where Edvard played the role of motor. Ann felt no need to get involved. His good side, being able to make small talk with peers, where the big words were left out, his smile, that was more than enough for her, and above all it worked as a softener. The Karlsson couple relaxed. When the refills were poured Ann tried to guide the conversation to Blixten, the one who maintained having seen Cecilia in Lisbon, but that didn't go well. Instead they started talking about a woman who had recently died.

"It's so sad. Did you know Olga Palm?"

"We met a few times," said Edvard. "Wasn't she a bit frail?"

"Diabetes. They finally had to amputate both legs. She liked Cecilia a lot. She would like to have been at the funeral. They always had a good relationship," said Gunilla.

"Cecilia worked for her son, Adrian," she continued. "They didn't always get along that well, but he needed her, he understood that, and had to hold back."

"Does he own a company?"

"Yes, something electronic, control systems in industry and such. Cissi was good at computers. They had to travel a lot."

Hotel Knaust in Sundsvall, thought Ann. Was he the one who'd written the postcard she read upstairs? It wasn't signed, but the sender was someone who knew her well.

"You said that he had to hold back, what did you mean?"

"He could be a little assertive," said Gunilla.

"Violent too?"

"No, no, not at all like that, but he has definite opinions about most things."

"Now he's probably in the Philippines," said Rune, "and he can stay there. Or was it Hong Kong?"

"He'll come to the funeral, of course."

"You think so?" his voice dripping with contempt. At once he became fifteen years older.

"Did Adrian and Cecilia have any kind of—"

"Never," said Rune. "That man!"

Edvard gave Ann a look that was hard to decipher. She chose to change tack. "Blixten talked about someone named Casper, is that anyone you know?"

"Casper?" Gunilla said hesitantly, sneaking a glance at her husband, who seemed however to have lost interest in the conversation. He stared stubbornly out the window. "No, not as far as I remember. Would they have been in contact?"

"That I don't know," said Ann, "but he was surely acquainted with both Cecilia and Adrian Palm, if I understood Blixten correctly." The lie passed Ann's lips without a problem; embroidering a little extra was an old occupational injury.

Ann got the idea that Gunilla Karlsson was concealing the truth. The name Casper had sparked something in her, an alarm bell had rung, Ann had that feeling anyway. That was probably an old occupational injury too, mistrusting a statement.

They said thanks for the coffee and got ready to leave. "Do you want to see a fine old photo?" Rune Karlsson asked, and it was obvious that he was addressing Edvard. He had not yet let go of the memories from before. "My brother Martin is in it too."

They went into the living room. Gunilla made a face which could mean just about anything, but gestured for Ann to follow along. Rune pointed at an enlargement of a photograph which was hanging on the wall. It depicted the Karlsson family, he explained. Mother and father, and five boys. They were lined up in front of a boathouse. Two pairs of oars hung on the wall. "You see how it has changed," said Rune. Perhaps he wanted to point out that the sea level was considerably higher then, or that it was a time when the family stuck together, was forced to. But it was a photo that signaled security, it occurred to Ann, while Rune pointed and listed off the names. He himself was standing to the far right, holding one of his brothers by the hand. Sweden in the 1950s, in the periphery of Gräsö. No extravagance, but in many ways an idyll, as Ann had understood from Viola's stories.

"You see," Rune Karlsson repeated, and his voice whistled a little, "then there was farming and a fishery to talk about. Then there was a life to talk about."

"And you do that pretty often," said his wife, but without any sarcasm in her voice, more like a factual statement.

"Now it's just claptrap with the island. All the goddam summer houses. All the goddam speculators."

He droned on in that vein, turned toward Edvard, whom he clearly saw as an ally, even though he wasn't a native of Gräsö. Ann felt that she'd heard it all before and lost interest. She looked around. On the opposite wall was the prize collection, lots of trophies in all conceivable sizes. She read some of the plaques but without actual interest. Gunilla Karlsson did not comment at all on the glass case which housed the careers of two successful athletes. Ann thought that was a bit strange.

Next to the case was a serving cart in two levels, both filled with bottles and a couple of carafes, which Ann studied with more interest. It looked expensive and a bit lavishly ostentatious, as if they wanted to show that they regularly traveled abroad and made sure to supply themselves from the duty-free shop, but perhaps didn't consume at the same rate. It was a cart for entertaining, but Ann got the impression that the living room often echoed vacantly. They did not stand out as enthusiastic socializers.

"Fine picture," Edvard said in front of a framed photo that was next to the liquor cart. He came closer and read out loud: " 'Khumbu Glacier,' where is that?"

"Nepal," said Gunilla Karlsson, putting an arm around Ann's waist as if to lead her out of the room.

"My brother, Sven-Åke, was there, but that was long ago." The sigh from Gunilla was obvious.

"Is he a mountain climber?"

"Then yes, they were searching for the man who conquered Mount Everest."

"The Englishman or the Sherpa? Had he disappeared?"

"Neither of them," said Rune. "There was a pair who did it long before." Then a story followed about two other Englishmen, Mallory and Irvine, who according to Rune, climbed the world's highest mountain in the 1920s, but then died on the descent. Mallory's body had been found in the 1990s.

"Sven-Åke worked with the Nepalese. He lives there now. Has a wife and three children."

"Interesting," Edvard said, and appeared to mean it.

"Very sweet children," said Gunilla.

"I have that kind of family," said Rune. "They all left Gräsö. I'm the only one who stays put. You can imagine how sad our dad was."

"But your brother Martin then, he was in Forsmark and seemed rooted there?"

"You think so, but then he'd wandered around on the seven seas for thirty-five years. He was simply forced to come back to Sweden. Cancer. That goddam paint the shipping companies used was the death of him, but he never wanted to admit that. He lived here for maybe a year, then he was done."

"It's too cramped here, too much village," said Gunilla. "Martin got to see a lot, he was content with his life."

"Cramped!?"

"Let's go out," said Gunilla. It was evident that she had heard the complaints before and wanted to tease her husband a little.

"Content with his life," Rune Karlsson muttered.

The Karlsson couple followed them out into the yard. When Edvard got into the car, Rune took a few steps closer to Ann.

"Stop snooping in our lives!" he hissed and turned on his heels. Gunilla was already standing on the stoop with her hand on the doorknob. Had she heard what her husband had spit out? Had Edvard heard?

They sat quietly in the car. Ann counted the oncoming cars. She'd done that since childhood, when she went with her father on his rounds with the beverage truck in the summer landscape of Östergötland. She still remembered the record on the stretch Ödeshög–Borghamn: 137 vehicles, since then a magic number. Another was twenty-four, the number of mailboxes from her childhood home to the Konsum co-op. In that way she had created order.

Now there were twenty-two cars up to the turnoff to the campground, but order refused to present itself. Edvard broke the silence.

"They're bluffing," he said, and Ann smiled to herself.

"About what?"

"That Casper, for example, they know very well who that is."

"Did you see how tidy it was in her room, not a speck of dust."

"They probably want to preserve her memory," said Edvard.

"That's probably so, but it was more than a museum, as if she was expected at any minute."

"But it hasn't been that many years since she disappeared," said Edvard. "Your old cop buddy was completely wrong about the year. What did he say, 2009 or so?"

"Yes, he seemed a little confused when we last spoke too. But it was in 2015 that she disappeared."

"He's starting to get dementia, they say."

"Aha, that explains it," said Ann, and it hurt her to hear that. Her father had gone the same route.

"I have to stop by here about something," said Edvard. He had talked about a job at the campground. There was always something for him. They met three camper trailers on the short stretch.

"Are they starting to leave?"

"Yes, little by little, but most will stick around a while longer."

In that way order was created, context. Ann liked sitting in the car on the way to a job he would eventually get. They were together on the way. He was thinking lumber and concrete, she counted car campers. And in the background an encounter with a couple of parents who missed their daughter. Ann knew that they would continue to process the experience at home with Cecilia. Could she, despite Rune Karlsson's parting words, return? Of course, anything else would be official misconduct, if she were to be official. Perhaps he could be provoked?

"When is the funeral for Olga Palm?"

"Saturday," said Edvard.

"It would be exciting to see her son, Adrian, if he were to show up now from the Philippines."

"Are you going there?"

"I can hang around a little outside the church."

"You can't just hang around outside Gräsö Church," said Edvard.

"I can," said Ann, and some of the past job satisfaction seeped in like a picture from before, that too a funeral, even if she didn't remember all the details. Would she ever be able to return to her old job, if they even wanted her? No, probably not, she'd always told herself the times she'd thought about the question. She would never want to work anymore as a police officer. Now she was making cheese at a farm creamery in a little village outside Gimo and was completely content with that.

Two

The house smelled of mold. It was raining into what had once been the living room. She had set a bucket on the floor. The little bedroom was in better shape, even if the ceiling panels had large damp stains and were buckling considerably. The cot was pushed into a corner, where something was scratching and gnawing in the wall, deathwatch beetle she thought it was called, was it a kind of wood-boring beetle? It made a sound like a ticking clock, counting down. The wallpaper was from the 1960s, the blind was always down. A chair served as a nightstand. There was a candle on it. That was the only source of illumination. Nowadays she hardly read anything, and she was afraid of light. She did not want to be seen or heard.

She charged the phone and the computer in the car. She barely used the little propane hot plate, boiled noodles, some soup, or a can of ready-made food. There were biscuits in a tin, instant coffee, a bottle of Amaretto and a little glass on a low bench painted green. She stored a little wine in a cupboard. On the table was the kerosene lamp that she remembered from before.

Darkness and a kind of peace rested over the house. Late summer was sneaking up, embracing the trees and thickets that crept closer and closer, and which with time would completely take over, the house would collapse. In fifty years only the old iron stove, weathered brick, and cracked roof tiles would be evidence of a settlement. Hilding's Croft. She had no idea who Hilding was, perhaps no one knew any longer. As far as she knew the cabin was owned by the old man who was called the Dutchman, who for many years had been bedridden in a nursing home in Öregrund. He would definitely not be stopping by.

A family from Gävle had rented it years ago for a few summer seasons, and on the narrow road through the forest she had met the daughter in the house, a scrawny girl whose name was Rafaela. She was dark-haired, a little shy, but gradually more and more lively. She spoke only Spanish with her parents. It was as if they had a secret language. They had socialized for three summers, almost daily. Cautious games at the edge of the forest, on the rocky ground south of the cabin, but never alone by the sea. Rafaela's mother had forbidden that. Sometimes she thought about her former playmate, what had become of her, the way you do. She had even dreamed about her. She would have searched on the internet if she only knew her last name.

The first days had been difficult with the memories that poured in like raw fog, the increasing darkness, and not least the unaccustomed silence. A week or so ago a big city, now a peripheral island in a sparsely populated country. She heard the sea like a gentle murmur, sometimes at a distance the sound of cars, otherwise nothing. Now it felt better, she could even relax, not to mention feel comfortable, even though the strange feeling of being involved yet still an outsider still dominated. She was living in a vacuum and would surely do so for a long time to come, perhaps always. She had tried to avoid thinking about the future the past few years, and succeeded relatively well with that, lived from day to day, went in and out of relationships with an ease that initially had surprised her but soon became a lifestyle. For long periods she could see herself as carefree, above all the time in the little village in the Alentejo stood out in retrospect as the happiest since childhood.

Now she was living a double life. The wig was on a chair. It was not of particularly good quality and had already started to lose its style. She ought to set it on the wig stand a little more often, but it served its function. Along with the smoke-colored glasses and the formless, nondescript dresses it had worked, no one had shown any sign at all of recognizing her. At the supermarket in Öregrund she'd run into a couple of old acquaintances and they hadn't reacted, even though they were standing in the same line at the register and had opportunity to observe her. On the ferry, summer visitors and Gräsö natives she'd known her whole life looked at her like anyone at all, a stranger. To a certain extent she was. She was even a stranger to herself. For several years she had played a game, made lying, evasions, and frequent departures into a way of life. On one occasion, in Portugal, it almost got out of control. On her daily walk through Estrela Park she had seen Nils Lindberg on a park bench. "Blixten," of all people! It was completely unlikely. A man who would only with great reluctance go over to the mainland before was sitting on a park bench in Lisbon! With her face turned away she'd hurried past, almost running up to the trolley, but heard his call. Shocked and on shaky legs she had squeezed into the overfull trolley. Her distress must have been noticeable, because immediately an older man offered his place and gratefully she'd sunk down on the seat.

After that she never returned to the park, where she loved to walk. The relative sense of freedom she'd had was gone, and she understood that she would have to move. She could get a ticket to South America or Asia, but she wanted to wait out Adrian.

She was in no way forced to stay away from Sweden, but it had turned out that way and she understood after a while, when she thought about it, that it was actually good for her long-term goals. Now it was time to put the plan into action!

The ready-grilled chicken and the plastic container of potato salad were on the table. She ought to eat, but had lost her appetite, picked with the fork in the oily salad, sat there and looked without seeing out the kitchen window. A spider was crawling on the windowsill. That was the company she had.

Happiness and betrayal. Death and flight. Loneliness and revenge. Those were the word pairs she had to relate to. It had been a struggle, but deep down she was strong, she knew that.

She stood up to break her train of thought, left the cabin and walked down to the water. The strait was restless. Casper had disappeared there in the deep. Never found again. It was over four years ago and the sense of loss had not diminished, which surprised her. He'd been a treacherous piece of shit, but a charming one.

She peered over the water toward the islands and islets in the northeast, where Norr-Gället and Kullaskäret were. Her parents had taken her there many times. She knew every reef in the sea and every stone on the shore. Her father had done strength training and swam between the skerries, while her mother meditated in seclusion. It was good for archery, she maintained, but Cecilia suspected that it was mostly to get away, escape the demands from husband and daughter. She herself had built an endless number of stone towers on the shore. Higher up in the terrain where the ice had not reached there were probably some still left as memorials and certainly invited speculation from visitors these days. She could not recall that she ever had company her own age with her. Gunilla had always had a hard time with noise and children's shrieks, and Cecilia could rarely bring home playmates. That was probably why the memory of Rafaela was still so alive; in her family it could get noisy.

Cecilia understood in retrospect what her upbringing had done to her, the rigid system with a kind of daily obligation to tell what she'd done and intended to do, and how it affected her relationships with other people. It became even clearer during the years in Portugal when her parents could not interfere in her life in the least. At first she had automatically asked herself what Gunilla, and above all Rune, would think about this or that she was doing. Then gradually this had receded, she felt increasingly rebellious, and thereby free. Her contagious laughter had been heard more and more often on the streets of Lisbon and in the alleys of the village of Serpa.

Rune had always had an enormous need to control, lists should be made before a visit to the grocery store, before trips, before invitations to parties, for most of the family's activities, everything should be followed up and checked off. Carelessness and oversight were not permitted. Her home-work quizzes were torture, likewise in her teenage years his scrutiny of her circle of friends and boyfriends.

Early on Cecilia realized that he secretly read his wife's text messages and email. He had never found Cecilia's passwords, otherwise he would have snooped in her conversations too, she was convinced of that.

Now he had no control over her and his frustration must be immense. He knew that she was alive but not where and how, and not who she asso-ciated with either, who she was sleeping with.

The stone that she picked up from the edge of the shore was black but veined with light streaks. She let her index finger run over its uneven edge. It was with stones like this she had built towers. The round ones were slimy and smooth and impossible to build anything sensible with. She crouched, picked up stone after stone, but built no towers and instead set them out on the ground like a cross.

In a few days there would be a funeral. She suspected that her worry and failing appetite came from that. She would get to see them all, old friends and acquaintances, her parents likewise. Maybe Blixten too, the most re-cent of the islanders who had seen and recognized her. The question was whether he would do so again. Adrian would be in top form, he loved to be at the center.

Must he die? That question had been grinding in her head for a long time. Yes, she had answered every time so far, and now that Olga was dead there were no obstacles.

Three

Against all odds Nils "Blixten" Lindberg still had his driver's license. There was no way to count all the times he'd driven under the influence on Gräsö, but luck, loyalty in his circle of friends, and not least the lack of police checkpoints had rescued him, and others, from accidents and a suspended license. It had happened by divine providence. He'd made a few visits into the ditch and the vegetation, on a few occasions a tractor had been needed to tow the vehicle, an uninspected Simca pickup of indeterminate age. The last time things had gone a little awry was on a tricky curve on the road toward Malmen. Fortunately there was a tractor in the vicinity; it was around the time for boat launching.

The island had long had its own laws, which were not always in line with the Kingdom of Sweden's. In principle that had changed over time; social control and the islanders' need to look for work on the other side of Öregrundsgrepen strait had step by step sobered up the permanent residents, in any event on the roads. That also applied to Blixten.

For that reason he was on the ferry with his bicycle. Always on the port side. Always with a cap from Lantmännen in Piteå on his head. Almost always a couple of bags from the state liquor store in the panniers on the side of the rack. He looked a little decked out, could almost be mistaken for a summer resident, but the lack of anything pastel-colored in his attire decided it: He was a native of Gräsö, the island where he was born and where he would die. About the latter no one could know for certain, but the risk that he would kick the bucket on the mainland was not impending. He spent most of his time on the island. There were exceptions; his trips to Lisbon were without a doubt the most sensational he had undertaken.

The visits in the Portuguese capital had to a certain extent changed the direction of his life. Outwardly he was the same, few could have observed any actual change. In principle he had the same movement patterns as before, quibbled with his friends about the same things, kept to the same diet, but inside Blixten the bodily humors had been rearranged. Whether the healthy humors had taken over was unclear.

His mother, who lived in a cottage in Klockarboda, had obviously noticed it. "I'm the same as always," Blixten had curtly and a little crabbily dismissed her questions. She was not exactly worried, mostly uncertain about what it all meant. Maybe he'd met a woman, she thought, and that was correct.

It had happened in Lisbon. He'd gotten a tip that resulted in him applying for a passport for the first time. It was his brother Axel who, when the darkness lay deep over Vidsel in the far north of Sweden, had capitulated and agreed to a trip to Portugal. He and his wife had spent a week in Lisbon and according to Axel had an unexpectedly good time. There in the crowd he'd seen Cecilia Karlsson; he was in any case "almost certain" that it was her. That was enough for Blixten. Axel was never drunk, usually levelheaded, and almost always trustworthy.

The place was Estrela Park, and that was where Nils Lindberg immediately made his way after having checked into a hotel in Rato. After that he'd spent considerable time at the outdoor café in the park. There he made a mistake; he had consumed far too many Sagres beers, becoming inattentive and slow on the uptake. The other mistake was that he had mentioned to Folke Åhr that he'd seen Cecilia. They were neighbors on the island, Blixten looked after his house during the winter and performed minor services. Now he had evidently talked with another police officer, admittedly also a former one.

While he was slightly amused about the stir, it made him a little crestfallen. Over the course of the years he had fairly well succeeded in suppressing the memory of Cecilia Karlsson, but he was all too often reminded of her. It happened every time Åhr came by. And now it would be hashed over again. Ann Lindell was the name of the woman who wanted to "exchange a few words."

This time he would speak his mind and in no uncertain terms. He left the ferry and cycled up the hill toward the church. Meeting at a cemetery, what an idea! No one who could be taken for a former police officer was visible. There was only Marja pulling weeds between the gravestones. She looked up and waved. That little gesture put him in a better mood. He leaned his bicycle against the wall and at the same moment a car turned onto the little parking lot.

"Nice that you could come" was the first thing the woman said after introducing herself. She did not look at all like he'd imagined.

"Nils, right? Or Blixten?"

"Don't matter."

"Shall we go in and sit down?"

"I'd rather not, I have packages," said Nils, pointing toward the bicycle. "Theft-prone goods." He did not want to be sitting on a bench. It would look arranged, as if they'd made a date. If they stayed standing in the parking lot it would look as if they'd run into each other by chance.

They made small talk about the summer, the weather, and the fact that they both still had vacation days left, before Ann led the conversation to Cecilia Karlsson. He told her about his visits to Lisbon. Basically repeated word for word what he'd said to Folke Åhr.

"I like Lisbon and Portugal," she said. "Especially the wine."

"I don't drink wine."

"I've been in the park where you saw her."

She did not question his information whatsoever.

"It's nice there," said Nils.

"What were you doing in Lisbon, do you have friends in Portugal?"

Friends, he repeated silently to himself and shook his head. He was longing more and more to open the pannier on the bicycle.

"How do you know Cecilia?"

"We went to school together and then . . ." What more could he say?

"She's a beautiful woman."

"How do you know that?"

"Photos," the ex–police officer said with a smile.

"Yes, she is . . . good-looking."

"You traveled there because you thought she would be there, was that so?"

"No, not at all . . ." How much did she know about his life, that he'd never been abroad before, that he'd been in love with Cecilia since middle school, that his few relationships with other women had gone nowhere?

He went into the graveyard through an open gate where he would have preferred to run away. She followed, as if they were taking a walk together.

"If you were to guess, I mean, you've known her since you were little, why would she voluntarily disappear?"

"I don't know," said Nils.

They looked at each other. The fact was that the ex-cop resembled Cecilia a little bit.

"I don't know," he said again. She observed him in silence, and he thought he glimpsed a flash of understanding, even sympathy, in her eyes.

"But I've thought about Cecilia, I even talk with her sometimes, as if she were with me. That sounds crazy, I know, but we had something together," he said, and it was as if the words like shimmering soap bubbles lazily floated away and evaporated, burst.

She reached out her hand and touched his shoulder. A brief touch, no hugging, no pressure, simply this gesture of, well, what? He looked around. Marja was bent over with her rear end in the air, hacking at the ground frantically. No one else was around.

"We hung out together a little a long time ago," he said, and the longing for a drink came like a hit in the solar plexus.

She nodded. "I know how that feels. Being away from the one you love."

"I have to go," he said.

"Do you live nearby?"

"Ten minutes by bicycle," he said.

"How nice to escape the car," said Ann Lindell.

"Why do you ask about Cissi? You're not with the police anymore."

He remembered a news story, it must be ten years ago, where they wrote about a tough detective from Uppsala. She was probably not that tough.

"I don't like mysteries," she said.

"Maybe she doesn't want to be found?"

"It may be like that, but even so you're searching . . . we're searching."

"I know her, you don't."

She nodded.

"There lies a Gräsö personality," he said, pointing to a grave.

"Two," she said.

"Yes, it's true, he was married to Helga."

"Viola is buried a little farther away."

"Did you know her?"

"Yes, she was a remarkable woman, a fine person. Edvard, the man I'm seeing, lives in her house."

He remembered how there was talk about Edvard Risberg, about how he came to the island many years ago, that he left everything on the mainland and rented a room with Viola.

"I stop by here sometimes. Here they lie, all the relatives that I recognize so well. Gräsö was peculiar, folks were peculiar, even the language. I've heard recordings of Gräsö dialect and you would have a hard time understanding what the old people said. They were poor, but folks didn't know anything else."

They stood silently awhile. His worry had subsided.

"My grandmother was like that," he resumed unexpectedly. "Sometimes it was hard to understand what she was talking about. She's buried over there." Blixten pointed toward an older part of the cemetery.

"And your grandfather?"

"Him! He's still alive but Mom has forbidden that he should be buried next to Grandmother."

"Does he live on the island?"

"No, nowadays in Öregrund. I remember him as nice sometimes, at least when he was in the smithy. He was incredibly skillful. People came from far away. If you see a beautiful forged candlestick on the island it's probably Grandfather's work."

"I think Viola had a pair," said Ann. "Maybe they were bought from him."

"Or a present. In his cups he could be generous just as well as violent. You never knew."

Once again there was silence.

"What kind of work do you do?" she asked.

"Landscape care," he said and thought it sounded good. "I restore old plots of land, do inventory, clear and such."

"For who?"

"For all conceivable landowners. Sometimes it's the county that pays."

"You can see that you work outdoors," she said, but did not explain how.

"I have to get going."

"Why did she disappear, do you have any idea?"

She truly had an ability to change the subject. He shook his head.

"Did she meet a man, do you know? There was someone named Casper, were they together?"

"Not a clue, we didn't have that much contact," he said, trying to sound convincing, but heard how thin it sounded. "As I said, I didn't know that much about her life then. When she left, I mean."

"Who was Casper? What was he like?"

He shook his head.

"No, I don't know that much."

"You know quite a bit about old times, about people who are buried here, but not about a man who perhaps was together with Cecilia," Ann Lindell observed. She'd seen right through him.

The sound of the ramp of the ferry striking the ground made him look up. He took a breath, sighed.

"Yes, I guess I'll be lying here one day," he said, and at the same moment the urge came back.

"Ride home, have a glass," she said, "and keep in mind that the two of you are surely going to meet one day."

He took a few quick steps toward the gate, turned just as quickly and extended his right hand.

"You know how it feels," he said.

She nodded.

"Sometimes I think that we have to live differently," he said, turned toward the cemetery, where the leaves of the trees trembled from a gust from the sea, the only movement that opposed the stillness that had settled over the place. "It's a short time we're granted," he continued with a worn phrase. "And . . . this flailing . . ." He let go of her hand.

"Cecilia was gorgeous," he resumed after a moment, strengthened by Ann's expectant posture. "When we were on a school trip to Uppsala I got to touch her. She was the one who wanted to, she was eager, I was mostly scared that someone would discover us, some custodian or minister. It was inside the cathedral. To organ music. That's how it started. She was almost always in the mood."

He smiled at the policewoman, straddled the bicycle, and pedaled away.

Four

Ann Lindell watched Blixten disappear northward, vigorously pedaling his old bike. His parting words about what happened in the cathedral had been unexpected, but actually not that surprising. She had experienced that before, how perpetrators, witnesses, and relatives of crime victims had been recalcitrant to start with, to then become eagerly talkative.

Almost always in the mood, she silently repeated his words. He'd looked satisfied when he told about what had happened in the church. His words also suggested that there had been a continuation to the touching.

Nils Lindberg had felt a need to explain himself, why he went to Portugal twice to trace a woman who'd been swallowed up by the earth. For him it was not just a mystery of disappearance, but more a story about love and loss. It was a story that had its start already in teenage years, which his anecdote so well illustrated. That was the background against which his life many years later would be played. If the mystery of Cecilia were never solved, he was in some respect probably lost.

Ann walked around the cemetery, stopping in front of the stone that told about the tragedy on Christmas Day 1877 when fifteen persons from Örskär perished. They had sailed north from Svartbäck on their way home after the early Christmas morning church service. The wreck was found on Boxing Day outside Uggleudden. Ann remembered Viola's dramatic story, how they found a sailor, Gräsman, who bound himself to the mast and even in death held the lighthouse keeper Alm's twelve-year-old son by the hand.

Now she recalled those two as she silently read the names of the deceased and tried to imagine the cold in the water. It didn't go so well. Drowning must be one of the worst things.

Those who voluntarily drown themselves must be more than inclined toward suicide. Ann got the idea that it was a way to punish yourself, by giving yourself a painful and drawn-out death by suffocation with lungs filled with water and a growing darkness, where the body was surrounded by water.

But the victims in Örskär wanted to live. Most of them were young. Was there a God then for the survivors? Ann was doubtful.

She left the cemetery, trying to shake off the feeling of discomfort that had overtaken her. It fit together with the thoughts about the drowning deaths, but also with Nils Lindberg's obvious dependence on and longing for alcohol, something she had no problem identifying and understanding.

The phone interrupted her thoughts. Edvard. He asked if he was disturbing her, and she said that he wasn't at all. Weeks, months, and years had passed when she'd longed for a call from him.

"I've found a Casper," he said. "One with cee."

"Where is that?"

"He was an old buddy of Adrian Palm."

Ann heard in his voice that he had more to tell. "And . . . ?" she said.

"He's missing too. A month before she disappeared."

"Where did you hear this? What else do you know?"

"I asked around a little. You know Robban, related to Victor, Viola's friend, the one who . . ."

"I remember him!"

"Robban keeps track of things. That Casper wasn't from the island. I don't know anything more. You'll have to talk with Robban."

"Does he still live in Victor's old house?"

"Can you still find the way there?"

Robert H. Sillén—The One and Only, it said in neat letters on a plaque mounted on the wall next to the front door. The paint on the wall was flaking, the door leaf mottled with moisture damage, and the frosted glass was cracked. It appeared as if nothing had been repaired for a long time.

Inside the house, music was playing. There was no doorbell or knocker. Ann Lindell knocked, at first a little carefully, then more firmly. No reaction. She pushed open the door, called "Hello," and stepped into the hall.

"Oh baby, you know what I like . . ." a voice roared through the house. "This is the Big Bopper speaking . . ."

Robban was his usual self when he looked out from what Ann remembered was the kitchen. "Good, huh? Those of us who are a little older have the sense to appreciate classic music."

"Hi, Robban, it's been a while."

"I understood that you'd be coming."

He inspected her from top to toe. "You've lost a few kilos, I see."

"Not you."

"Come in and we'll have coffee. Don't all police do that all the time?"

"I'm not a police officer anymore."

"You make cheese outside Gimo, thank God for that," said Robban, who kept track. "Wait, I'll turn it down a little."

They sat down at the kitchen table. Most of it was the same since Victor's time. Victor had been Viola's partner, without living together, for eighty years. They never really worked it out, but between them was nurtured as deep a friendship as was possible between two such decided individualists. They were the most beautiful couple Ann had encountered. Now they were gone, but something of Victor probably still lived in the walls of the house.

They made small talk for a while. She felt at home, a sudden and over-whelming feeling came over her. She liked Robban, the house, what he said, and how he said it. Through Edvard she was a part of Gräsö. She never visited her birthplace in Östergötland, no one could guess that she was from there, the dialect had been smoothed away long ago, likewise the feeling of home she'd once felt. She had no siblings, her parents were dead, there were a few cousins, one of them was a friend on Facebook, that was all. Uppland had become hers, and then not least Roslagen.

Robban lived in the American dream. He wore jeans, boots, and a soiled Stetson hat, purchased during a visit to Graceland. He played only American music—soul, blues, and country—and now he'd discovered Spotify, he told Ann.

"Casper," she interrupted at last. "Who is Casper?"

Robert Sillén grinned. "I wanted to see how long you could contain yourself."

"Why did he disappear?"

"Casper Stefansson worked with Adrian Palm in Stockholm. I think that he was actually the one who ran that company. Palm latched on, after a while he took over. Casper moved abroad. Everything was going smoothly. Cecilia and several others were hired. She was shrewd. Everyone knew that. Casper Stefansson came to the island, probably to visit Adrian. It ended with him renting a cabin."

"You met him?"

"A few times. Adrian, Blixten, and I used to drive to Hallsta and check out the speedway, and Casper came along sometimes. Sometimes we hung out at home with Adrian to watch Formula One races."

"What was he like, Casper?"

"A charmer," said Robban with poorly concealed contempt. "He thought he was some kind of James Dean, but he aged quickly. He was a little older."

"How well did you know Cecilia?"

Robban gave her an indecipherable look, then looked to the side, as if he was embarrassed.

" 'One in a Million You,' " he said. "That's an oldie but goodie too," and Ann understood that he was talking about some song from the past.

"The Southern states is where the real USA is. The North is just steel-works and shit. Larry Graham is from Texas."

"Robban! That's sweet, but tell me more about Casper."

"A person should find a woman, but now it's probably too late. A person should go to Thailand and screw some fifteen-year-old. That's all the rage now. There's a whole gang of Swedish refugees down there who don't understand a bit of what the natives are saying but babble about Lucia celebration, that supposedly it's prohibited. I saw a program on TV. They call themselves Friends of Sweden."

"Yes, that's sad," Ann felt forced to agree. "But Casper."

"He lived in Kallboda for a few summers. Talked strangely."

"What do you mean?"

"As if he had a chair leg shoved up his ass, if you know what I mean."

"Not really, but he was from Stockholm, wasn't he?"

"Exactly!"

"Was he together with Cecilia?"

Robert Sillén smiled.

"But you're from the south, right?"

"Ödeshög."

He considered this fact. Possibly he had difficulty placing the town.

"Casper Stefansson disappeared like a paycheck. His car was left behind and there was a dog out barking in the yard."

"What happened?"

"Fishing," Robert observed. "He was probably drunk and fell in."

"And it was at the same time that Cecilia disappeared?"

"It was around then. About a month before. It was in May. The boat was found, it had drifted all the way down in Högklykefjärden. It was a little motorboat. I'd fixed the motor, an ancient Penta. In the boat were fishing tackle and a bucket for fish."

Cecilia Karlsson had disappeared at the end of June four years ago.

"But was he really a fisherman, someone who went out and caught herring?"

"Not really, he was the sort who rented a yacht and fought to bring in a two-hundred-kilo marlin. He would brag about that sort of thing. He was a diver too, he often talked about coral reefs, cave diving, and such. He had boats somewhere in Asia that he rented out."

"Familiar with water in other words," said Ann.

"I understand where you're headed . . ." said Robban. He looked distressed, as if he'd been reminded of all the mean things people are capable of doing.

Ann waited. "Was there any herring in the bucket?" she asked at last.

"Once a cop, always a cop, huh? You ought to ask Åke Brundin, the cop. He was the one who took care of it all. And he was convinced that what happened to Casper was about being drunk at sea. There was a liquor bottle in the boat with a few drops left."

Ann knew Brundin very well. They had worked together on several occasions. He was a good policeman, even if she thought he wouldn't make too much trouble for himself for a lightweight from a Stockholm suburb who had probably stumbled over the railing.

"Fingerprints on the bottle, do you know anything about that?"

Robban grinned. "Listen, relax. Have you ever done that?"

"It has happened," said Ann, who was starting to get irritated at Robert Sillén. In the background, country music was playing, there was someone who risked losing his ninety acres of land, that much she understood of the lyrics. She found herself listening more carefully. Robert observed her, perhaps he awaited a statement.

"There were only his fingerprints, I think. Casper with a cee, he was precise about that," Robban said when the song died away. "My darling left too, but she didn't go off with a salesman."

"What do you mean?"

"The song," said Robban, making a gesture toward the living room, where the country music was starting up again.

"So what was he?"

"A pharmacist, can you imagine anything shabbier?"

That made Ann smile. "So what else?" she tossed out.

"Olga Palm is dead."

"I know that."

"Maybe Adrian will show up, if only to keep an eye on the inheritance. He was her only child."

"Cecilia," Ann attempted one last time. "Tell me something."

"She's dead. She took Casper's death hard, unexpectedly hard, and followed him into the water. That's the way you die here, if you choose to go in voluntarily. Yes, the old men shoot themselves in the head, like Edman for example, but Cissi didn't have a shotgun."

"Her parents think—"

"Hope doesn't die, that a missing person will return one fine day," said Robert, and Ann got the idea that he meant his stray wife.

They went out in the yard together. They stood quietly a moment. "One thing about Cissi," said Robban. "She was good-looking but there was something more about her."

"What was that?"

"There was something in her appearance, she radiated tons of those pheromones. Men notice and see that sort of thing, believe me. Perhaps it wasn't so good. There were many who misunderstood. Some thought they could get it on with her, but she wasn't that type, not a slut, if you understand."

A shaggy dog came shuffling. "I took over Caesar," said Robban. "Casper's mutt," he added when he saw Ann's uncomprehending expression.

They observed one another as if to measure the other's quality. Robban was a hodgepodge of many of the characteristics and opinions she encountered so often in single men. Yet there was something genuine in him. The jargon he'd adopted, and the bitterness that occasionally seeped out, was his way of processing middle age and the fact that perhaps he would never get to experience the romance his music so often spoke of. Perhaps he didn't even want that, it struck Ann.

"One more thing," he said. "I don't believe in that bottle in the boat. He didn't drink liquor. I never saw him have a shot or a toddy."

"So what did he drink?" Ann asked, even though she suspected the answer.

"*Vin ordinaire,*" said Robban.

"But if he were desperate and wanted to drown himself, then maybe a little stronger goods could give him courage."

"Casper was brave. Upper-class, of course, but he didn't usually back down. Once he'd decided on something he didn't hesitate."

Ann got into her car. Robert H. Sillén was still standing in the yard. She saw in the rearview mirror how he bent his neck and with one hand stroked his thinning hair.

In the car she tried to summarize what she knew, and what she was guessing. Many pieces, and the majority were missing, she thought. That had been her work, her passion, working puzzles. Perhaps a thousand pieces, sometimes many more. She felt the feeling from before. She would go to the funeral for Olga, and there she would probably encounter one more piece, her son, Adrian. Could she ask him about the letters, and thereby reveal that she'd read them? Could she ask about that "misadventure" at the Hasselbacken restaurant that was mentioned in one of the letters?

She'd read the text from the four postcards several times but had become no wiser. They were like concise text messages. Some expressed longing, others were more everyday: "See you on Friday"; "Don't forget to bring with you . . ." or "What a nice time we had . . ." No other names were mentioned, no places other than Hotel Knaust in Sundsvall.

She came up to the highway, had to wait, a long row of cars had driven off the ferry and were now heading north in a column. She counted them, then turned and accelerated.

There was something extremely old-fashioned about it all. Who sent snail mail these days? Was that an expression of a kind of romanticism, a stage in a flirtation? If Adrian did send letters to Cecilia, then perhaps he also wrote letters to his mother, Olga? Ann would like to get hold of other documents by his hand to compare the handwriting on the postcards.

She decided to ask Adrian, perhaps without directly mentioning that she knew about the existence of the letters, but with a few white lies it should be possible to coax something out, not least about Casper Stefansson.

"Piece by piece," she said out loud, and suddenly saw herself as an active police officer on Gräsö. How many inhabitants did the island have, seven hundred? In the summer that number doubled. In the best of all worlds there would be a police officer stationed on the island. Now the nearest police station was in Östhammar, and the small force there had a large geographic area to cover.

She could become a parish constable, move in with Edvard and live the rest of her life on the island. Daydreams, she understood that. The reality looked different.

"Men," she said then. They were all men, and of a certain sort. Single men: Casper, Adrian, Robban, and Blixten Lindberg. And then a woman in the center of interest: Cecilia.

Five

"The cost is two thousand, three hundred fifty kronor per year. And then there's VAT."

"But you get mail delivered at home for free," said Ann Lindberg. "And then you have to send out a mail carrier in all kinds of weather."

"What do you mean?"

"With a post office box you all can stay indoors, with lots of boxes in front of you and just throw in the mail, and then the customer takes the trouble to go pick it up. And it costs me three thousand. That's what I mean."

"Just under."

"What do you mean, just under?"

"The cost is just under three thousand kronor."

"Okay, I'd like box number 339. That's my lucky number."

"Unfortunately, that one is taken," said the postal official after some rustling of papers.

"Is your office on Björkgatan in Uppsala?"

She got the complete address, which she noted. *Sammy gets to fix this,* thought Ann, while she more or less politely concluded the call with Nordpost. Perhaps her old colleague at Violent Crimes could produce the name of the person renting the box. It was likely that Cecilia Karlsson had terminated her rental. It would be interesting to know when.

"You don't give up."

Edvard was sitting at his favorite position, Viola's old place at the kitchen table, with a view over the strait. The house was the last outpost on the narrow gravel road, then the sea started. It was a classic Roslagen home, a two-story log house built in the early 1900s. It was fishing that once paid for the logs and timber, the magnificent sun porch and the ornamentation. Viola had been the last in an ancient Gräsö family, too headstrong to start a family, despite being courted. But Viola resisted, rejected all proposals, perhaps she dreamed of Victor, who was equally headstrong, and remained single.

Edvard had come there by chance when, during his escape from the mainland, from home, family, and work, he spontaneously turned off the highway, drove to the end of the road, got out of the car, and asked if there was a possibility of renting a place to live. Viola had looked him over, perhaps realized his qualities, and pointed to the top floor. When she later died, between age ninety and a hundred, he inherited everything.

"It irritates me that Cecilia had a post office box in Uppsala. I'm going to ask Sammy to check if and when she stopped paying for it."

"Can you do that sort of thing? Snoop, I mean. She hasn't done anything criminal, has she, she just disappeared."

"If you only knew what the police do."

Edvard smiled. "I've understood a few things."

"I think she killed Casper Stefansson, pushed him in the water, and staged a drowning accident. Arranged a bottle so that it would look like he was drunk on the water. You know that he was a diver? Someone like that doesn't just drown."

"And then she took off for Portugal?"

Ann nodded.

"That will be hard to prove."

"Perhaps there are witnesses," said Ann lightly.

"Do you know that it was Blixten Lindberg who found his boat in Hög-klyke? There'd been a northerly wind for several days."

"What was he doing there?"

"Dredging some old beach meadow by the strait. He does that sort of thing."

"Is he capable?"

Edvard gave her a quick glance. "That was an unusual question coming from you, but I think so."

"I'm going to take a walk," said Lindell, getting up from the table. She wanted to think in peace, but also leave Edvard alone. She'd understood for a long time that he needed solitude more than she did. He had taken a week of vacation, she had understood that as generous, and they'd been together intensively the last few days. She had deliberately adapted to his rhythm and needs without feeling slighted or ignored. If she was too intrusive he withdrew, she knew that from before. She had intended to call Sammy Nilsson, and she had come to understand that Edvard could be a little jealous of him, so the call could just as well happen out of earshot.

She herself had a week and a half left before cheese making awaited. Before this she wanted to get answers to quite a few questions. She walked down to the sea. It was late summer and perhaps the best time of the year. Many of the summer visitors had left and the water temperature was decent for swimming, about twenty degrees Celsius in the little bay below Edvard's place.

Sammy Nilsson was downright dismissive of her suggestion to check on box 339. "I don't want to be some Stasi agent who harasses innocent people," he said. In general he sounded sullen and tired. Ann assumed it had to do with his divorce. She suggested that they should meet, but the response was a vague "we'll have to see when that works." After the call it struck Ann that the connection to her old job and colleagues was thinning out more and more. She remained standing on Edvard's dock. A swan pair with three half-grown cygnets glided past by the small reef which at low tide stuck up like a lizard's back, and which Viola had called her own pantry, but it meant less and less, the perch had mostly disappeared. In the beginning of Ann's relationship with Edvard they would row out with fishing rods and return to Viola's kitchen with half a bucket of fish, whose filets immediately went into the frying pan.

Where was the linchpin in this story about Casper Stefansson's probable drowning death and Cecilia Karlsson's disappearance? Had anything criminal even happened? Was she simply a superannuated cop who for lack of stimulation was rooting in other people's lives and misfortunes?

She had to decide, and that would happen after the impending funeral of Olga Palm. *It will have to be that way,* she thought. *If nothing solid emerges then I'll drop the whole thing.* She had a sense that otherwise Edvard would get tired of her and she did not want to risk that for anything, now that they had resumed contact.

A movement caught her attention. A sea eagle came gliding at a low level over the water. Sweden's largest bird, she had recently learned. It came closer and closer. Ann felt how her life in one stroke became a little lighter, and with the eagle's help she let herself be carried off for a moment until the cell phone vibrated in her pocket as a reminder of real life.

It was Gunilla Karlsson. She apologized in a torrent of words that immediately put Ann off. *Get to the point,* she was prepared to interrupt, just when Cecilia's mother suggested that they should meet.

"How did you get my number?"

"I called and asked Blixten."

"I see, and why should we meet?"

"I'm worried about Rune," said Gunilla Karlsson.

Afraid of him, in other words, thought Ann, but did not say anything, forcing the other woman to continue.

"He's acting more and more strangely."

"And how shall I help you with that? There must be others you can turn to?"

"I don't want to go to the police."

Ann observed the eagle that sailed on higher and higher. *A police question,* she thought, *not something for the psychologist in other words.*

"Can we perhaps meet in Öregrund? I can treat you to a cup of coffee, we can sit down in peace and quiet . . . without anyone else listening. It shouldn't take that much of your time."

Ann hesitated a moment, and then said, "When and where?"

Six

The weather forecast spoke of seventeen degrees Celsius and drizzle. That suited her fine. She decided on a dark, wide coat she'd bought in Porto, which made it possible, with stuffing, to increase her body mass and transform herself into a butterball. Together with the wig, a broad-brimmed hat, dark glasses, and a different way of walking, that should fool everyone, she was sure of it. She had practiced walking with small steps and not the long strides she normally took.

There was one problem. She could not change her voice, but if she stayed in the background and adopted a slightly dismissive attitude it would surely go fine. If she were to be asked how she knew Olga Palm she would take a handkerchief out of her coat pocket, lower her head, and pretend to be crushed by grief.

Cecilia Karlsson came to the church at the last minute. It was a conscious decision. The parking lot was full. There was a throng of people dressed in black in front of the entry and many had certainly gone into the church as the rain picked up. Umbrellas were opened. That was just fine. She parked along the road on the hill leading down to the ferry terminal, got out of the car, opened her umbrella, and walked toward the church. *Small steps,* she repeated silently to herself.

No one paid her any particular attention. An elderly couple nodded, but that was probably more out of habit. She stood at the outer edge of the group, partly hidden by the umbrella, took off the glasses which might seem suspect in the rain. She sneaked a glance at the funeral guests, a few she recognized immediately, others were unfamiliar. Adrian Palm was standing in front of the church entry. He was four years older than the last time she had seen him. His hair had started to turn gray and he seemed shorter. He played his role well, one moment affected and dejected, the next heartily welcoming, shaking hands with everyone. A younger woman got a kiss on the cheek, and with one arm he herded people into the church. *Speed up a little,* he seemed to be saying, *so we can get started and get her down in the ground as quickly as possible.*

In no way did it feel upsetting to see him. Cecilia was mentally prepared. The years abroad had strengthened her, she'd had time to analyze her life, what and who called the shots for her. Adrian was undeniably one of those who had ruled her life. You hear about master suppression techniques; Adrian knew most of them. Perhaps that was required if you wanted to run a business with hundreds of millions in sales. On the internet she had followed Adrian and his company. It was blossoming, he must get credit for that, and had expanded outside the country's borders, with offices in Copenhagen and Hamburg, and as of a few months ago in London as well.

It had taken a couple of years in Portugal to understand what had formed her, years of doubt and soul-searching, and a little self-pity. Maybe not formed, she thought, more like deformed. She now saw herself as a victim, not of circumstances but instead because of the men who explained the world to her. Constantly explained.

More and more people were making their way into the church. Cecilia took the opportunity to slip in under cover of a group of elderly funeral guests, who she believed were coworkers of Olga. She grasped a woman under the arm, pretended to support her, as if she were a confidante or friend. The woman smiled gratefully at this gesture of consideration.

"That it should rain on us. Miserable. Olga, who had such a sunny disposition," said the woman. Cecilia tried to put on a friendly face behind the rising inner tension and nodded in confirmation that she agreed. Adrian's mother really had been like that, someone who shone like a sun, warming her surroundings. What Adrian always concealed behind his accommodating and good-hearted attitude was hardness and calculation, which could definitely not be blamed on his mother's intentions and influence.

She heard his voice behind her, looked around for a seat at the back of the church, turned to the left, and sank down on the pew. He passed in the middle aisle. His seat was naturally at the very front, where he slowly made his way as if the sorrow made him helpless. *Games,* thought Cecilia. *He hasn't changed.*

Someone had chosen hymn 249, perhaps it was Olga herself. It thundered out of the organ pipes, and the congregation joined in with a mixed voice, the verses sank and rose as if the funeral guests had to take a breath, uncertainly making their way forward between the familiar words: "Day by day . . . He whose name is strength and counsel both . . ." Cecilia bowed her head, reminded of Olga, but also brought back to her own life on the island and solemn moments in the church. Perhaps she no longer believed in any God, but the words unraveled threads from the fabric of her person.

Carefully she let her gaze wander over the necks of the congregation. So far she had not seen her parents but assumed that they were there somewhere in front. She toyed with the thought of making herself known. How would they react? Rune would of course turn stiff and mute, then furious, incapable of expressing anything other than pent-up rage at her hiding and years of silence. Gunilla would surely stammer out questions about "why," combined with laments about her daughter's shameful betrayal.

After Casper's disappearance and probable death in the strait they had openly insinuated that she'd been in the boat and was directly or indirectly behind his death. It was a peculiar, slightly amusing experience that her parents so unreservedly thought her capable of such an action, she who otherwise always stayed out of the way. She had responded with mockery, even though inside she was dark with regret and loss, and her hatred of them had grown and came up like bile. She had started preparing her flight out of the country. *Free yourself,* she'd repeated again and again during the early summer of 2015, *and punish them.* Yes, she had wanted to hurt her parents, and there were two widely separate reasons.

"Help me, Lord, no matter what befalls me / To take from your faithful father's hand" echoed in the sanctuary as the congregation took courage and in a strong voice sang out as if so that Olga would hear the words there in her casket.

Then she caught sight of them. Rune, straight-backed, and who despite his strong and beautiful singing voice surely was only mumbling along with the verses, while Gunilla, aware of her screechy voice, sat with bowed head and her hands clasped on her lap. Crushed. Not in sorrow over her old acquaintance's death and burial, no, it was her own life that was ransacked every time they moved among Gräsö islanders. That's how it was. No medals or distinctions from the arenas of archery fields and running tracks could dispute that they were being punished by their daughter, declared incompetent and not worthy of her love. They had failed with their only child. She had frustrated their ridiculous hopes for her and thereby in a way crushed their honor and pride. This had slowly become plain to Cecilia during her time abroad.

Can you stop loving your parents? Yes, she had finally answered herself at the little neighborhood place in Serpa where she almost daily could study a family of half a dozen members that actually appeared to function. The restaurateur couple almost stood out as caricatures, created for a pleasant family film: he with a considerable roundness, boisterous and hearty, and she short and slender, always in the background with a guarded look. Their children came and went as they wanted, Cecilia had never understood the distribution of work and the schedule, but it evidently worked; the food came to the table, jokes and laughter by turns, but also private, quiet conversations that were negotiated in the inner parts of the restaurant.

It was there, at "The Heart," which was the name of the restaurant, that she came to the insight about her own heart's beating, her own rhythm. She no longer loved anyone. To stand before this abyss and stare down into a frosty and lonely darkness was obviously frightening, sometimes horrible, but the insight also provided a kind of relief. She explained herself. Her upbringing was explained.

The ceremony continued. The officiant gave his eulogy. Hymns were sung. Someone read a poem by Pär Lagerkvist. She recognized it. Olga had read it to her so many times that she knew it by heart, and she read along, silently to herself, while the tears ran.

Adrian was sitting in the first row. She liked seeing how he started sobbing. She'd never seen him cry. She remembered his hands best. She sank into the memory while the traditional rituals continued.

Suddenly it was all over, the organ thundered, people stood up, and the casket was rolled away on a little cart through the church. Adrian took the lead, and the line gradually formed. Cecilia was taken by surprise and became hesitant, getting up and sneaking away was not a good idea, she would get everyone's eyes on her. Instead she tried to do as little as possible, hunched over, looking down. The casket passed. Gräsö natives and summer visitors passed in review; a strange mixture of anxiety, body odors, and perfume rose up from the procession. She suppressed the urge to look up, see Adrian at close quarters. She wanted to study her parents, had they aged much? The music sounded disquieting. Scattered low voices were heard, a child laughed, the line moved slowly forward, and she was the last one to stand up and join it. Before she reached the church entry she put on the glasses. Adrian was caught up in conversation with an elderly couple who had been neighbors of Olga. That suited her very well and she could slip away, working her way forward and away. She stopped and turned her head, inspected the congregation that was starting to break up. There they stood! Rune who despised formal attire but was careful about convention was dressed in a dark suit. Gunilla was wearing a light coat that Cecilia had bought in Stockholm. It made her a little upset, *She could have asked first* was the thought that first flew through her mind.

Rune was a little bent and Gunilla was a bit more wrinkled, but otherwise the two looked like they had the past ten or fifteen years. Their athleticism had been beneficial as they grew older, superficially at least they were a relatively healthy middle-aged couple.

Cecilia felt nothing. She had looked forward to, perhaps feared, the moment when she would see her parents again, but everything was blank inside. That disappointed her, she wanted to feel some emotion, a little something in any event, because this nothing was probably even more evidence that her emotional life was damaged forever.

She left the cemetery with dainty steps. Outside the gate a group of people was standing. Cecilia caught a few words about coffee, there would be a gathering afterward, she had assumed that. With bowed head she tried to slip past unnoticed but felt how they were scrutinizing her. She was a strange bird and those sorts were subject to inspection on the island, and then there was the very human element that you wanted to know who had participated. A funeral was a farewell but also a confirmation of belonging, you wanted to be able to gossip a little. Behind her back she heard Blixten's voice, it was unmistakable. Had he recognized her? Would he come running after her like he did in Lisbon?

The car was a short distance away and this was a painful stretch to cover. She cast a hurried glance backward. Blixten was looking at her, it was obvious. There were two alternatives: Either she joined the ferry line, she saw the ferry docking and would not need to wait long before she could leave the island, or else she could drive in the opposite direction toward her hiding place, but then she would have to pass the church and thereby be subject to a new inspection.

She decided on the mainland. There were only a dozen cars that rolled on board the ferry. Once again she felt split, to leave the field alone or be warmed with the others.

On board the ferry, during the few minutes the crossing took, the old hatred flared up again. She knew that it was consuming but the feeling could not be suppressed. She had hated ever since childhood but didn't understand then what it was an expression of. For a long time she blamed herself, looked at herself with her parents' eyes, above all Rune's demanding and often openly critical gaze. *Perform*, it seemed to say, not "live," "play," or "desire," but instead "perform," and for a long time she did. She always had the highest grades and the best reports in school. On the running track she had not inherited her father's explosiveness and sharp elbows for the eight-hundred-meter, but probably the endurance. She became a long-distance runner, kept at it, lap after lap. There was nothing beautiful in her style, instead her running gave a painful impression. When she was sixteen years old and ready for national junior championship, she stepped off the track for good.

For several hours she drove around the roads of north Uppland without a plan or destination. She passed towns that she had visited as a child and let herself be inundated with memories.

It was a high price she'd had to pay to attend the funeral, but she was compelled. Olga was the person who had meant the most in her life. As the wise woman she was, she had seen Cecilia's worries and taken on the young girl, told her about play and desire, about self-esteem, about men and love in a way that Cecilia had never encountered, neither before nor later. She had read poems by Nils Ferlin, Karin Boye, Pär Lagerkvist, and Dan Andersson, talked about that there was something beyond the hills. It had been so shockingly different from her home's narrow and controlled world that to

start with it had been difficult for Cecilia to take in. Carefully Olga had untied many of the knots that made Cecilia's youth an inexplicable mystery.
She started to take things for herself, to help herself. She took courage. She
started to smile instead of looking at the ground. She started swaying her
rear end instead of being ashamed of it. She started to win, even in the short
races. Rune had not understood much, many times he'd been furious at his
daughter, tried to stop her, but the process was irreversible.

A year after her disappearance abroad Cecilia had called Olga. They
talked for a long time. There were no fiery and reproachful questions about
how and why Cecilia had been hiding, no criticism. "Tell Rune and Gunilla that I'm alive," she had said, "but not how and where."

After that they had spoken once or twice a month. Olga kept her informed about what was happening on the island, what Adrian was doing,
how the company had grown quickly, and that he visited Gräsö less and
less often. She also told Cecilia that her parents mutely received the word
that she had called and used Olga as a go-between.

"I actually took transportation service to their house. I thought such
news must be delivered face-to-face." Rune had left without a word.

"She's ashamed!" Gunilla Karlsson decided. "That was why she called
you and not home."

"This is probably the last time we can talk," Olga had unsentimentally
said at the end of July. "Now that they've taken the other leg too I don't
want to live any longer." They said their goodbyes. "Can I ask someone to
call you and let you know? Maybe Nygren, the retired minister in Öregrund, you remember him, don't you? He's good, we keep in touch and he
has duty of confidentiality." That was how three weeks later Cecilia found
out that Olga had passed away and when the funeral would happen.

It was late evening when she returned to the cabin. She opened a bottle of
wine, set out a glass and a plate with cheese, lit a candle, and sat down in
the kitchen. A decision must be made, and soon at that. Should she immediately leave the island and Sweden, or stay behind and carry out what she
had intended? She ached inside from the indecision and agony. How long

should she stay on the island? There was probably quite a bit to arrange after Olga's death, estate inventory and all that sort of thing.

Late in the evening, after having emptied the bottle, she sent a text message.

Seven

Nils "Blixten" Lindberg was both shaken and irresolute. A day and a half had passed and again and again he had replayed the scene outside the church. He had skipped the gathering with coffee and driven home. After a few minutes on the internet he produced the owner of the vehicle, a car rental company. When he called he was met by a recorded response: "We are open weekdays between 8:00 A.M. and 7:00 P.M., Saturday between 8:00 A.M. and 2:00 P.M., closed on Sundays."

Now it was just past eight o'clock on Monday morning. The results were skimpy; the only information he got was that the car was rented to a woman. The lie that he'd been in an accident and wanted to make contact with the driver hadn't worked as he'd wished and believed. "Inquire with the police" was the answer he got. "Naturally we do not give out names of our customers, but I can confirm that the woman is about thirty-five years old."

He clicked away the call. Cecilia would turn thirty-four in November. He would never go to the police. If she found out she would never want to see him again. There was another possible solution: He could turn to a former police officer.

He turned in toward "Viola's," as people still called the place, even though she'd been dead for ten years, but stopped immediately and stayed there for a few minutes. He hesitated about intruding, but Ann Lindell seemed relaxed, and she could always say no.

It wasn't cool to disturb people that you were only superficially acquainted with, ask them for favors. Edvard didn't make it easier. He was standing in the farmyard and was anything but accommodating. "She's on vacation," he said curtly.

"She came to me," said Blixten Lindberg, "and now I'm coming to her."

"Shouldn't you be going to work?"

"I can do that more or less as I want. I'm going to plow the ditch and meadow for the Man from Skåne who bought the Dutchman's place. The alders will probably still be there tomorrow."

They'd had some contact before. Edvard had helped him on some jobs when he'd fallen behind. A few years ago he gathered up and took away brush south of Mörtarö, and did it quickly and well, it was apparent that he'd been a farmworker. Once he had operated a rented chipper. They'd gotten along well, but then it was about work.

"She ought to let go of that Cecilia," Edvard said at last. "Maybe you too."

"I think she's in Sweden," he tossed out as bait. "Maybe even on the island."

"What, have you seen her?"

"I'd rather talk with Ann. I can come back later if this isn't a good time."

It struck him that maybe she was still asleep.

"Wait," said Edvard, stomping off. He had swallowed the bait. It did not take long before Ann Lindell came out.

"Would you like coffee?"

He shook his head. "I need your help with something." He told her that he thought he'd seen Cecilia Karlsson and how she quickly disappeared from the church. "I wrote down the license plate number. A rental car."

"Where was it rented?"

"In the Stockholm area, a small company, not one of the big brands that you recognize."

"And they won't tell you who rented it?"

"Quite right," he said, smiling. He liked this cop more and more.

"Does she have a valid driver's license?"

Ann turned toward Edvard, who was standing on the stairs to the porch. It looked as if he both wanted and didn't want to take part in the conversation.

"She reported both driver's license and passport as stolen and renewed everything two weeks before she disappeared. Folke Åhr mentioned that he had checked up on that. There is a theft report registered in early June of 2015. That strengthened the thought that she was not the victim of a crime but instead that it was a planned disappearance."

"She liked Olga a lot," said Blixten. "I don't really know how that came about, they weren't related, and I think she wanted to be at the funeral."

"I was there too," said Ann Lindell. "But I didn't see anyone who resembled Cecilia, and I looked carefully at everyone."

"She was in disguise and had a wig, but there was something that convinced me that it was her."

"What was that?"

"Hard to say," said Blixten, looking embarrassed for a moment, as if he'd been caught in something shameful. "Her way of moving her shoulders and then when she looked back . . . she sought my gaze somehow . . ."

"What's the name of the company that rented out the car?"

"I wrote down the registration number and all the info."

"Now is when the fun begins," said Ann. "Thanks, I'll see what I can dig up."

Eight

"Are you going to sell the house?"

"I don't know, don't think so."

They observed one another. Cecilia was wearing her wig. That surely bothered him. He probably felt betrayed, that during the funeral he'd fallen for a disguise.

"How many people know you're on the island?"

"No one."

"You came for my mom's sake?"

She nodded. *And your sake,* she wanted to add, but kept her mouth shut.

"I'm sorry it turned out the way it did," he started with the expected verbiage. He was his old self, and tried to explain like so many times before, as if the lies could be transformed into truths if you simply repeated them often enough.

Talk away, you, she thought, strangely passive, calm before his nervousness. A picture from Serpa in Portugal came unexpectedly to her, the

"The Heart" restaurant one evening in May, table on the street, a little coolness in the air, the women pulling their coats around their chests, the men wearing knit pullovers and dark caps, the lovely stone pavement, the murmur and the laughter.

"You're going to die." The words tumbled out of her mouth.

"What did you say?"

She shook her head.

"Where have you been?"

"Here and there. Abroad mostly."

"Many people have wondered. I've wondered."

He fell silent. They were standing in the parking lot at Gräsö Inn. The suggestion was hers. She had parked down by the ferry and taken the path up. She didn't want him to see her car.

"Have you seen Rune and Gunilla?"

She overlooked the hint. "And what about you? You travel around the world. It works out fine, right?"

It seemed as if he appreciated the question, that was his turf, and he started up the verbiage again. A lot had happened in four years, she'd already understood that, but the extent of his plans for the future were still astounding. It was partly a different language that he spoke, it was noticeable that he wanted to impress, as if to say: *It's going quite fine without you.* That actually didn't concern her, but her irritation grew. She stopped listening.

"And Casper, do you think about him sometimes?"

Her question made Adrian lose the thread of his self-praise. "What do you mean?"

"It was probably his idea from the start, I mean when you got the contract with Tetra Pak? Without that maybe everything would have stopped, and you'd still be sitting in a basement office in Östhammar. For that reason alone you ought to give him a thought."

"There is a witness," said Adrian.

"What do you mean?"

"Blixten saw two people leave the dock by Kallboda. Casper was one of them."

It was a blow to the stomach but she managed to keep a straight face.

"And the other person?"

"Blixten was probably drunk. You know how he gets. When I asked a week or so later he denied everything, that he'd seen anything at all. But he was there by the strait, he was the one of course who found the empty boat later."

"Why should he cover that up? If he did see two individuals."

"Maybe he didn't want to squeal."

"Squeal" sounded completely wrong in Adrian's mouth, someone who always tried to sound a little more refined than he was. She wondered why he even brought it up. Certainly to shake her up, that's probably what it was. He loved to confuse, and in that way get the advantage. It struck her that perhaps Blixten really had seen the whole course of events. It was not impossible in any way. She must deal with him, she must find out.

Adrian suggested that they should drive over to Öregrund and have a bite to eat. She rejected the suggestion.

"We have to talk," he said.

"I don't think so."

"I have a few things to tell you."

Once again this insinuation. She tried to sneer but felt that it didn't go that well, the talk about Blixten and what happened at Gällfjärden four years ago had shaken her up properly.

"I'm going to visit Rune and Gunilla too. There were a few things that Mom wanted them to have."

"If you say a single word that I'm in Sweden I'm going to kill you."

He stared mutely at her. Finally she had managed to disturb his arrogant expression.

"You're not well," he forced out.

"That may be." She took a step closer to him, put her hand on his crotch and took hold. He cried out.

"I have a few things to talk about too," she said. "What is the statute of limitations for fraud?"

She let go. The fact was that she felt a shiver of arousal. Maybe him too?

A little pain, a little lust. Like life. She remembered their moments of de-sire and passion. It had been intense, she had to admit that. Neither before nor after had she loved so wholeheartedly, so recklessly.

"You want to, right?" she said, smiling. "You want to fuck me. Say it. That's the only thing you want. You don't want to tell me anything, not have a bite to eat, just check into a hotel in Öregrund and fuck me."

She was standing quite close, let her breath warm his face. He took hold of the back of her neck with one hand, breathing heavily, defenseless be-fore her attack. She touched him again, this time playfully, and felt his bursting sex between her fingers.

"Never again," she said, smiling. She released herself from his grip and backed away.

He swallowed and looked around. A middle-aged couple came walking, headed for the information board that the municipality had set up. They pretended not to see the performance.

She turned on her heels and went her way. "How many years?" she re-peated loudly before she disappeared into the grove between the yard and the church.

Nine

There was no point in calling Sammy Nilsson again. He had refused to investigate the post office box in Uppsala and would certainly not be interested in checking out the car rental agency. Ann read the name of the company and address in Solna. Should she go there directly and try with a ploy, pretend to be investigating a traffic accident? But who would believe such a story, that a police officer drove such a long distance to check on a trivial offense?

"Don't you know any traffic cops?" Edvard asked from the stairs, as if he'd read her musings. "If there are still any of those left?"

Then it struck her that perhaps Åke Brundin at the police station in Östhammar would help her. He'd investigated Casper Stefansson's accident and of course knew about Cecilia's disappearance.

"You're good to have around sometimes," she said, fishing the phone out of her pocket. Brundin's number was stored, and he answered after a couple of rings.

"Oh, it's you," he said, and Ann could really see how he was smiling to himself.

"Do you have a moment?"

"Does this concern Cecilia Karlsson?"

"How did you know?"

"Folke Åhr called and told me that you ran into each other in Portugal. I didn't really know if it was true or not, because he was truly babbling about everything."

"He does that, more and more often, more and more," said Ann, who did not want to mention the suspicions of Alzheimer's.

"I think he's starting to get senile," said Brundin.

"Two things," said Ann, who truly did not want to babble. "A post office box in Uppsala and a car rental in Solna." She explained the connections, and her former colleague listened without interrupting. When she'd gotten to the point he was silent a moment.

"Doubtful," he said at last. "I can't start a private investigation just like that."

That was the response she'd expected. Anything else would be surprising. He was an honorable policeman.

"What if a witness calls you? Nils Lindberg is his name, also called Blixten."

"I know who he is," Brundin said curtly. "But how does the post office box come into the picture?"

"I saw an envelope, several actually, at the Karlssons' home. Cecilia's parents, that is."

"Thin."

"I know, but there's something to this, I'm almost certain of it." She let him think a moment.

"We've known each other a long time," she resumed.

That was what she could say, refer to: that she'd been a good investigator and that they'd collaborated well before without fuss. "You remember the dismembered woman?"

Of course he remembered, likewise the arsons in Ann's village the year before. "*I'm* not senile," he said.

"If anything emerges you'll get to take over, of course." That was bait as good as any. "I think Cecilia is alive and that she may have had something to do with Stefansson's death. You wondered yourself at the time, four years ago, didn't you?"

She shut up, mustn't jabber too much, and it was extremely doubtful that Brundin had wondered. He'd been quite sure that it was a drowning accident in a state of intoxication, that was what she'd heard anyway.

"I'll think about it."

Ann gave him the number of the post office box and the information about the car rental agency in Solna. "One more thing," she said before they ended the call. "You're not looking for a constable on Gräsö, are you?" The response was a hearty laugh.

Edvard was still standing on the steps. "The old Ann Lindell in top form," he said, and what made her even happier was that he smiled. An opposite reaction would have been completely possible, even likely.

"I'm going home to Tilltorp for a couple of hours. I'm missing a few things."

"Cheese maybe?"

Ann laughed. "No, not cheese. You'll see later. Do you need anything?"

"Yes," said Edvard and looked at her seriously. "You'll see later."

Ten

Who? The first thought was Rune. It was a purely reflexive reaction that came from many years of monitoring and control, but she realized immediately that it was unlikely. What would he be doing in the cabin? Who had any business there at all? She decided that it was chance that brought a visitor there who peeked in through the window. The tracks were clear in the fine-grained sand that Cecilia had sprinkled in front of the windows. Someone had stood there, walked around a little, and perhaps in the crack below the blind discovered something that attracted interest.

She rounded the end of the house. The cellar door was untouched, the lock she had placed intact. She went around the house two times and tried to discover anything that would indicate that the intruder had managed to get in.

Unease. Thought of immediate flight. Who? Had someone seen her turn down the little road, which nowadays resembled a broad, overgrown path,

and gotten curious? She'd been careful, looked around as she approached
the drive, which was isolated, far from any settlement, the traffic sparse. A
couple of times she'd waited, slowed down, let a car pass, before she quickly
turned in.

Perhaps it was a mushroom picker? She'd seen that the yellow chanterelles had started to peek up. Some exercise fanatic who was out for a run?
She worked her way through the various possibilities.

There were footprints only in front of one of the windows and that made
her a little calmer. While she walked back to the car, which was parked in
a thicket a good ways from the house, she toyed with the idea of leaving.
How would she ever again feel secure and calm in the cabin? She walked
back indecisively, inspected the tracks again. She compared them with her
own size 38. The prints were considerably larger. Flats, maybe running
shoes.

She crouched down and inspected the gap under the blind. It was possible to glimpse the wig stand in the room. The propane stove was clearly
visible, likewise a number of cans, the package of biscuits on the table
as well. Whoever had peered in understood that someone was inhabiting
the house, at least temporarily. That was bad. Curiosity had perhaps been
aroused. Would the intruder come back?

She kept the lights off, moved in the darkness with the greatest caution.
Now and then she cracked open the door, peered out in the darkness, listened, but heard only the wind and the sea, perhaps an owl in the distance.

She made tea but let it stand, instead poured a glass of wine and drank
slowly but deliberately. There had been occasions in her life when wine served
as a soporific. Now she took care of herself, poured a second glass but then
corked the bottle again and put it away. She could not get drunk.

If she were to leave the cabin now, where would she go? There was no
simple answer. She could get a room at Gräsö Inn, a thought that struck
her when she met Adrian in the parking lot outside the hostel. If she had
to stay longer perhaps the cabin would be a bit too spartan, she reasoned to
herself. She knew the proprietors, she'd seen a couple of the farm's people

at Olga's funeral. The question was whether they would ask for identification, or would they simply see through her disguise?

The night was restless with sleep that came and went. The deathwatch beetle gnawed its passages in the wall, *tick tick*. With her ear against the wall she could clearly hear its insistent work. *So strange,* she thought, *we live so close to each other, perhaps only a few centimeters separate us. You count down. I count down.*

She got up several times to look outside. The darkness was truly compact and it would get worse when autumn came, but then she would be far from Gräsö.

At dawn she had decided. *Adrian must die.* With that thought she fell back asleep and then slept heavily for several hours, but was wakened by a strange sound. It took a while before she understood that someone was knocking on the door. She flew up, looked around in confusion, tiptoed out in the kitchen. A knife was the only thing she had. She seized it on her way to the minimal hall. Put her ear against the door. Another knock, harder this time, with the conviction that there was someone in the house.

"Hello," she heard someone call. A woman. "Hello, is anyone at home?"

Cecilia thought that she recognized the voice, or rather the tone, but who did it belong to?

"What do you want?"

"I'm looking for a cabin to rent."

"This one is occupied, go away!" Cecilia screamed in a voice that was shriller than she'd intended. She simply sounded afraid. There was silence for quite a while. She stood stock-still, breathing shallowly, squeezing the knife in her hand.

"Cecilia, is that you?"

Eleven

It bothered her that Gunilla Karlsson was so nervous and scattered. She didn't like that, never had, it was as if foolishly enough she always placed higher demands on women. She had the desire to tell her to stop picking at the napkin. It had been folded any number of times.

"He gets up at night, walks around."

"Outside or inside?"

"Both. Once he was gone when I woke up, and I had to start searching. Then I was really worried. I found him in the skiff. He was curled up in the bow, looked like a little bundle."

"Cold and a lot of mosquitoes," said Ann.

"That sort of thing doesn't bother him. Mosquitoes and gnats don't affect Rune."

"Why, do you think?"

Gunilla Karlsson crumpled the napkin, ruling out with emphasis any origami. Ann observed her clenched hand, felt how the tension was rising.

"He holds on to things," the brief answer came at last. Ann waited. There must be more, she thought.

"He didn't like it that they were going to move to Italy. You knew that, that she'd quit her job and they were going to leave that summer, Cecilia and Casper? Rune was against it, of course."

"That's not particularly hard to understand," said Ann.

"I know that Rune met with Casper."

Gunilla Karlsson let go of the napkin, pushed it away, gave Ann a glance. What was there in her tormented expression? Fear, calculation, guilt, and shame, all in one perhaps?

"It was right before Casper disappeared. I was at a gathering for archers. We have an association, we arrange small competitions and parties. I'm on the board. I wasn't at home, but I found out later."

"What was that?"

"That they argued. The mail carrier heard them and was a witness to it all, how Rune screamed and threatened Casper. It was unpleasant, he said. Rune whom he knew as a sensible fellow was completely crazy."

Ann stood up to get more coffee. She wanted to give Gunilla a little breathing room, but it was clear where she was headed. After she had retrieved the thermos of coffee and refilled the cups she took matters to their logical conclusion.

"Do you think that your husband murdered Casper Stefansson?" She did not wait for a reply but instead went back with the thermos. "You said that the mail carrier knew Rune as a sensible person, but you don't?"

"We've had a good life for a long time, but sometimes I'm scared," said Gunilla Karlsson, and thereby gave an indirect answer to Ann's question. "It has happened that I've left for a time. I usually take the car and just drive a little until he's calmed down. Once I drove to Uppsala and stayed overnight with an old friend. She knows what it's like for me and convinced me to stay. After that Rune was calmer for a while."

It was a threatened and frightened woman's story. Ann had heard variations of it far too many times. "Why does he take his anger out on you?"

"The slightest thing," said Gunilla, "but often it has to do with my archery, that I'm away from home. But I have to get away sometimes! I have to breathe, do you understand?"

Ann nodded but without any great enthusiasm. She would rather hear stories about happiness and trust. There had been a little too much of the opposite in recent years. Even so she could feel sympathy for the woman on the other side of the table. Her wandering, apologetic gaze confirmed that she felt divided talking about her marriage, her husband and the fear she felt.

"Cecilia, what did she say? She must have noticed it."

"When she was at home Rune was like a lamb." The mockery in Gunilla's voice was unmistakable.

"And you didn't say anything?"

"A little maybe."

How soiled everything is, it struck Ann. Everything suggested that Gunilla Karlsson was a victim, even if the other part hadn't been mentioned, but the exposure of a family's shabby distress was not pretty.

Ann turned her head and looked out over the cemetery on the other side of the street. Some children were playing between the old black crosses. What could she say? Should she drill even deeper into the Karlsson family?

"Is there something you want to get out?"

"What do you mean?"

"You wanted to see me. Is there anything else that is pressing on you, that must be said?"

"There's a lot, but it's not easy. I thought it would be nice to talk with a woman with experience. We're about the same age too."

"Is it because I'm a former police officer that you wanted to see me, talk about your husband, gossip a little? You think that I still have contacts, that I would whisper in some former colleague's ear."

"What is that? What do you mean?"

"Whisper that Rune is a violent man."

"I just wanted . . . maybe I'm a little scared. I thought we made good contact," Gunilla Karlsson said defensively, and Ann regretted her words at once.

"I understand," she said, "but I probably can't help you. Maybe you have to make contact with others, professionals I mean. What you've told me doesn't sound good. And you shouldn't have to be afraid in a relationship."

"Thanks," Gunilla said submissively, standing up. "Thanks for taking the time."

Despite everything she left the bakery café with style. It was probably in her marrow, to straighten up, raise her head, look purposeful, sail away and out.

Ann observed the crumpled napkin, wondered what the woman's words were about. Was it a cry for help or did she simply want to get an ally in a heartless family drama and indirectly put pressure on her husband? Because surely she understood that Ann would be affected and perhaps look at Rune with a changed eye.

It wasn't beautiful, but that was life. She smiled to herself, stood up, called "thanks so much," and went out into the fresh air. She stood there, observed the children's play over the resting place of the dead, turned right down the hill, right again, and headed for the entry to the state liquor store.

Twelve

"Hello!"

No response. She hated not knowing where he was. It had gotten worse recently. He made himself invisible in the house, did not make himself known, as if he was amusing himself with a cat-and-mouse game. It felt as if he wanted to say: *This is how it can be if you don't behave yourself, you'll come home to a deserted house.* Maybe he wanted to provoke a reaction, observe her in secret before finally appearing.

The best reaction of course was to not care, but she didn't like that. She wanted to be aware, not let anyone attack her from behind. She listened toward the top floor but it was silent there. He basically never went upstairs during the day. If he wanted to rest awhile he lay down on the sofa in the kitchen. She sat down in the kitchen, more irresolute than ever. Had she managed to convey what she wanted to the ex–police officer? What surprised her was Ann Lindell's somewhat hard and dismissive attitude. Ann had seemed receptive and reasonable when she and Edvard visited, had she been mistaken? Gunilla Karlsson decided that it was the old work style that had come out. As a detective you were probably forced to be a little tough.

Was he down by the dock? She went out in the hall. There were the boots he almost always had on when he went to the water. She opened the front door and peered out, but there was no movement, no sound that could explain where Rune was.

She had come to hate the farm more and more. The silence. The isolation. He on the other hand was content. He could sit in the same spot and stare for an hour or two. "I'm philosophizing a little," he might say, but never uttered anything sensible later. If you ponder such a long time something substantial ought to come out, she thought, but no. He made his rounds, as she assumed his father and those before him had also done. Then it was justified when the farm was full of livestock, there was feeding or mucking, milking or grooming to do, fences to be looked after and gates opened and closed. Now it was just infantile to parade around like an estate owner.

Did she also hate her husband? Yes, maybe, even if "hate" was a strong expression. He had gotten old and it had happened quickly, accelerated the past few years. His previously so lithe and muscular body had collapsed. If they were to arm-wrestle maybe she would beat him. She still practiced archery and actually thought she had gotten stronger in old age.

He exercised less and less, only went for a run now and then, and had lost his flexibility and potency. The past year he hadn't even tried to force himself on her in bed, surely aware how meaningless such an approach would be, and she was only grateful for that. *I get mine anyway,* she thought, with a smile.

After a last look over the farm she closed the front door but at the same moment opened it instinctively again. It felt as if she must have an easily accessible escape route, a silly thought of course, but she couldn't suppress the feeling. Did he want to harm her? Hardly, but on the other hand he was so unpredictable that you could never know for sure.

She heard a faint clicking sound and she stood quite still, but it stopped at that. Once again silence prevailed in the house. It struck her that maybe the sound came from the cellar, which she hadn't checked. She pressed one ear against the door. She could definitely hear something, diffuse sounds that she couldn't attribute to anything. She slowly opened the door. The lights were on. He was there! He never left them on, he'd nagged about that for years, how many kilowatts it would be in a year.

"Rune?"

No response. She called one more time, this time louder.

"Here!" His voice sounded as if it came from the underworld. It always echoed eerily in the cellar.

"What are you doing?"

"Are you home now?"

What an idiotic question, she thought, but his voice sounded happy anyway, in any event not upset or angry, so she decided to go down. He was sitting at the worktable in front of the gun cabinet. One of the rifles was laid out before him.

"A little gun care," he said without giving her a look. She understood now that the clicking sound she'd heard came from when he tested the trigger. She'd seen and heard it previously. She was not unfamiliar with gun care in itself, she was after all a shooter, albeit with a bow, but there was something adolescent about his fixation. His father had been like that, she'd understood. His old M9 was still around, so Rune could be excused for that.

"The question is whether I still don't think that my old M98 is better. I have to adjust the pressure on the new Mauser but I don't dare do it myself. Maybe I dare, but I shouldn't. It can easily fire off a shot . . . an accidental shot."

He gave her a quick glance before he continued tinkering with his rifles. He had thoughts about the appearance of the butt and the recoil on the M12. She had certainly heard it all before, but kept her composure.

"Pity that Cissi never got interested in hunting," he continued.

"Not in the bows either," she said, deadly tired of the talk. "Are you hungry? I can—"

"No, absolutely not," he interrupted her. He twisted the old office chair a quarter turn so that they were facing each other. The gun rested on his lap. "Do you see other men?"

He smiled, as if the whole thing was an amusing game and not a death-blow to their marriage and life. The direct question put her off balance, and she understood that was the intention.

"I know that you're sleeping with others, so you don't need to answer. I've known it a long time. I think that was one of the reasons Cissi ran away."

"That's horrible!"

He shook his head. "Having a whore for a mother can't be nice."

She turned on her heels. "You get one more chance," he said when she reached the stairs.

Thirteen

It was a fine day with radiant sun and clear skies; you could feel that autumn was waiting around the corner. He removed alder and willow from the ditch. The landowner wanted to quickly get the stumps removed too and Nils Lindberg would come back with the backhoe loader, but it would have to be when the ground held a little better. More trunks fell and formed a long row along a stretch of perhaps eighty meters. He took pride in having them fall neatly, preferably at a ninety-degree angle to the ditch. The road that ran along the old meadow would facilitate the transport. Maybe it was an idea to chip.

The chain needed to be tightened, fuel and chain oil filled up, and Blixten turned off the saw. So far it had gone quickly and well. His nickname had come from this, the work pace he was able to maintain, often despite hang-overs and regret that tore at him inside. Without work outdoors he would have gone under, he understood that very well.

He sat down on a log, pulled off his helmet and visor, observed his task, and smiled in his solitude. He had been guaranteed work for a month, maybe longer. The client was a summer visitor who'd bought an estate, yet another Gräsö home that became a summer residence, but the new owner seemed fine. He wanted the fields to be restored, talked about grazing animals.

"That's probably good," Nils Lindberg said out loud, it was a habit he'd acquired. "But the hair grass has to be removed first." The entire old meadow was littered with tufted hair grass. He inspected and tightened the chain and then gave it a pat. There was nothing as reliable as a well-maintained chain saw.

From his low position he stood up with some effort. Thirty meters left and after that he would follow the gravel road up toward the farm. The ditch was tolerable with only scattered alders but totally clogged by meadowsweet that had started to spread more and more. There was work to do.

In the middle of the day a light rain swept in from the northeast and just as quickly disappeared. By then he'd made it up to the farm. The land-owner had called him in, offered him lunch, and talked uninterruptedly about all his projects. Blixten did not say much, aware that most of it would drag out in time or never be realized, but he had to admit that Jens Thörn was uncommonly clear for coming from the mainland. Skåne besides.

"Was it 'the Dutchman' you all called him?"

"Yes, his name was Hollander."

"I'm finding a lot of junk in all the outbuildings."

"He collected everything. Went to all the auctions, bought things no one else bid on. He was special."

The Man from Skåne appeared to consider this. "I am too," he said after a while.

"Then you'll fit in well here."

"There's an old cabin in the forest."

"Hildingstorp, yes, it should probably just be torn down." He had to tell Thörn what he knew about the place.

"I'm thinking about repairing it. I actually drove down and checked."

"If you want to renovate I know good people."

"It looked like someone was living there."

"That was long ago," said Blixten. "Summer visitors."

"But there were fresh groceries on a bench."

"I see, strange," said Blixten.

"A little farther down there's an old villa, down toward the sea."

"You probably can't call it a villa. That's the Karlsson place, it's been there for ages."

Blixten fell silent, thinking about Cecilia, but was reluctant to tell the Man from Skåne about how she disappeared four years ago and about her parents who since then had become more and more withdrawn. There were those who said that Rune Karlsson was starting to completely lose control.

"What do you think about sheep here?"

"Maybe," said Blixten, prepared to drop the whole thing, but regretted it immediately. A kind of tired anger came over him. "You were talking about Highland cattle too, have you read something about that? Do you have any experience with grazing animals?"

"Not exactly," said the Man from Skåne.

"It's a little damp in certain places. Sheep don't like that."

"Is that so?"

"Here you can let Highland cattle go, they don't wear down the ground as hard when it's a little damp and tricky."

"But sheep would look better," the landowner objected.

The afternoon passed. After the ditches he had to take out the trimmer. The Man from Skåne wanted it cleared closest to the house. He talked about a potato patch and raspberries. A new cultivator was strapped on a trailer. Jens Thörn was full of ideas. And money. That was why he could prattle so much, thought Blixten.

He thought about whether he should drive down to the Karlssons' since he was in the vicinity anyway. He'd helped Rune and Gunilla with reed eradication and then they'd talked about beach meadows that ought to be reclaimed. He could take that as a pretext for a visit.

Said and done, after stowing the tools in one of the many sheds that the Dutchman had set up once upon a time, he drove the less than a kilometer to the Karlsson place.

Rune was standing by the flagpole.

"We'll probably never raise the flag again," he said as Blixten got out of the car.

"Is it starting to rot?"

They talked flagpole and dredging of beach meadows awhile.

"Anything new?" Blixten said, fishing. He didn't need to explain what he meant.

Rune shook his head. "That damn Adrian Palm," said Rune, getting that dark look and the involuntary twitches in his cheeks that many took as signs of a dormant madness. "It's his fault!"

"I think it was something else," Blixten objected carefully.

"Bullshit! The only consolation is that he's going to die young."

"What do you mean?"

"You can see it in his eyes. He's sick, really bad off."

"Should I take down the flagpole? I have the little Stihl with me."

They looked one last time up toward the top of the flagpole. The gold glistened. "I felled it up by Blötan. Fourteen meters. I dried and processed it carefully. It's been around for many years, I remember that we raised the flag when Cissi graduated from high school, but now it's time."

Blixten went for the chain saw. "What about the ball at the top?"

"Think if you'd known then what you know today," said Rune Karlsson.

"The ball?"

"Forget about it!"

After half a minute the job was done. The spruce trunk had fallen for the second time.

"There's one more thing you could help me with," said Rune, "down by the smithy."

"Okay, let's take a look," said Blixten, even though he would rather go home.

The smithy was a good distance away from the house. It was unusually large for a small farm, but Blixten knew that there was a long blacksmith tradition at the farm, which Rune also talked about on the way there.

"My old man was handy but it was above all my grandfather who was a good smith. But you know that, your grandfather was an expert too."

Before Rune could expand too much on the story, Blixten asked what needed to be fixed.

"You'll see," said Rune. "The roof tiles are starting to wear out, it's raining in. I thought we could put up a tarp at least temporarily. It goes quicker if there are two of us." He pointed at a light tarp that was on the ground. "I have two ladders."

The whole thing was done in a few minutes. They stood silently awhile.

"Do you have any contact with your grandfather?" It was an unexpected question and Blixten didn't know what it was really about, and he hesitated as if there might be some doubt about the answer. "A really grumpy old man, but what a touch."

"No, I haven't talked with him in ages," said Blixten.

"Well, of course not," Rune said a bit defensively, as if he realized that he had stepped into sensitive territory.

"Did you know that Casper guy?" he continued. "The one who drowned?"

"I knew what he looked like and maybe a little more. We went to the speedway sometimes. How is that?"

"That retired cop Lindell was asking about him."

Blixten saw how the uncertainty about Cecilia tormented the other man. He got no peace.

"How did she look there in Lisbon?"

"The same," said Blixten.

"What is she doing in Portugal?"

"She'll come home one fine day," said Blixten, feeling uncomfortable. "I'll cut the pole up into smaller pieces and pick up the shards from the ball, some animal might get injured."

Fourteen

For long periods they sat silently, Rafaela surely just as astounded as she was. It was more than twenty years since they'd met, since they played with each other, but the contact was immediate.

"It's so strange to be here again."

Cecilia reached out her hand and grasped Rafaela's. They smiled at one another as if they shared a secret together, even a conspiracy against the adult world. They were transformed again to young girls.

"We had fun," said Rafaela. "You meant a lot to me. And now you're renting our old summer cabin. That feels right."

"I'm not renting it. I'm here without permission."

"How did you get in?"

"The key was hanging in the outhouse like it always was."

"Wow, that can't be true!" Rafaela's laughter again carried Cecilia back to childhood, with Rafaela's and not least her father's antics.

"What happened with your parents?"

"Papa died a couple of years ago, liver cancer. Mama moved to Umeå. She has a sister there."

"I remember him as happy all the time."

"Yes, he had that role, but exile wasn't easy. He came here of course as a teenager and had seen enough of life in Chile, I mean under Allende, to feel that split. For Mama it was easier, she didn't remember that much, she said anyway."

"Who was Allende?"

"The president that the military murdered. My grandparents on both sides had to flee the country."

"I didn't know that. You never talked about it."

"We were kids, we should be protected. And yours?"

"They're alive," said Cecilia.

"Your dad wasn't exactly cheerful, was he?"

"No, rarely."

She had a desire to tell Rafaela everything, more than the hints she had offered so far.

"He crushed me" was what she came out with at last. "And the worst thing is that I've inherited quite a bit from him. Especially his crazy sense of order. I can go crazy when logic stumbles."

Rafaela reached out her hand and placed it on her thigh. They were sitting on a couple of rickety garden chairs along the west wall, where the sun reached at times.

Then it burst. Like a raging spring river came part of the story, the flight from the island and Sweden, and that she'd come back for a funeral. What a relief! Getting a girlfriend just like that. Someone who had the sense to let silence speak.

"I don't want to hurt anyone," she said without thinking, but it felt as if Rafaela could take it.

"Your dad?"

Cecilia shook her head. "Adrian is his name. And now there's a green light when his mother is dead and buried. She was my best friend." She told her friend about Adrian and his company, how they had worked together.

"Before you say more you must know something. I'm a police officer."

"Police? But why?"

Rafaela ignored the question. "And he treated you badly?"

"I know how it sounds, as if everyone has been mean, but it's not like that. But he tricked me and many others. Above all Casper."

"Who is that?"

"Who was that, rather. He was my great love."

"Is he dead?"

"He died in the water in Gällfjärden."

"Do you want to talk about it?"

"There's not much to say. He's gone, and it was Adrian's fault. He toyed with all of us. I will never forgive him."

"And now he's going to be hurt?"

Cecilia nodded.

"This doesn't sound good."

"It's hell and has been for several years."

"Have you talked with this Adrian, I mean more recently?"

"We've met, but he would never admit anything."

"Isn't the logic limping a little now?"

Cecilia did not reply, but stood up instead.

"Where do you live?"

"In Öregrund."

"And you want to rent something on the island? I'll give you a couple of names, two people who know everyone here."

"Please do," said Rafaela.

"But don't say anything about you getting the names from me."

Rafaela observed her.

"I haven't done anything wrong," said Cecilia.

They parted with the feeling of something unfinished and wounded. The conversation had taken such a turn. History had thundered into their story, and that was fine as long as they kept to childish games, but the story about the adult years had exposed her in a way that was disturbing, as if she were a lunatic. And then that business that Rafaela was a police officer. That didn't feel good. Cecilia wondered if they would meet again, as Rafaela's back disappeared between the spruce trees. Probably not.

Fifteen

Fourteen years ago. A stab of loss and desire passed through her, a shiver that started in her belly and was transmitted through the groin like a contraction. They had been on the mainland for a going-away party, someone was moving south. They came back with the ferry that left at midnight, and walked home to Blixten's house. He was one of the few in the gang who had his own place.

"I ought to get home, Rune will wonder—"

"They think you're sleeping over in Öregrund," he interrupted her. "You don't need to be worried. And how would you get home?"

"A car always comes by," she said, but without conviction. She was tired and then she did want to go with him. She wanted to. Blixten had always been good, considerate. He was the first guy she'd been with who actually asked what she wanted. They plodded ahead in the summer night.

———

Now she was standing at the same entrance ramp, fourteen years later. She remembered that night with sadness. It was the last time. They had obviously met many times since but never slept together. She really didn't understand why. Maybe it was his seriousness that bothered her, his focus on her, he simply got to be too much. It was as if he erased himself.

A few years later they ran into each other on one occasion outside the pizzeria in the harbor. They went in together. Always marinara with extra shrimp. He'd explained that he was still in love with her, always would be. She didn't want to listen, she didn't want this persistent courting, she didn't want a man who with no resistance lay down flat before her, like a cocker spaniel begging for treats. She'd tried to explain. He hadn't understood.

Should she feel regret? How would life have turned out if they'd left the pizzeria hand in hand? No, it didn't work that way, she knew that very well, but still. He'd always been there, ever since grade school. He would never betray her.

She put the gear shift into drive position. He was still living there, had even bought the cabin he'd rented previously. It happened right before she left. That alone. Continuity. Still living there.

"You" was all he said.

"Are we alone?"

Blixten nodded. She took off the hat and wig. The sudden movement and the sight of an unmasked Cecilia made him jump.

"I'm like a downed tree in the forest."

"What do you mean?"

"I don't know, it just came to me. I'm just lying there, like an old fallen oak tree."

"You're still living here, in other words."

"Even oak logs rot," he said.

She smiled. "You've changed, gotten bigger."

"A lot of work. I saw you."

"I understood that. No one else recognized me."

"You're just as beautiful, more beautiful."

She felt how she blushed. *Don't say anything else,* she thought, *I want to carry my anger a while longer.* It struck her that they could disappear together. He would never judge her.

"You were at Gällfjärden."

"I'm there a lot," he said.

"Sorry," she said. "I left you. Maybe I should have stayed."

"It doesn't matter. Nothing has changed. I'm the same." He smiled, laughed a little, as if it were a joke.

They observed one another. The wind was singing in the rowan trees where the many berries testified to last year's heat. He had told her that many years ago, how nature piggybacked on the year before, that nothing came quickly, like people in general believed. There were so many explanations; it was the spring rain, it was the mild late spring, it was the fruit moth that flew the wrong way, but the trees didn't only count days but rather months and years backward.

"Do you have anything to drink?"

"I actually have a few bottles of wine," he said and went into the house. She thought she saw a new certainty in Blixten. She took off her coat, sat down at the garden table.

He came out with a bottle and two glasses. "A Barolo from 2012," she observed.

"It may taste vinegary, it's been in the pantry for four years," he said.

"Storage is only a good thing. Do you know what an Arborina 2012 costs today?"

"It wasn't cheap."

"This is one of the best wines you can find. Where did you buy it?"

"I asked a guy at the liquor store in Gränby if they had any really good wine. They had to order it. This was the best, he thought."

She understood that he'd bought the wine with calculation. "You thought that I might stop by?"

"I was hoping for something like that, but then you disappeared."

They raised their glasses. "But now I'm here," she said, bringing the glass to her mouth to conceal how moved she was.

"That wasn't bad," he said, looking through the ruby-red wine.

"What did you see?"

"How you crossed the strait. But I haven't said anything."

"You believe that I pushed Casper into the water?"

"I don't know," he said, emptying the glass and setting it down carefully. She saw that he had an injury on his hand that was bandaged expertly. "You went ashore at Norr-Gället."

"That's far away."

"I always have the binoculars with me. But listen, it doesn't matter to me, not really."

She poured more wine.

"I bought three bottles," he said.

"So it doesn't matter that I killed Casper?"

He gave her a quick look. "I'm sure you had a reason," he said at last. "And that's a long time ago."

"The statute of limitations for homicide is twenty-five years, right?"

"That may be," he said.

She had never seen him so sure of himself.

"Adrian said you'd seen something, that two persons went out on the strait."

Blixten looked up in surprise. "Maybe I said something to him, but never what I really saw."

"You didn't want to squeal," she said, repeating Adrian's words.

"You've changed," he said.

They drank in silence. The bottle would soon be empty.

"You can help me," she said, wondering how she should continue. "Adrian has to be gone," she said at last straight out. If he could swallow one murder, he could probably take one more.

"Gone? Gone as in dead?"

She nodded.

"Forget about him. He's history."

"Gone," she said and smiled.

"Should I kill him, is it something like that you mean?"

"You don't need to, but you have to help me."

He stared at her. "You're serious."

"In Hildingstorp there's a deathwatch beetle that ticks. At night I put my ear to the wall and follow the countdown. Tick tock, Adrian dead, tick tock, Adrian dead, it scratches."

"Cissi, forget about Adrian, he's not worth thinking about."

"Then we can go somewhere. Portugal, for example," she said, putting on her best smile.

He slowly shook his head.

"It wasn't me," she said.

"What do you mean?"

"It wasn't me with Casper in the boat on the strait. If you saw two individuals."

"I saw you."

"Were you drunk?"

"Stone sober, I was working, clearing the shore of sea buckthorn for a summer visitor."

"Perhaps it was me you wanted to see. You wanted me to be the one who took Casper's life. Do you have another bottle?"

He got up without a word.

"I was with Olga that afternoon, helping her clean the house. She was going to get a visit from a care planner, home service or something, and she wanted it to look tidy. You know how she was. Get the wine now!"

Could he be so wrong? The distance was great, she was right about that. For the umpteenth time he replayed the scene that day in May 2015. The sun was in the southeast and created a luminous glitter of waves in the fresh northeast wind. Two silhouettes in the boat which after a sheer northward with foam around the prow moved past a known reef and headed for the southern tip of Storgällen. It was an imaginary line that all the natives followed. The two figures went ashore. It took a few seconds before they disappeared from his field of vision, but for him it was enough: The one who was moving was Cecilia.

It was in the morning, so her talk that she'd helped Olga in the afternoon was in itself no evidence of her innocence. She could very well have returned to Kallboda and pushed the boat out in the strait so that it would drift away and then driven her car to Olga's, but he understood that his story would not mean much in a legal proceeding.

He stood with the bottle in one hand and the corkscrew in the other and looked out over his own farmyard, trying to fully take in that she was actually sitting on his garden chair. He still remembered that morning the last time they were together. Before she sneaked away. He could take that, she was only twenty years old after all. He'd been forced to accept it. Now she was back, but for how long? She stood up, looking around as if there was something that worried her. He hurried out.

She observed him as he poured more wine. "I thought I heard someone," she said.

"No one ever comes here," he said. "Where are you staying on the island?"

"Hidden," she said. "Not far from where I grew up."

He suspected where but didn't want to press her. Maybe she would talk about it voluntarily, and it really didn't matter.

"You can hide yourself here."

"What did you do to your hand?"

"I cut myself on a flagpole ball." He hesitated over whether it was wise to talk about where it happened, but then it struck him that he had to try to shake her up. He must get her off balance, get her to leave not just the wig and hat but also the mask that she was holding in front of her apparently controlled face.

"At your parents' house."

"When were you there?"

"Today. I just talked with Rune. I got the sense that Gunilla was away. I cut down the flagpole which had rotted. He talked about when you graduated from high school, how he raised the flag. I remember that day too. You had the best grades of anyone I knew."

She sat with her head lowered, fumbled with her hand across the table, found the glass, raised her head and looked at him, brought the glass to her mouth and slowly took a sip of the dark wine. It resembled a religious ritual.

"It was hell. Rune complained that I didn't have the highest grades in all subjects. You messed up, he said."

He'd heard her tell the story before.

"Rune thinks that Adrian is going to die soon. Do you know whether he's sick?"

She shook her head. "So Rune is alone in the house?"

"I think so. He mentioned something about her visiting a sick relative for a few days."

Cecilia took another sip.

"It's only about sickness and death," he said. "Have we forgotten all the rest? The beautiful." He made a gesture toward the rowan branches weighed down with berry clusters, a sign of nature's generosity, then let his hand work its way toward the wine bottle, an expression of nature's willingness to help people get started, and stopped with a meaningful gesture with his hand toward her.

"Stay here tonight," he resumed. "You can't drive. We can pretend a little."

She smiled and he sensed that she liked that, pretending. Maybe she'd done that for years since she'd gone into hiding. He felt how his stomach muscles were quivering with tension.

"I'll get us some whiskey," he said and got up.

"You're transparent, Nils," she said.

"Is that good or bad?"

She smiled in response. He could see how her intoxication had increased. Had she eaten anything at all?

"Let's form an alliance," she said.

He turned around on the steps. "Let's forget the others tonight, can't we?"

"We have to plan," she said, still with a smile on her lips. "But go and fetch your whiskey now."

Sixteen

"Brundin called. It was Cecilia who rented the car in her own name, showed a driver's license, and paid in cash; she maintained that her bank card had been stolen."

Edvard seemed moderately interested, but asked for how long anyway.

"One more week," said Ann. "What is she doing here on the island, or in Sweden?"

"The funeral," said Edvard.

"Yes, but one more week."

"Maybe she has other things to take care of while she's in Sweden anyway."

"Where is she staying?"

"Maybe on the mainland," said Edvard quietly. He was sitting in the garden leaning over a table with a dismantled chain saw, rooting among the parts. "It's annoying how things can disappear."

"Someone ought to check hotels and inns."

"Why? There's no reason. She probably hasn't done anything, staying away and going around in a wig isn't illegal, is it? And the post office box?"

"That would take a little longer, according to Brundin, formally it's a little trickier. He'd gotten a call from a colleague in Gävle too. A woman who knew Cecilia when they were little. They played together. This colleague had run into Cecilia and was worried about her. She seemed confused, talked about hurting someone."

Edvard looked up. She had finally managed to get his interest. "Where did she run into Cecilia?"

"She didn't want to say. She didn't want to betray the confidence, she told Brundin, but wanted to keep him informed anyway."

"What a fucking mess," said Edvard. "I'm starting to get tired of this person. She does seem completely out of her mind."

Ann took a few steps toward the car, but was still indecisive. Edvard observed her from the corner of his eye. "I'm going for a drive," she said at last, but didn't say where.

"Do that," he said. "You need to get out a little." The ironic tone did not escape her. They were on vacation together and maybe they ought to do something together too, but on the other hand he was sitting there fooling with a chain saw. She knew that there was no turning back, she wouldn't give up until she'd met Cecilia Karlsson. What kind of person was she? Hearing that she might hurt someone was ominous. There was also something unspoken that was sick in this drama. Ann had seen it before, signs that something wasn't right, with a creeping sensation of approaching destruction.

"You again?" he said with ill-concealed irritation. Rune Karlsson had come out on the steps when she drove in between the gateposts.

She decided to go on the attack directly. "Your daughter has been seen on the island." In a way it was admirable that he didn't visibly react, showed no sign of any surprise or emotion, but then she caught sight of his hands around the railing, and understood that the self-control took its toll.

"Who are you to tell me that? Someone who comes around with loose talk and gossip."

"I understand that you're upset," said Ann Lindell, "but as a former detective I've seen a few things, and I think I understand when things aren't as they should be." She made that sound more dry and formal than she'd intended.

"What do you mean?"

"I believe Cecilia wants to harm someone."

He let go of the railing, and swallowed.

"Adrian," he said, going slowly down the steps and up to the little morning coffee table that was by the facade, sat down, and indicated with a hand gesture that she should sit down too.

"Your wife?"

"She's not at home."

"Adrian?"

"The very one," said Rune Karlsson, and she saw how sad he really was. She discovered in one stroke his loneliness too, which she'd sensed at the previous visit but couldn't identify. He was missing not only his daughter, he was missing the time with good fishing and bird hunting, when the bellowing from cows and heifers could still be heard on the small farms, but also when a few minutes on the running track to the cheers of the spectators explained the world. He was starting to get up in years, and he reminded her of a couple of the older men in her village outside Gimo, men who struggled against time that was relentlessly ticking.

Then came his story. She was careful to let him decide for himself the direction and pace. She sensed that he was a man who liked to be in command, and that was fine as long as he let go and relieved the inner pressure, as long as he delivered, as Sammy Nilsson would have expressed it. She had plenty of time.

Adrian Palm was not a good man, malicious actually, he began, and Ann understood that he exaggerated to prepare the way for an extreme conclusion. Adrian had recruited Cecilia when she had just turned twenty, after she'd come back from a six-month stay in London. It was generally known that she was knowledgeable and had a rare analytical ability, and that she was in demand on the labor market. "She could get any job at all," he went on in praise of his daughter.

"But she chose a company here?"

"Yes, we agreed that it was best that way, then she could keep on living here too."

He looked out over the lot and she followed his gaze. A flagpole was lying on the lawn. Then he resumed his story. She had quickly become important to the company, indispensable, and while Adrian traveled around making customer contacts and selling his systems, Cecilia held down the fort on the home front. They had an office in Östhammar. There were no eight-hour workdays. She was often exhausted when she came home, simply to eat a little something and then continue in front of the computer.

"In 2013 the company had a major breakthrough, including a contract with Tetra Pak in Skåne. It was due to Cecilia. Completely. But she didn't get any credit for it! And Casper actually helped out too, he knew people at the company."

He fell silent. *Get to the malicious part,* thought Ann.

"He seduced her." There was a streak of bewilderment in his voice, even though the insight must have come to him years ago. "Then it ended."

"Was she sad?"

"It was . . . she had difficulty showing her emotions. Superficially she tried . . . but he dumped her, I think. And then something happened. They had a serious falling-out."

Ann waited for him to continue.

"It was that Casper."

"But when I asked last time you didn't know any Casper."

"That was for my wife's sake. I wanted to put an end to all the talk. She gets upset easily."

"Why did Cecilia and Adrian become enemies?"

It seemed as if he closed up again, he sucked in his lips, tensed his jaw muscles, and looked away demonstratively, but after some time for reflection the answer came spitting out in staccato tempo.

"Casper had arranged some more contracts. You know he was really loaded. He didn't really need to work. He liked to sail and dive. But he helped out. Ingratitude is the wages of the world. Then he disappeared in the strait."

Get to the malicious part, Ann thought again.

"Adrian pushed him in. He wanted to be rid of Casper. And Adrian was unscrupulous. He will walk over dead bodies."

"You think that, but is there anything that supports such a thought?"

"Gunilla talked with Adrian, it was when the boat was found. He just laughed and said something about Stefansson having gotten into water over his head for the last time. An evil person."

Ann suspected that there would not be much more than that. Talk, loose talk. Rune walked away, stood by the fallen flagpole.

"Blixten was here, cut himself on the ball. Worse luck."

"And Casper Stefansson, what was he like?"

"Maybe he deserved it," said Rune Karlsson after staring out into space for a long time. "I don't know, maybe he toyed with Cissi too. I was used to fair means but that sort of thing no longer applies."

"Was there any doping when you were competing?"

"Oh yes, I was in Montreal in 1976 and then in Moscow in 1980."

"Exciting," said Ann, who did not follow track and field and definitely not his achievements as a runner.

"Sometimes she goes away and then it feels as if my legs don't carry."

Ann thought at first that he was talking about Cecilia, but understood quickly that this concerned his wife.

"It was that way when she competed too, she continued with archery until just a few years ago. She needed it, but I didn't really know what she was up to. I didn't like it."

"Where is she now?"

"With a cousin who's not well."

"I thought about that business with Casper—"

"I think Adrian hid money in the West Indies or somewhere in those banana countries that have a hundred inhabitants but a thousand banks. And Casper didn't like that. He didn't need to finagle, he was rich anyway, always had been, inherited I don't know how much, but Adrian was an upstart and scared of losing his wealth."

"And you think that Casper threatened to expose the whole thing?"

"Maybe it was like that."

"Did Cecilia know about it too?"

"That's pretty likely."

"Did she get scared, do you think, I mean if Adrian was so unscrupulous?"

"I was acquainted of course with Martti Vainio. We spent quite a bit of time together at the world championships in Helsinki, and after that. We had a lot in common, but he went to jail for doping later."

"You competed against each other?"

"No, no, he was a long-distance runner. But I mean, who can you trust?"

Ann observed him in a partly new light. It was obvious that he was tormented and afraid. But of what? Aging, Ann decided again, and having to approach old age and death without really knowing where his only child was, but maybe something more.

"Cecilia told us that she and Casper were going to move, maybe abroad. He had a house in Italy too. That was only a week or so before he disappeared."

"And quit the company?"

He nodded. "Quit and move. We were worried, of course."

"Did you tell this to the police, to Brundin? About the moving plans, I mean."

"No, it didn't have anything to do with the matter, I thought then."

"But now you do, why is that?"

"It was something that Olga said . . ."

"Adrian's mother?"

"She came here to tell us that Cissi had called from abroad, that she was doing fine, that we didn't need to be worried. We started talking about what had happened. Olga had overheard a quarrel between Casper and Adrian. They were standing in the yard and Olga was sitting inside by an open window. They argued about money, always about money . . . about the move to Italy and . . . about Cissi. Adrian was livid, she was important to the company, but he was jealous too, that much Olga had heard, that Casper had 'stolen' Cissi, as Adrian expressed it. She was in demand in every way."

Ann thought the conversation was over when he silently disappeared into the house. Shortly after that she heard the toilet flush.

"I take diuretics," he explained, and Ann was struck by how a person can change moods. He sat down again but this time on a low stone wall that ran out from the house, as if despite his readiness to talk he wanted to mark a certain distance. His hands rested on the wall. The slender fingers drummed on the surface. It looked as if he was in the starting block prepared to take off. He gave her a quick glance before he continued.

"That was when Casper threatened to expose the millions that Adrian had concealed. 'A single word about Malta,' Adrian screamed, 'and you're dead!'"

"You didn't talk with Brundin even then? That was actually a serious threat."

"A week later he disappeared in the strait. But no, we didn't talk with anyone. Adrian was Olga's only child after all."

"Now she's gone."

"Now she's gone," Rune Karlsson repeated with an ambiguous expression on his face; sadness in his eyes and the wrinkled forehead, combined with a scornful smile.

"And Cissi is in Sweden."

"If you see her, say that I want to talk with her."

"I'll tell her that."

"Do you know what's worst? Not knowing if she's doing fine. She's strong, I know that, but maybe she's lonely and desperate . . . maybe not always, but . . . that's when I would want to . . . do you understand?"

Ann nodded.

"I would like to see her. But maybe not here." He looked around as if he was judging the suitability of meeting his daughter on the home court. "We could have coffee in Öregrund, like we did when she was little. She loved feeding the sparrows on the courtyard. Have you been there?"

"At the bakery café by the church?"

He nodded and stood up with an expression as if he had suddenly lost interest completely. The conversation was over.

"Thanks for the chat, it was nice of you to take the time," said Ann, and the warmth in her voice must have surprised him, because he looked embarrassed, perhaps because he remembered his parting words at the previous visit.

Seventeen

Thirty-two million, almost to the krona, that was what he could secure if he now chose to flee, go underground, go up in smoke, evaporate, vanish for good. He'd amused himself by using all the expressions he could think of, but at the same time was painfully aware that "running away with his tail between his legs" was a more truthful description.

He was scared, to put it simply. Now this was no longer an S and M game like they'd been involved in once upon a time. It was a matter of life or death, he understood that, he'd read it in Cecilia's eyes. She was capable of just about anything, she had a motive and perhaps also the means. She was no nitwit, and once she'd decided she would proceed to deliberate, well-planned action.

In parallel with the fear his anger had also grown. Should he let a lunatic from his past rule over his life and direction? She had left Sweden and the company, betrayed him, so who was she to whine? What she knew he'd taught her during the almost ten years she was his employee.

In the old garage, which had basically stood unused since his father died twenty years ago, were the documents, all the codes, the contacts, the account information. There were the millions. By connecting to the internet with a few keystrokes he could get the process started. It would be over in a few minutes. He was no corrupt oligarch from South America or the Philippines lugging suitcases filled with US dollars, no, he let ones and zeroes do the job.

To justify being in the garage so often he'd parked an old Kawasaki there that he tinkered with when he visited his childhood home. Now he didn't need to playact, he could come and go whenever. Sometimes he suspected that Olga had known about the hiding place. Not because he thought she snooped, in practice that was impossible after she lost her right leg too. She had been bedridden, waiting to die. That wasn't something that upset him, he understood her attitude very well. No, no snooping from her side, but certainly hints that he was concealing some of his business and transactions.

Socialist hag, he'd thought many times, and she had been that her whole life, a committed Social Democrat, but they don't make types like Olga Palm any longer, now they're all equally bad, everyone made sure to take as much as they could. He had also shouted that out in a heated discussion, and that outburst had actually disturbed her, silenced her. Now he felt a little guilty. It wasn't her fault that the crooks had taken over the show. It wasn't her fault that he'd become a bandit, when she had always preached solidarity and the value in "the public" running schools and hospitals, and that it must cost tax money. No, it was the "spirit of the times" that seduced him. There was a green light to enrich yourself and forget about others.

The motorcycle was tricked out and gleaming. He would be able to sell it for a good profit, if you didn't count all the hours he'd expended. Maybe the One and Only Robban would be interested? No, he would want a Harley-Davidson.

Adrian Palm stood with one hand on the handlebars of the Kawasaki. It struck him that maybe he could buy Cecilia's silence. Everything and everyone was for sale. What would she cost? A million? Two? On the other hand, what guaranteed that she wouldn't take the money and then snitch to the authorities?

Could he take her on a boat ride? He laughed but felt how the cold immediately made itself known, as if he had an intense fever inside. After their meeting at Gräsö Inn he had first had the thought: *You want her like before, take her,* but he knew that was unrealistic, wishful thinking. *Drown her!* was his next impulse, but he rejected the idea immediately as macabre. But now it stood out as a conceivable alternative. She was the only actual threat to his future well-being.

He left the garage, closed the double doors behind him, stood there staring at the green-painted panel that had long had to withstand the north wind. With one hand he stroked the rotted wood where the paint had flaked. Suddenly the tears came, a kind of sorrow. "Olga and Verner Palm," he mumbled, "of blessed memory," a phrase he'd heard once long ago, but not since. The language thinned out as life proceeded, he'd thought sometimes, but perhaps not that often, the new words elbowed in and demanded their place. It was the new that had made him wealthy, it was undeniably so, but still . . . still there was the memory of their words and actions, Olga and Verner, he could never let go, but even so he must erase them. He blamed the funeral, the effect it had had, all the old friends and acquaintances who spoke so warmly about Olga, but looked at him with neutral gazes at best.

He went to the other side of the garage simply to see that the old chair was still there. Verner's. It wasn't. And how could he think that! *I have no son* was his next thought, *no one who is going to miss the chair on which I once enjoyed the south sun.*

Drown her! The desire to kill welled up. He wanted to destroy everything that chained him to the island, make a clean sweep, never to return again. It was an equally frightening and enticing fantasy. *There's no one here now who loves me.*

Where was she keeping herself? He would find that out. He must be the one who was a step ahead, directing. Was she staying on the island, and in that case where? Probably not. It struck him that perhaps her parents were hiding her, but he rejected the idea immediately, he knew her that well. What friends did she have? Blixten Lindberg was probably the one she was closest to. For all these years he had faithfully trotted behind her, like a tired old Saint Bernard, constantly sipping the cognac. He was the one who claimed to have seen her in Lisbon, maybe it was true that they'd made contact down there. Who else would have told her that Olga was dead and when the funeral would be?

Blixten. Adrian had been at his house, at parties when they were very young and later when they went to check out the speedway. There was only a side road to his house, but you could get there unnoticed through an overgrown road that ran through the forest almost all the way up to Rönntorpet. As thirteen-year-olds they had joy-ridden mopeds together. Now he had the Kawasaki.

But I do love her! We can flee together. She can learn to love me. Hadn't he seen the lust in her eyes when she took hold of him at the parking lot at Gräsö Inn? He recognized that look so well. That hand.

She could kill you every day. Like the gigantic spider in Manila which for several days sat stock-still on the wall with the cockroach in its embrace, and sucked out the innards. Fascinated, he had studied it. It was like hanging out with an old friend, a strange feeling of having an eight-legged comrade in the toilet. One morning it was gone.

Eighteen

There was a song about giving a woman a morning, "I give you my day," the stanzas from the song had become vague, but those that he remembered returned as a wordless humming to Cecilia. She was lying stretched out in the bed, the sheet draped like a half shroud, with one hand over her exposed stomach and the other extended as if she was reaching for his body. She had told him about her worry in the cabin, that must be Hildingstorp he'd said, and she laughed and said, "Of course you understood." She had described the nights with the ticking of the deathwatch beetle which made her sleepless, and then all the wine they'd drunk, and that they made love during the night! At three o'clock in the morning they had staggered into the shower and then back into bed.

Carefully he pulled back the sheet. Her naked sex resembled a shellfish, folded and half open. Never before had he seen a shaved woman in real life, only in porn films. He got down on his knees by the end of the bed, leaned forward, and carefully kissed the lips, let his tongue play. She whimpered and in a half-waking state she spread her legs as he licked more and more eagerly. She smelled of a special sort of tea, something Indian perhaps, and tasted of honey.

He observed her and wanted to burn the image in his mind's eye forever; her soft, arched belly, the breasts that intermittently heaved and the parted mouth that whispered something he couldn't make out. "Keep going," she said louder, "I want your tongue."

When it was all over and she fell back asleep he left the bedroom on trembling legs. *If it could still stay like this,* he thought, but understood all too well that it was wishful thinking. Cecilia was not someone who gave in. "Compromise isn't for me, not these days," she'd said the night before when he tried to convince her to back off. He could sympathize with her intransigence but he also knew that it put obstacles in the way of a normal life. She was too big to fit in on the island, at Rönntorpet. He himself could very well imagine living on the island, continuing with his work outdoors, and if she was there it would be complete. A dream.

Her ideas were literally dangerous, verging on the unheard of, exceeded all human considerations, invalidated everything he took for granted. For him it was inconceivable to consciously injure another person, much less take someone's life. He had difficulty setting a mousetrap, and when it concerned killing an irritating insect he seemed like an orthodox Jainist.

The insight that she was a murderer frightened him, and much worse that she could repeat the whole thing, but over the years that had passed he had gradually accustomed himself to the thought that she had shoved Casper into the sea. However strange that felt, it was a kind of process that could lead to them reuniting, he and Cecilia. Stefansson had been a stumbling block that was kicked to the side and left an open path forward. Now it was Adrian Palm. "Then I don't need anything more," she had sworn. "Then we can live." He took that as a promise, and had silently repeated those words to himself during the early morning: *Then we can live. We.*

The coffeemaker had probably never hissed as generously as when it spit out the last steaming drops. The windows were opened, the bottles put away, the glasses washed, and the kitchen table wiped off. He had texted the Man from Skåne that he had a few things to take care of and would come a little later. "OK" had been the immediate reply.

They ate breakfast in silence. It did not feel at all unpleasant or even awkward. Occasionally she looked at him and smiled. He thought about that morning fourteen years ago when she left the house without even wanting to drink a glass of water, as if she'd become frightened of his nearness and their affinity. Because of course they belonged together, then as well as now. She moved just as gracefully as before, she was just as beautiful, if not more beautiful, her body was just as discomfiting and inciting as four years ago, fourteen years ago. The difference was that she had become stronger, that she didn't let herself be bullied, he had seen and understood that.

"Do I frighten you?" she asked suddenly.

He shook his head. "You attract me."

"Sometimes it can be the same thing."

"I'm happy with you, always have been, you know that. Ever since we were in the cathedral in Uppsala."

She laughed. "You were scared."

"But excited," he said.

"That can often be the same thing."

During the night he had tried to create an understanding of where and how they would live. She was clearly not averse to living in Portugal, but to say the least skeptical about Gräsö, even if she had not expressed herself categorically. Maybe it was the closeness to Rune and Gunilla that made her doubtful. Rune was a bit tricky, Blixten had always thought, but he was probably not a bad man. What Cecilia had told him, about how on the home front he had created a miniature version of a surveillance society, did sound frightening. "The only thing missing were cameras in every room," she'd said, but outwardly Rune had been okay, a little moody, always with definite opinions, but also generous. He had coached youth on the island in track and field, volunteered as a leader in the soccer club, despite the fact that he thought that soccer was for Neanderthals, and participated in volunteer work that would benefit the island.

Gunilla had apparently submitted. It was the general understanding that she adapted to his strict living patterns, but had archery and competition as her opening to another, certainly freer world. She had been successful and Rune had also basked a little in the glow. He never disparaged her performance, on the contrary, and that had strengthened the bond between them, Olga Palm had said so anyway.

They had been forced to adapt to a life without Cecilia, and Blixten could understand their frustration and grief. If they were to lose her again, if she went back to Portugal, the darkness would fall heavily over the two of them.

"That was a good breakfast, the best in a long time, but now I have to get going."

He did not ask where. They went to her car together. He repeated that she was always welcome. Suddenly she stiffened. "What was that?"

"What do you mean?"

"An engine sound," she said, staring toward the forest behind the house.

"My hearing isn't as good," he said. "I've probably been lax about hearing protection, but there's nothing in that direction."

"It was the sound of a car."

"There's no road," he said.

"Now it's silent," she said, listening attentively toward the curtain of scrubby bushes and underdeveloped trees, put her hand up when he wanted to say something. "I'm going now." She was in a hurry to leave. He looked after her, suddenly worried by her paranoia. This was not a good ending, he checked his phone, to eighteen hours with Cecilia. Togetherness that he could only have dreamed of before.

He wondered whether there was any logging in progress, but he knew that a thinning had been done a few years ago, and now there would be nothing to do in the forest for several years. The old forest road, where he'd driven mopeds twenty years ago, was basically impassable nowadays, so what was it she'd heard? Someone from Nordangärde or Österbyn, even if that was some distance away? Even from Muskargrund, although that was even farther away? There were quite a few summer visitors and maybe someone had a four-wheeler and amused themselves a little with forest rally? He decided not to call Uffe and ask if he knew anything. True, he took care of the tax returns, but otherwise they had no contact.

Where was she going? To Hildingstorp or somewhere else? He decided on the cabin. She'd said something about having to change clothes. From the cabin his thoughts went to Rune Karlsson again. He'd seen something new in his eyes, the sternness had given way to disorientation. Was he in the process of getting a little screwy, as some said?

An empty bottle was lying on the grass. He picked it up and observed the beautiful label and sent a thought of gratitude to the clerk at the liquor store in Gränby. Then it stung to dole out half a fortune for a little wine, and many times with a touch of bitterness he had looked at the three bottles in the pantry, but now it had paid for itself and then some. He was on the plus side, that's how it felt when he'd seen her surprised expression.

"Barolo will be our melody," he said, laughing.

"Are you happy?"

Blixten turned around. There stood Adrian Palm, dressed in a worn and thoroughly soiled motorcycle outfit.

"What the hell are you doing here?"

"I'm test-driving a little," Adrian said lightly, making a sweeping gesture toward the forest. "The Kawasaki runs like a spear. I was driving our old track."

If I kill him now and bury both him and the bike I'll really be on the plus side, thought Blixten. *Who would suspect anything?*

"Are you offering a cup?" Adrian asked, sitting down at the garden table on the chair where Cecilia had sat, and Blixten hated him for his unexpected appearance, for asking about coffee, and not least because he had provoked such a murderous idea in his head.

"Don't have time," he said. "Have to get going to work."

"I thought I saw a car take off. Was it the mail carrier?"

Blixten didn't reply.

"Fancy drink," said Adrian.

Blixten took a couple of steps closer to the other man. He could raise the bottle for a blow. Adrian sensed the thought, got up, and backed away.

"You've always been a coward," said Blixten. "Leave now."

"She's crazy, do you know that? And you're nuts to believe anything good about Cissi. I know her true self, you don't."

"Get out of here!"

Adrian had regained some of his nonchalance and nodded, as if to confirm his statement. "I know her," he repeated, "and you know how things went for Casper."

He turned on his heel and went his way, disappeared between the bushes, and soon the Kawasaki was heard revving up. Blixten raised the bottle and inspected the dregs.

Nineteen

"Hi, it's me."

"Yes, I hear that. What are you doing?"

"Can I come out for the weekend?"

"Home? Of course, but I'll probably still be on Gräsö. Can't you come here?"

"We have a few things to talk about. I was in Berlin this summer."

"Wait a second." Ann stood up and left the kitchen, went out in the yard where the reception was better, while she tried to understand where he was headed. They hadn't spoken with each other for several days and the last few times she'd heard in her son's voice that something was bothering him. Now maybe it would come out.

"Now I can hear better! Berlin, you said."

"Don't get mad now."

Erik had a marvelous ability to immediately provoke all kinds of emotions in Ann. He wasn't much for euphemisms, and usually that was good and liberating, but now worry and alarm bells were ringing.

"That depends," she answered, hoping that her reservation would come out clearly.

"I met a relative in Germany," he said.

"What? Someone from Ödeshög, Alice? She always has something sensational to tell. You shouldn't believe everything she says."

Ann's cousin was married to a German, and if she remembered correctly he was from Berlin.

"Not her. Not a cousin."

Erik's breathing reminded her of a very stressed witness or actually a suspect who was staring at the microphone of the tape recorder in the interview room.

"Spit it out now!"

"Don't get angry," Erik said again. "But I met my dad."

Erik was the result of an encounter with a man that Ann had never seen again, but on the contrary repressed and, to start with, cursed. She remembered that he was an accountant but not much more than that. The whole thing stood out as slightly desperate, from both sides. It was as if he'd never existed, he felt unimportant, but inside her the thorn had remained; that it was a one-night stand and not Edvard. He'd left her when she told him that she was pregnant by another man. She had also understood that Erik would wonder and she'd feared the day when he wanted to know who his biological father was.

"How did you know?"

"I actually have a half brother who is six months younger. We're a lot alike. We're even in the same grade at school. It was our father who understood first, when he heard who you were. He saw you at an information meeting at the school, you remember that one about drugs."

That fucking snake, thought Ann, but an outburst or a wrong word could be destructive. "Did he make contact with you?"

"Last spring. He had checked when I was born and calculated—"

"Is he certain? Are you certain?"

"Yes, Evert says that we even have the same gestures."

"Who is Evert?"

"My brother."

Evert and Erik, she thought.

"And you all met in Berlin?"

"Yes, he knew that I was going there. His wife doesn't know anything . . . about us, I mean . . . that Evert has a half brother."

Ann quickly understood the context. In Berlin they could meet in secret. A stab of jealousy. A flash of anger. A flood of sorrow that streamed through for all those years, thoughts about what could have been reality. With Edvard. No fucking accountant who pops up like a jack-in-the-box, no fucking Evert.

"Come out here to the island, we have to talk."

Erik did not reply.

"I have to calm down a little, you understand that, don't you? But I want to see you, talk with you. I'm not angry, just stunned, do you understand?"

"Understood," Erik whispered.

She could hear that he was not far from tears.

"Come out tomorrow. Take the bus. The weather is going to be great." They ended the call without anything being decided.

She was taken back to that day when she told Edvard. It happened at a healthcare clinic in Östhammar after an accident at sea. In heavy weather he'd gone out to salvage nets, Victor's nets Ann recalled, fell overboard, but made his way up onto an islet. When he was being rescued in a boat he'd slipped and broken his leg.

He had joked and everything would have been hunky-dory if she hadn't been pregnant. She told him straight out as he lay in bed with his leg in a cast. Ann remembered his account of how he crawled onto and clung to the slippery rock, thought about how much he loved her, and said the words that had ground in her head for all these years: *I can't live so far from you.*

The happiness had immediately been replaced by pain and despair when she told him that the child wasn't his. They ended up living far from each other.

Twenty

He looked behind him. It looked terrible. Pick-up sticks. As if an amateur had worked his way along the ditch. He tore off helmet and visor, opened his vest, undid a couple of buttons on his shirt, and let a little air in against his body. It immediately felt a little better, but still not good.

"Cecilia!" he said with his gaze toward the sky. The sun was shining just as intensely as the meteorological institute had predicted and actually promised. The flies celebrated around his sweaty hair and neck. He was tired, that was probably why he had lost focus. Then he suddenly smiled when he recalled that he'd gotten laid for the first time in God knows when. And with Cecilia at that. He closed his eyes and recalled the sight of her sex.

Pick-up sticks. Like life, everything in a jumble, crisscross, hard to clear up. Unnecessarily time-consuming. He wanted a beer! He wanted to snuggle up next to her again!

Are you prepared to pay the price? To see someone die, how does that feel? "You have to help me," she'd said.

Adrian, that bastard. The sneer on his face. Had he seen her?

The Man from Skåne who talked up a storm. Highland cattle. He was a peculiar man in a way. *Do such professors exist?* "I mostly do research," he'd said with a crooked smile, "about pacifism in an historical context." *Context, what the hell does that mean?* Now he wanted to live a little more peacefully. *Who the hell doesn't want that? Pacifistically.*

We'll leave! Portugal, or why not somewhere in Asia, where no one could reach them?

"Sustainable agriculture in the periphery," the Man from Skåne was constantly talking about. *I see, is that where I live?* "I distrust the vegans." *Who doesn't?* "Animal production would probably amuse me." Of course, but what about the profitability? *He doesn't even know how animals graze.* Or did he have old professor money?

He picked up the helmet and pressed it down on his head. The flies buzzed with irritation. *Should I tell Lindell that I've seen Cecilia?* He understood that life would never be the same. *Are there ditches with brushwood in Portugal?*

"I see, you're feeling rundown? Maybe you're coming down with a cold." The Man from Skåne sounded sympathetic but didn't seem overly concerned. "Go home, come back when you've recovered. The alders and aspens will probably still be there."

Blixten got into the Simca and drove away, uncertain where he should go. There were at least three alternatives. Down to Hildingstorp to check if she was there, straight home to have a beer and wait for her next move, or find Adrian and simply warn him that Cecilia was really on the warpath and get him to leave, preferably from Sweden. It would have to be that. With Adrian gone from the island, maybe her lust for revenge would subside.

The Kawasaki was outside the garage. A hose was curled on the grass like a yellow snake. The door to the house was open. Blixten got out of the car and waited. It was only a few weeks since he'd visited the Palm house, but he already thought that the place looked dilapidated. He recalled everything he'd done, everything he and Olga had discussed. A few years ago he'd helped her by sawing down a scraggly spruce hedge that Verner Palm had planted maybe fifty years earlier. Then they'd burned up the brush, grilled sausages, and had a few beers. Olga knew how work should be arranged. He had never taken any payment.

After a good while Adrian came out. He had of course seen and heard the Simca but hadn't been in any hurry.

"I remember the spruce hedge," Blixten began by saying. Adrian looked uncomprehending. "The one your old man planted."

"Have you come here to talk about old memories?"

"It was crappy in the forest, I see, but you've fixed up the bike well."

Adrian ignored the small talk. "What the hell do you want?"

"I want you to leave the island, and just as fast as you can. There's a great risk that Cissi will think of something really evil."

"Did she say that?"

"The best thing would be if you disappear."

"You come here like some fucking underling from the Mafia and give orders."

"Recommendations," said Blixten. "And as far as the Mafia is concerned you're probably closer."

"Go to hell!"

"Can't you ever listen? Go away from here."

Blixten left Solhem, which the house had been called since the 1940s, checked in the rearview mirror how Adrian stood there and stared. Should he maybe arrange a little fire? Maybe that would get Adrian moving. He slowed down, stopped and got out of the car, walked back a ways.

He saw how Adrian with deliberate movements wiped off the motorcycle, whose chrome cast reflections in all directions, before he pushed it into the garage, closed the door, locked and did what Verner and Olga had always done: pushed the key into a crack above the door.

Cecilia Karlsson was sitting on the same chair as the day before, with her long legs stretched out in a graceful position and her bare feet playing in the grass. She was wearing a white and red summer dress. The wig was on the garden table.

"I hoped that you would come home early."

"I split from the Man from Skåne, blamed it on a virus."

He wanted to go up and kiss her, or at least touch her, but wise from experience he held back.

"I shopped for some groceries, maybe not the world's best, but still."

A couple of bags stood in the shade under the table. Blixten took that as confirmation that she liked being at Rönntorpet, even if a future together appeared remote.

"I'm going to shower," he said.

"Me too," said Cecilia with a smile, and they went in together.

Half an hour later they were sitting at the table. It struck him how changed she was anyway. There was a calm about her that he had never seen before. Was it Portugal's doing? He asked her to tell him about the Alentejo, which she'd mentioned the night before.

"Serpa, that's my town," she began, and while they ate salad, cheese, and the thinly sliced ham and drank a Portuguese wine that she'd bought at the state liquor store in Öregrund, he got an exposé of the southern parts of the country.

"Let's go there," he said. She only smiled in response.

He told her that he had stopped by Adrian's. "I'm thinking about burning down his garage."

She looked quite flabbergasted. "That wouldn't be a good idea."

"I don't want to kill anyone or contribute to it. Not even Adrian."

"We will kill him," she said quietly, setting aside her utensils, pulling off a sheet from the roll of paper towels, and wiping her mouth carefully. Everything she did was performed with great precision.

"But burning down the garage we are definitely not going to do," she continued, and then told him why.

In many respects it turned out to be a beautiful evening. Blixten had never felt better. He sent Olga Palm a thought of gratitude, that she'd gone and died and thereby brought Cecilia to Gräsö.

"We're going to kill him, but not really," said Cecilia.

Twenty-One

I knew there was something! thought Ann Lindell, not without a feeling of triumph. It was as if she could have sniffed it out. He never went into their daughter's room, Gunilla Karlsson had said, so where would you hide things if not there?

Brundin's news came unexpectedly quickly; he had after all mentioned a lot of bureaucratic hassles. Based on how he presented it, a bit snidely, she understood that he too realized the complications.

"Who wrote to her?"

"Adrian Palm, I think," said Lindell. "He definitely had an affair with Gunilla Karlsson. Maybe it's still going on."

Brundin hummed a little. "There's a pretty big age difference."

"About twenty years," said Lindell. "She's probably about fifty-five."

"Fifty-three," said Brundin. "I did a little checking. She was very young when she had a baby."

"And she's kept the post office box, is that so?"

"Yes, Gunilla Karlsson started renting the box in 2009 and it's still in her name."

"Can Cecilia have used it?"

"Quite possible," said Brundin.

"Rune is a man who wants to keep track, from what I've understood. The post office box was a way to keep him unknowing."

"Love letters," said Brundin.

"That was long ago," Lindell observed.

"I have a hard time believing that it can be anything else," said Brundin.

"Money, maybe laundered," said Lindell.

They speculated a little before they ended the call, both aware that there would be more to come. Now Brundin's curiosity had been aroused, he was sitting firmly on the hook and would surely be willing to help her again. She had gained an ally.

Gunilla Karlsson was away, visiting a cousin who was sick. Was that true? Maybe only partly. Was she still having an affair? But Adrian was on Gräsö, wasn't he? The letter writer had talked about Hotel Knaust, and that she had a relative in the area that she could use as a pretext to travel to Sundsvall.

But did this have any bearing whatsoever on Stefansson's death, Cecilia's disappearance, and her threat about injuring people? The whole thing perhaps was a dysfunctional family and a shabby love story.

She wanted to discuss, look at things from different perspectives, and despite the contact with Brundin she missed her old colleagues and interlocutors. She had the imagination, time, and desire to dig deeper.

Edvard was in Östhammar getting supplies, which meant buying building materials. He had talked about what he needed, joint fasteners and God knows what. He was starting to gradually prepare to get back to work again. That felt good, then she avoided having to feel guilty.

Ann poured a glass of wine. At home with Edvard the bottles were in a cupboard in the old parlor. There was wine, but also dark rum, which was his favorite. She herself never drank hard liquor. She got memory gaps.

She stared out toward the strait, sipped the wine, and tried to discuss with herself. It didn't go that well. Who had Gunilla Karlsson slept with? Crassly put, that was what the whole thing was all about. Did Rune suspect anything or did he even know about the infidelity?

Ann took a few turns in the parlor and tried to remember how he had expressed things on her two visits. She stood in front of Viola's old walnut bookcase. One thing suddenly struck her, why had Edvard told her to check behind the books in Cecilia's room? Why this idea? An impulse from his side, or . . . she inspected the spines of the books. There were not many she recognized, she was not an avid reader. She reached her hand in behind a row of books, considerably fewer than at Cecilia's, and found the letters at once. She trembled, would she dare turn them and study the address, perhaps there were letters from his old life, that's probably what it was. Maybe old love letters from his ex-wife, Marita? Or from that red-haired hussy from Norrskedika that he went out with for a while. She counted seventeen letters. She turned the bundle, and got a minor shock. They were all addressed to her. The handwriting was Edvard's, she had no problem seeing that.

Seventeen letters that he had never mailed. Now his suggestion in Cecilia's room got quite a different meaning and weight. It was no impulse.

Seventeen letters that she had never received. All stamped, sealed. The top two were addressed to her current mailbox in Tilltorp, the others to the two addresses in Uppsala.

Could she open them? Edvard would be livid, she knew that. Maybe never want to see her again, never again want to write a letter to her. This was his secret, the secret compartment of his life. She suddenly got teary-eyed when she understood how much she must have meant to him anyway. She was the one he'd written to! Seventeen letters, seventeen years.

She inspected them one by one before she put the bundle back on the shelf. Could you open letters without it being detected? She had a former colleague who knew all about such things, but could she call and ask? *No, she answered herself immediately, the letters are Edvard's, don't mess up everything because of your curiosity.*

She poured another glass. She had read an interview with a former finance minister who evidently had problems with alcohol, and he'd warned people about starting to drink too early in the day. It was the only thing she remembered from the article.

She looked at the gilded wall clock that Edvard considered an honor to keep ticking and running, and strike every half and full hour. Viola would have wanted it that way, he'd said. He was a romantic. It was early for the second glass, but it was too much, first Erik's news about having met his father in Berlin and then the letters in the bookcase that would continue to worry her.

Could she ask him? She did not know, after twenty years of acquaintance, how he would react, and she could not bear to lose him again.

She tried to push aside the thoughts of Edvard. "Decide!" she said out loud. Either skip the post office box and the letters as irrelevant, forget about Cecilia, or continue snooping with the attitude that it had to do with Casper's death and Cecilia's disappearance. She leaned toward the latter. The whole thing was an infected story that stank and the secrecy—post office box 339—was one part, a piece of the puzzle. Could she make Rune Karlsson a conspirator or would he throw her out headfirst? There was only one way to find out.

Twenty-Two

He was not much for hugging, probably never had been, not even when he was little, but now Ann took him in her arms. Cars streamed past, to spread out over the island's fine-meshed road network. Some bicycling tourists were talking heatedly with each other. A truck loaded with lumber was the last vehicle to leave the ferry.

He released himself from her grip. "Hi, Mom," he said. "You look healthy." He had a singular capacity to give her encouragement, small compliments that were delivered quietly and naturally. It had always been like that.

They rode in silence to Edvard's house. *Who would start,* she thought. The tension that she felt after their conversation about Berlin and that ruined her night's sleep had let go. "You can never lose him," Edvard had said in the morning. He had taken the news about Erik's father with composure, even though Ann understood how much old grief it stirred up. Ann and Erik's close connection, despite all the shakiness, was in contrast to Edvard's relationship with his own two sons. He seldom talked about Jens and Jerker, they never called, and it had probably been a few years since they'd been on the island. That visit had ended with a quarrel.

"Let him decide the pace," he'd continued, a bit too wise in Ann's opinion. He was probably not the one who should give advice, but she had simply nodded.

Edvard had taken off early, expecting work, he'd said. That was fine, she got to have Erik to herself. Ann had prepared a second breakfast. Together they set the table on the sun porch. He had difficulty sitting right down and just talking, but with his hands busy making sandwiches and eating scrambled eggs perhaps he could relax and tell her about Berlin and the meeting with his father. Besides, he was almost always hungry.

"I'm not angry," she repeated her words from yesterday.

He nodded. "Should you be?"

She shook her head. "The important thing is you. The only important thing is you. Were you happy to find out?"

"Yes, of course. I've wondered."

"What was it like?" she asked, pouring a second mug of coffee. And Erik told her. It could have been a dramatic story, with an unknowing and then tormented father and a brooding son, who got the surprise of his life in his late teens.

"He called me last winter after a match I played. You remember that time I made four goals? He was there."

But not me, thought Ann.

"He wanted to meet. At first I got angry, but he seemed nice, calm somehow. We met later. Of course I was curious, you hadn't told me that much."

Nothing, thought Ann. There was nothing to say. Erik struggled with the words, which he could choose, and in what order they should come. It struck her that he was doing everything not to hurt her.

"You're so wise," she said.

"He just wanted to see me, hear me talk, he said."

"What's your half brother like, is his name Evert?"

"If you know that we're related we're very much alike. He's good, maybe not like me. He talks politics all the time."

"So you saw each other in Berlin?"

Erik nodded. That was the answer she would get, maybe more would come at some point, but did she really want to hear details? They gave each other a quick look. A measure of embarrassment was there, a slightly uncomfortable feeling. Would it be the result of the whole thing, that a wordless and troublesome barrier was raised between them? The unspoken, the unexplained, could find paths that no one wanted. It had been that way for twenty years with Edvard, years with shifting fortunes, where happiness and despair were mixed.

"Is there anything you want me to do?"

Her question surprised him, she understood that; it surprised her too.

"No," he said.

"Is there anything you wished that I should have done?"

It was thin ice, but it did not break.

"Mom, you've been good" was the only thing he said. She wanted to stand up, take the few steps around the table, and pull him to her, but instead she reached out her hand and touched his forehead, as if she were stroking back his bangs.

"Erik, you've been good. You've been my everything, you know that."

She wanted to say so much more, be wise and forgiving, but understood that would have to wait. Erik fished out a paper from his back pocket and gave it to her.

"Check," he said.

She unfolded the paper. It was a screenshot from a bank account, she understood that immediately. His name was there. The balance was almost 250,000 kronor.

"What is this?"

"He opened an account for me and deposited all the money. He did that last spring. He's an accountant or something and figured all that out."

"Why?"

"Support, he said. He wanted—"

"Was he trying to bribe you?" she burst out.

"No," said Erik with a voice that was close to breaking. "He just wanted to help out. He didn't know of course that I existed, not until he saw me at school, saw how like Evert I was. Dads should probably pay for their children."

"That's a lot of money. Is he that rich?"

"I don't know."

"But freeing up a quarter million . . ."

"His wife doesn't know anything, he said."

She would really like to get up from the table, drink unbelievable quantities of wine. Like Cecilia Karlsson she wanted to disappear. Why did he make himself known? Why the hell must men always behave as if they will save the world? For years she had struggled like a beast to keep herself upright, give Erik something that resembled a childhood and a tolerable upbringing. The anxiety that she wasn't sufficient for her child still sat like a black coating inside her. And then this accountant devil comes, writes out a check and plays responsible.

"It doesn't feel cool" was the only thing she could say.

"I haven't touched the money," said Erik.

"Has he asked about it?"

"A little," said Erik.

And what the hell have you said, she wanted to scream out, *what the hell have you told him about your alcoholic cop mother, who moved out to the countryside to clear up her life?*

"I know a lot," said Erik. "I've understood a lot, even if you don't believe it. I'm proud of you," he said. "I mean that you succeeded. You were a good police officer, Sammy said so. And your boss called me several times. He said the same thing."

"Ottosson called you!?"

"He said such nice things about you, that you were his favorite. I liked him, wanted to hear more, but then he died. And my friends were jealous that my mom was a police officer. You were in the newspaper. You almost died one time."

Ann could not stop the tears that ran down her cheeks.

"I bragged about you," Erik said, sobbing. "I don't care about the money. I can send it back."

Ann slowly shook her head, as if she had a hard time taking in everything that was coming out.

"We can go somewhere," said Erik. "You do want to go to India."

"India?" He nodded. True, she had talked about India, but that was years ago. She looked at him, new tears squeezed out.

"You remember that?"

"We saw elephants on TV, they moved logs, it was like some industry, and you said that you wanted to see elephants. They went to a river then and bathed, got scrubbed. Do you remember?"

"I remember the elephants," said Ann.

She would always remember that moment, she understood that. The happiness that he existed welled out uncontrolled, seized her. She stood up, rounded the table, got down on her knees, drove her head against his chest.

"Erik," she said. He held her, his rib cage heaved in violent spasms. Everything was won, all the bad was overcome. His words had melted down the darkness. Now she could live, free of sorrow, intoxicated by life, by the love for her son.

"Shall we go down to the shore?" he said.

They took the old path, the one that Viola's grandparents had once worn down. "I want to know the names of the flowers and trees," he said.

"What do you mean?"

"The names," he said. "What they're called."

"I don't know that much," she said.

"What about Edvard?"

"Yes, maybe. He knows quite a bit, but mostly about wheat and rye and such. You know that he was a farmworker before?"

"He's told me."

"He's good at weeds too," it occurred to her.

"Like you," said Erik, and she didn't understand, guessed what he might mean but chose not to ask.

The strait was unexpectedly still. The northeaster was otherwise often present, sometimes like an amiable ripple, sometimes like a frothing and angry old geezer that you wanted to throw out. Those were Viola's words.

She remembered happy days by the sea with Edvard, but hesitated over whether she should say anything. This was Erik's moment. Instead she talked about Cecilia, and he listened attentively as usual. He had always done that when against her better judgment she talked about work, detective work, the suspects, those arrested and jailed. It had been her way, many times unconsciously, to link him to her. Now she understood that he had told quite a bit to his friends. They'd been envious that his mother was a cop.

"This bush is called seaberry, that I know," she said, pointing at a scraggly bush.

They stood on the dock. Edvard's little aluminum boat was bobbing there and the wooden gig he and the legendary Gottfrid Andersson had built together. She and Edvard had taken many outings in the archipelago outside Gräsö, spent the night in sheltered bays, a couple of times Erik had been along.

I actually have only one mission, she thought, putting her arm around his waist and leaning her head against his shoulder. She perceived him as stronger than ever. It was exercise, obviously, which he went in for passionately, especially after there was speculation that in the winter he could take a regular place on the Sirius A team. He was successful in the bandy arena, he had developed a special move, they talked about making a "Lindeller," where he burst forth on his left side. It wasn't beautiful when he moved ahead on the ice, she couldn't think that, it looked vague and sloppily loose-limbed somehow, but it seemed to fool the opponents. He staggered through, got past, turned unexpectedly toward the center or delivered a pass that cut through the defense and reached a teammate. It was an audience-flattering style he had, the blue-and-black cheering section, the west side as it was called, wanted to see more of him.

A sudden memory came to her and she sobbed, in a peculiar mixture of self-pity, shame, and love for her son.

"What is it, Mom?"

"Nothing, I was just thinking about when you were little."

The memory was one of many but perhaps the most painful: She wakes up, looks around in confusion. Erik is sitting at the foot of the bed, observing her. Doesn't say anything. He's between three and four years old, he has stopped wearing diapers during the day, but still uses a night diaper. It's been removed. It smells of feces. He is naked except for a pajama top. It's Sunday, it's past ten in the morning. She staggers out in the bathroom. The toilet seat is soiled. He has tried to wipe himself. Toilet paper is knotted up on the floor along with the diaper, which is heavy with pee. She vomits in the sink, and when she turns around Erik is standing there.

"Don't think about it."

"It's a torment. I wasn't a good—"

"We're here, we managed. Sometimes you play really crappy matches, but then another round comes."

They left the dock, followed the shoreline a ways. "Far out there a man disappeared in the sea," she said, pointing toward the horizon. "There are those who think he was pushed in."

"What do you think?"

"No," she said after having considered her response a moment. "He was a diver and I have a hard time believing that he drowned, even if he was drunk. I think that he was dead when he was dumped in the sea. Or else he's buried on some island out here. Or living in the Philippines, not giving a damn about anything or anyone in Sweden."

Twenty-Three

From the boulder they had a good view. Like so often there were memories connected with even the most insignificant heights. People sought out peaks that rose over the surrounding landscape, even if only a few meters, and it was that way too with the little hill south of Adrian Palm's house.

Blixten told her that he'd gotten drunk there for the first time in his life. It was after school let out in June, he'd completed eighth grade and that would be celebrated with beer. Adrian was there, Thynell and Fabian Larsson too, as well as some sort-of friends who were summer visitors, about whom he didn't remember much of anything. No girls, just a gang of peach-fuzzed, boisterous teenage boys. Adrian's father had just been buried and his mother was visiting a sister on the mainland.

Cecilia smiled secretively but did not say anything. Blixten felt a stab of jealousy, maybe she'd been with Adrian at the same place. They'd hung out together a little starting in high school.

He felt like an awkward hayseed. Cecilia had talked about Portugal,

about culture, goat cheese and wine and all sorts of things he knew nothing about, and then he brought up getting drunk as a teenager. It struck
him that a lot of things fit together, how threads ran back to their common
childhood and upbringing, baggage they had to drag along whether they
wanted to or not, and that it determined a lot of what they undertook later
in life.

"My old lady barked like a bandog, but dropped it later, never said another
word," said Blixten, who could not forget that night a few decades ago. "I
came home late, I'd had an accident with the moped and scraped up my face.
She was good. She is good." It was as if he wanted to avenge himself. Cecilia
constantly badmouthed her parents, so it would do her good to hear something different. His father hadn't been much and disappeared early from
the family and the island. Today no one knew where he was and Blixten
didn't care.

"There he is," said Cecilia, crouching down. Adrian locked the door, remained standing for a moment on the steps, as if he was trying to remember something, before he straddled Olga's old Crescent. A cat suddenly
appeared and Adrian bent down and gave it a pat before he pedaled away.

"He's taking the bike?"

"He's going to the bar."

It looked peculiar, how Adrian wobbled away on the gravel road, with
his dress shirt flapping in the wind, someone who was worth millions and
could take a taxi back and forth without putting a strain on his finances.

"Why doesn't he take the car and stay at the hotel in Öregrund?" said
Cecilia, who had evidently been struck by the same thought.

"Olga would never accept that kind of wastefulness," he said.

"Olga's dead," said Cecilia.

"For us, yes," said Blixten, watching Adrian disappear at the curve by
Storfuran, where Adrian's father had set up a bench. He'd liked resting his
legs. "Maybe he's going to visit someone on the island."

"He has no friends here," said Cecilia.

"Friendship isn't required for a visit," said Blixten, thinking that sounded
wise.

"Shall we?" said Cecilia. He nodded but was still not convinced that they were doing the right thing, uncertain what it would all lead to. They made their way down to the house, the path led between thickets of wild roses where the rose hips shone like small lanterns. Blixten pulled off a rose hip and stuffed it in his mouth, let his tongue run over its smooth shell.

The garage was weather-beaten. The sheet metal roof had taken on a rust-brown shade and the windowsills had almost no paint left. A red elderberry was growing crookedly close to the wall and by being put in motion by the wind left arcs of scrape marks on the facade. *I should have helped her more,* Blixten thought as he let his gaze pass over the lot.

"How do we get in?"

Blixten just smiled, reached up, and took out the key from the crack in the wall. "The key's been here since time immemorial."

"Time immemorial," Cecilia repeated, seeming to savor the phrase.

"I cut the grass for Olga when Adrian wasn't here, and that was most of the time of course."

Blixten turned the key, opened the door. An odor of gasoline struck them.

"Now let's kill him," Cecilia said, slipping in. He followed, closed the door, and reached for the switch to the fluorescent lights in the ceiling. Cecilia walked around, passed the motorcycle and inspected benches and fixtures, picked up a paper bag from IKEA, and stood in front of a cabinet filled with boxes of varying shapes and ages.

"Somewhere here are papers, maybe an external hard drive, maybe a computer, maybe compact discs."

"Lots, maybe," said Blixten.

"We'll search, you take that side and I'll take the cabinet." She started with a carton marked "Sony," set it down on the floor and opened the lid. Blixten watched. "Get busy," she said.

He'd been in the garage many times, retrieved tools and equipment when he helped Olga with various chores. He had never encountered anything unexpected, but on the other hand he hadn't searched. He started with the workbench, cluttered with tools, cans, and packages. He inspected it all and occasionally cast a glance at Cecilia, who doggedly and systematically was going through shelf after shelf.

Blixten doubted that Adrian was hiding anything in the garage, it seemed much too amateurish. Without great enthusiasm he started pulling out the drawers of the bench. There was quite a bit of old junk that he understood was from Verner's time, shoe trees, well-used tools with worn wooden handles, and cans with screws and bolts in every size. Finding a hard drive in that mess seemed unlikely, but he loyally continued his search.

After twenty minutes of searching in silence they stopped for a moment. "Nothing," Blixten said. He felt uncomfortable, with dirty, greasy hands besides. Cecilia inspected lumber that was stored on the trusses. "I've checked," he said. "There's nothing above the boards. Just dust from Verner's time."

"I know there's something here," said Cecilia. "Olga was certain."

"Maybe he's moved it, whatever that is."

"She saw him go out here with the computer. And why would he do that?"

"That was probably long ago."

"Last summer," said Cecilia. "That was one of the last things she said to me, that her son was a swindler and that he hid things here. And you know how he is, he doesn't trust anyone. He would never rent a safety-deposit box, never store sensitive information at the office. Here is where his secrets are."

He observed her, admitted she was partly right where the description of Adrian was concerned, but was still doubtful.

"Maybe there's a hatch somewhere. Does the garage have a cellar?" She suddenly looked eager, inspecting the cast floor.

"No, no cellar. Never has been."

"Maybe he hacked out a hole," she said. "Check under the bench!" It was her last hope, he understood, and obliged her, getting down on his knees and looking under the bench. The space was perhaps fifty centimeters.

"Here's a flashlight," she said, setting an antique object on the floor. He let the lamplight play across the floor. He saw it immediately.

"There may be something," he said, and she also got down on her knees.

"Look," he said. "It's dusty everywhere except right here." It was clearly visible in the glow from the flashlight.

"Those are marks from Adrian," she said. "He reached in, set something here."

"In that case it's gone," said Blixten.

"Shit!" Cecilia exclaimed.

In a way he was satisfied. They could end this. He'd seen her growing eagerness and sensed what that could lead to. She could go too far sometimes, he knew that from before, she never gave in. If she now understood that the garage no longer contained anything important, she would have to let go. She wasn't stupid, of course, it wasn't possible to conjure up things. She got to her feet.

He looked around under the bench one last time, reached his head in a little farther, mostly to give the appearance that he wasn't leaving anything to chance. He lit up the frame of the bench, the bottoms of the drawers.

"Do you see anything? Is there something?" Cecilia's eager voice testified that she perceived something in his body language, perhaps he had unconsciously tensed, perhaps she interpreted his silence as confirmation that there was something under there.

He crawled out. There were five rows of drawers. He pulled out the one farthest down in the middle of the bench. It was filled with old instruction books and warranty certificates, he'd already browsed through the pile. He pulled out another drawer and set it alongside.

"Do you see? The bottom drawer is shorter."

She sank down beside him. He reached his hand in, felt around. Of course it was like that. The drawer was cut off and the space that had been created behind was blocked. Cecilia took hold of his head, turned it toward her. "You're a genius," she said, and the smile she gave him crushed all his worry.

He searched with his hand all the way back but suspected that it was from under the bench you could get at the secret compartment. He lay on his back and wriggled in under the bench. Two small nails held a plywood base in place. He pulled them out and loosened the plate. Along with it came Adrian's secrets.

Twenty-Four

The darkness had slowly but definitely settled around the house, but the porch was illuminated with a dozen wax candles. From outside it surely looked spooky, or else cozy, that no doubt depended on the observer. It was Edvard's idea that after dinner they should have a glass there, and Erik had arranged the candles. Edvard drank beer, Ann wine, and Erik juice. Edvard told them about his next job. He often did that well, could make it sound interesting, even if it concerned something as trivial as an addition to a summer house.

Ann watched his hands. She liked them. They were not especially forceful considering what they had to perform, but expressive. He used them in inspired moments almost in a southern European way, gesticulating. She understood that he was satisfied to get started on work again after the break. They'd had a period of everyday togetherness, and he'd managed it, that was the way Ann suspected that he viewed it. There was a promise in this. She was well aware that she soon must retreat to her cabin in

Tilltorp, he needed his solitude and she had cheese vats waiting. The little farm creamery was getting more and more customers and she was needed. Simply that, to be needed in the production of cheese.

Edvard fell silent, went after another beer. Erik looked at her and grinned. What did he see in Edvard, in her, and their multi-year but ever-so-tangled relationship? She had often wondered that, almost always with a guilty conscience, prepared that at any moment he would really take her to task, explain that in the future he never wanted to have anything to do with her.

"It was good that you came," she said. "It was good that you told me." That was the summary of his visit, and he seemed to agree. That was how she interpreted his gaze and the gesture with his hand.

"I'm going to my room," he said.

"I hope the internet works tonight," she said.

Edvard came back. He smiled at Erik, who was clearing the table. "Take my glass too," said Ann. As he plodded up the stairs Edvard laughed. It was as if he was on uppers this evening.

"You're stirring the pot," he said, opening the beer.

"What do you mean?"

"First I saw the One and Only Robban on the ferry and then Blixten at the ICA store. Robban talked away as usual. A cousin of his had seen Adrian with a woman at the parking lot by Gräsö Inn. They were arguing and the woman boxed Adrian in the crotch, or something like that. Robban's cousin is a fundamentalist and a bit high-minded so he didn't go into details. In any case they'd had some kind of squabble as it appeared."

"Was it Cecilia?"

"Maybe so," said Edvard. "In principle there are probably other women who would like to unman Adrian, but a lot suggests her. It can be worth testing his reaction, if you were to run into him."

"I'm thinking about dropping the whole thing."

"You're not thinking that at all," said Edvard.

"And Blixten then, what did he have to say?"

She got the feeling that Edvard was an informer who was talking with his police contact for payment.

"He did some nice shopping. Somewhat odd things for him, if you ask me. I saw everything he set out on the conveyor belt at the register."

"Shopping list from Cecilia?"

Edvard laughed. "Drop it!"

Ann wished that the wineglass had gotten a refill, but now it wasn't possible to change her mind.

"I recognized his beat-up Simca too," Edvard continued. "I parked next to it and on the passenger seat was a box full of wine. I don't think I've ever heard that he drinks wine."

"Consumption habits are changing on Gräsö, from moonshine to ripasso," she said.

"There's a settling of scores going on," said Edvard, putting a word to what she'd been thinking. But about what? Between whom? Here passion with Cecilia was in the center, here was money, lots of money, in the form of Adrian, and a family drama a few miles north with surely more than one skeleton in the closet.

They sat facing out toward the August evening, as if in the darkness they were trying to decode what was happening.

"Is Cecilia dangerous, do you think?" he said to break the silence.

"Yes, maybe," said Ann, thinking about other women she'd encountered during her years with the police. Otherwise it was men who dominated her work but she'd seen enough of women's calculation and capacity, a kind of decisiveness that male perpetrators often lacked. For the men it was the flaring jealousy, the spontaneous anger, many times steered by alcohol or drugs, that led to the act of violence.

"How is she thinking?" said Ann. "She hides out for several years and then turns up. Unexpectedly for everyone."

"Maybe not for everyone."

"How so?"

"Olga Palm's funeral. How did she know? She must have had a contact who kept her informed, and I don't think it was Blixten."

"No, not him," she said. "But after that, what is she doing here? She doesn't seem to want to see her parents." She told him about Rune Karlsson's plea that she should tell Cecilia that he wanted to see his daughter, at Lundeborg's bakery café in Öregrund, but now it was called something else, was it Wilma?

"I was actually at old Lundeborg's funeral, that was many years ago. Viola was acquainted with her and she was eager to attend, even though she despised churches. That's the only time I saw tears in Viola's eyes, and that was when they played the first hymn at the funeral."

"What hymn was that?"

"The 'Old Pastoral Hymn,' " said Edvard after getting up and opening the double door of the porch out toward the darkness. "A mournful melody. When they played it in the church it was as if I could hear my grandfather talking."

Ann did not know the hymn. On the other hand she knew a few things about the grandfather, Albert; a farmworker, a legend, who by means of an old gramophone, 78 rpm records, and worn dictionaries learned several languages. She also knew that with a frightful blow he caused a man's death on Rue de la Goutte d'Or in Paris in the 1940s. What Edvard meant was unclear, and she did not want to ask. She observed his back, the graying hair, his hand on the door handle. *There was a lot of talk about funerals,* she thought.

"I'm going to take a walk," he said, and when she saw his shadowlike figure disappear out of the pale light from the porch, she was struck by a horrible thought: *Is this what death looks like?* A living person who acts, speaks, dreams, and loves slowly dissolves and goes into an eternal darkness. Ann became anxiously afraid that Edvard would follow the path toward the sea and disappear in the depths. It was a completely unmotivated fear but grounded in the insight that it was just that fragile. She stood up, wanted to run after him, but instead she went in and poured a glass filled to the brim with wine.

Twenty-Five

They walked in silence. That's how it should be, in Blixten's opinion. He went first, he knew the route from long ago, eager to get home but just as anxious not to push the pace so that Cecilia got winded. He listened to her breathing and slowed down. She laughed, as if she'd seen through his thought. He loved her comments and laughter, always had, but for just as long he'd been afraid of her willpower.

It was about half an hour's walk from Adrian's house to Rönntorpet and the path partly passed through a patch of older forest with sections of puddles and marsh. The ground smelled of mushrooms and he thought he could also detect chanterelles in the moss. He wanted to stop, turn around, and say that someday they would have to come back with a basket, but kept his mouth shut, because he didn't want to give the impression that he'd planned anything with her, not even mushroom-picking.

She giggled behind his back again. He picked up the pace. She'd said something to the effect that they had a night job to look forward to. The cell phone's display showed 9:42. Was Adrian still at the pub? When would he understand that he'd had visitors? They had photographed all the documents from the hiding place under the workbench, it turned out to be hundreds of pictures. They had noted addresses and telephone numbers to banks and financial institutions in several countries. In a couple of cases Adrian had written down names of contact persons, some with a plus after, others with a minus sign. Blixten had not understood the significance of everything but Cecilia had become increasingly excited. It was there and then the chuckling started.

He opened one of the wine bottles he'd bought in Öregrund. Still without really having commented on what they'd found at Adrian's, Cecilia stood for a few minutes with the glass in her hand and looked out the kitchen window. Blixten waited. What occupied her thoughts? Was it decisions that must be made? Was it perhaps memories from the past, when she and Adrian had worked together, that showed up?

She turned around. "Now we'll crush him," she said and sat down at the table. She opened the computer and started it. "Now the deathwatch beetle will start ticking."

"What are you doing to do?"

"Snoop," she said in a lusty tone. "Adrian will be broken with a fate worse than death for him: drained accounts."

"That's criminal," Blixten objected, mostly to have something to say.

"Do you think he'll report it?"

"And where will his money go? There must be millions."

"I don't know . . . we'll have to see," said Cecilia. Despite her vagueness, Blixten was convinced that she had decided long ago.

"But hiding things in the garage, that seems so crazy."

"Adrian knows that the information on a computer can be traced as easily as anything. He wants to have manual processing, so to speak."

She tapped on her phone.

"Why do you hate him so much?"

"He took Casper from me."

"You think that Adrian murdered him?"

"Of course, who else?"

Once again Blixten replayed the scene from that Monday four years ago: the boat that crossed the strait, two figures who went ashore and disappeared. The one forever. Would Adrian be the one who returned? No, thought Blixten, you can think a lot of things about Adrian Palm, but he was no murderer. Not that coward. And could he have seen so wrong? There were two alternatives. Either he should ask her to leave the house for good, and thereby crush the dream that he'd nurtured so long, or else he should play along, protect a murderess, and contribute to other crimes, for it must be theft, hacking, and surely much more.

I'm selling myself, he thought, *and without having any guarantees at that. Maybe she's only using me and then she'll go her way.* He observed her determined expression as she went through the images on the phone and transferred them to the computer.

"Millions," she said suddenly. "Pour another glass, please."

"I can fix a little something to eat, I went shopping."

She looked up and gave him a look that seemed to say: *How can you think about food?*

I'm selling myself, he thought again, reaching for the bottle to fill her glass. He would not drink anything himself. The night would surely be long and he wanted his head to be clear.

The stress from snooping around in the garage and now the expectations about what they'd found had made her feverishly eager and focused. It was as if the thermostat had been turned up several notches. He could understand that, but he had a harder time with the lust in her eyes. There he glimpsed pure revenge and schadenfreude, perhaps greed and even a little madness.

"If it goes like I think, I want you to visit Adrian first thing tomorrow. Early."

"What should I say to him?"

"You don't need to say anything."

Twenty-Six

The alarm came at 6:21 A.M. and reached two fire stations, Öregrund and Östhammar, as well as the fire department in Söderboda on Gräsö.

Oskar Lidh, who was chief at the Öregrund fire station, reacted routinely and quickly, doing everything by the book. He found satisfaction in that.

A few minutes later he and two colleagues were departing in a fire engine. They were followed not long afterward by a Ford Ranger, so now they could form a complete smoke-diver group. The ferry was on the Gräsö side but had left the island at once and the fire engine and the Ford could almost immediately drive on board. A passenger car took the opportunity to slip on too. There was rumbling from the ramp and before the booms had closed behind them the ferry had set out. There was a strong west wind and the crossing would take six minutes.

Vidar Persson, who was out on his daily walk with the dog, observed it all from a distance. He took out his cell phone and called his daughter, who was a police officer. "Inform your colleagues," he said. She was not terribly happy to be wakened on a Sunday morning. "I'm sure they know about it," she said. "Now I want to sleep." She ended the call. Her conclusion was correct. Her colleague Brundin at the agency in Östhammar was already in the car, just passing Norrskedika at sixty kilometers an hour over the speed limit. He enjoyed passing the community at high speed. He'd never liked the village, on the contrary, it was too spread out, giving a Norrland impression. When he left Highway 76 and turned right toward Öregrund he had five, at most six minutes to the ferry landing. A couple of minutes behind him a command car from Östhammar fire station rushed at equally good speed.

"I'll be damned how the wind is picking up," said Oskar Lidh, who was the driver of the fire engine.

"No personal injuries," said his coworker Åke Nilsson, who had telephone contact with the informant, who was also the property owner. "The garage is about twenty meters west of the residence, a wooden house from the 1920s." They all knew what that meant. The wind was coming from the west.

"We have maybe eight, ten minutes to go," he said into the phone. "Don't do anything about what's burning. Do you have a water hose outside? Pull it out and spray the wall of the house that faces toward the garage, do you get that? Keep an eye out. If you have valuables in the house carry them out, that's all you can do. We're coming soon, try to stay calm. Whatever you do, don't go into the garage!"

He ended the call and told the other firemen that the property owner maintained that there were valuables in the garage. "What's his name?" asked Oskar Lidh, who had decent personal knowledge where the permanent Gräsö residents were concerned.

"Adrian Palm."

"Oh, shit," said Lidh. "Maybe it's a Rolls-Royce or something? That guy has money."

Once on board the ferry, which Brundin shared with the command car from Östhammar and an ambulance, he called Ann Lindell. That was not something he had to do but somehow he felt obligated to inform his former colleague. He liked her, more than she perhaps understood, for Brundin was not one to make a big deal about things.

"Cecilia Karlsson," Lindell said immediately. Brundin chuckled. "So once again we meet at the scene of a fire," he said, convinced that she would jump into her car and take off for Adrian Palm's house. Edvard could inform her where it was located.

He arrived just in time to see the fire engine from Öregrund using its five thousand liters of water to extinguish the fire. A charred motorcycle was sticking up in the center of the garage, which was a smoking wreck. The fire had spread in the grass east of the garage, a couple of pine saplings had caught fire, but the house hadn't been affected. Brundin recognized Adrian Palm immediately. He was standing in a bathrobe talking with one of the firemen from Öregrund and one from the island's fire department who had been called there via SMS. Brundin recognized him from before and they greeted each other with a nod. Brundin went up to him.

"You were probably the closest," the police officer observed.

"Yes, it was almost like I arrived before the arsonist," said Herman Viktorsson with a grin.

"So you think it's arson?"

"Dead sure," said Viktorsson, but gave no reasons for his conviction.

"Of course it's arson!" said Palm. "You're police, right?" Brundin nodded. "Find that crazy woman Cecilia Karlsson then! She's the one behind this."

"You think so?"

"I know so. She hates me."

"Have you seen her recently?"

The question put Palm off balance. "No, not exactly, but I mean . . ."

"Would she have come here on a Sunday morning to burn down your garage, and in that case why?"

"She's capable of such things, or else she's used some errand boy."

"Let's go over here," said Brundin, carefully taking Palm by the arm. He did not want to have too many ears close by, as he understood that there was something concealed behind Palm's hints. Viktorsson was a good fellow, but he liked to talk.

They walked toward the house. At the same moment Ann Lindell came driving up. Brundin waved but continued walking away with Palm.

"I mean, maybe she was before, but I don't know her these days."

Brundin inspected him for a few seconds. "So you don't want to point her out directly?"

Palm stopped, looked back at the charred garage. Brundin understood his agitation very well and that then you could make thoughtless statements, but this was something else, he was sure of it. "I must understand what you mean and what you're saying," said Brundin. "Has she contacted you? Threatened you?"

Palm coughed, certainly because of the stinging smoke from the fire. He shook his head as if he couldn't trust his senses.

"Have you seen her at all in four years?"

"No," said Palm. "For me she doesn't exist."

"Some henchman then, errand boy as you say, who could that be?"

"I don't know, but she has always had people that she wrapped around her finger, who obeyed the slightest hint. She's a dangerous person."

"By people you mean men, but there isn't anyone you want to point out, if I've understood you correctly?"

"No, no one," he said.

"Can you think of anyone else who . . ."

"No, I don't have any enemies on the island," said Palm. "Maybe it's some lunatic."

"Is it a warning, do you think?"

"What do you mean?"

"I think you understand."

Palm took a breath and staggered away. Ann Lindell came up instead.

"The early bird gets the worm," she said, shaking hands. "Thanks for the tip."

Brundin understood that she didn't want to ask what had happened, did not want to seem too assertive in a matter that was actually no concern of hers. He told what he knew.

"So what do you think?"

"He maintains that he doesn't have any enemies on Gräsö," said Brundin, and with that statement he hinted that he distrusted the assertion.

"Money always creates envy," said Lindell.

"Likewise passion," said Brundin.

"Yes, that was it! Easy as pie," said Lindell. Brundin laughed. They understood each other.

"Electrical defect? A rag with linseed oil?"

Brundin shook his head. "Lidh from the fire department said he thinks someone poured gasoline all around the garage. Strong smell of gasoline over the whole fire surface."

"Not from outside?"

"No, inside the garage. And Palm is certain that it was locked."

"Was there gasoline in the garage?"

"At least two cans, according to Palm. For the motorcycle, the lawnmower, the chain saw, and maybe a few other things."

Lindell looked around. "Risky to come here by car, the risk of being seen is pretty great, even on a Sunday morning."

"My thought too," said Brundin. He was glad that he had "called in" Lindell, not because she'd offered anything so far he himself hadn't thought about, but the exchange of ideas was stimulating in itself. "There are three properties on the road here, two look like summer houses."

"I asked Edvard about that before I came here, he thought too that there was only one year-round resident, a truck driver. He lives in the middle house."

"Yes, you see," said Brundin, as if to confirm his own thoughts about the importance of exchanging ideas.

"A lovely morning," he resumed. "It would be nice to go out on the water, if it weren't blowing so hard."

"I'm thinking about Casper Stefansson. He was pretty well off, who was his heir?"

"Three nieces and nephews," said Brundin. He perceived it as a test question from her side, that he had checked on what motives there might be to take Stefansson's life. "There was a will."

"What kind of person was he?"

"Superficially a rich brat, someone who never really needed to exert himself, but I think that most people misjudged him. Olga was fond of him. He was here fairly often."

"And Olga had good judgment?"

"Most people think so, and she was probably not easily fooled," said Brundin with a smile. "The nieces and nephews inherited, yes, but there was an exception, a house in Piedmont in Italy."

"Who got that?"

"Cecilia Karlsson, can you believe that? The problem was that when the estate was going to be distributed, it look a long time because there were so many papers that had to be produced and no one could be sure when she had disappeared that she really was dead."

"She was never told that she became a property owner in Italy?"

"Don't think so," said Brundin. "From what I understand the house is still being managed by a local company, who already had that job before Stefansson disappeared in the waves. They rent it out, get a cut of course, but the rest is being held in trust awaiting a solution. The house has a beautiful setting, I've heard."

"You believe that he fell in on his own steam, so to speak?"

Brundin shook his head. "That's what I said externally, but I worked a long time on the idea that he was murdered."

"And?"

"That post office box made me think." said Brundin, striding away toward the smoldering garage where Oskar Lidh was waving. After some hesitation Lindell followed him.

"Gasoline," said Lidh. "Opened jeep cans." He pointed into the black mess that constituted the garage. "Three of them. Maybe one that contained diesel, you'll have to ask Palm. That's enough for a fire. It all started in there."

"Arson," said Brundin.

"That's my suggestion," said Lidh, and Brundin took that for granted. "Six o'clock on a Sunday morning," he noted.

"Have you seen anything else here that surprises you, I mean any sooty detail that sticks out that perhaps shouldn't be found in a garage?"

Lidh let his gaze travel over the remains of the fire, then shook his head. "Only Palm can answer that, but for me there's nothing in particular."

They turned toward the house, where the owner was sitting on the steps with his head resting heavily in his hands, an illustration of fatigue and despair.

Ann Lindell turned on her heels and walked away. Brundin looked after her. "She had a nasty experience with fire," he said. "She came close to dying many years ago. Your buddies in Uppsala had to smoke-dive and carry her out of a burning inferno."

He had heard from colleagues that it had taken a long time for Ms. Lindell to recover. The flames had scorched her hair and skin, but perhaps mostly her peace of mind.

"Maybe you can find traces in front of what was the door. We haven't tramped around that much, there was no reason," said Lidh. "We let the water do the job. Palm was here of course, so we assessed that there was no danger for life."

"Considerate," said Brundin, who was filled with a kind of gratitude for the firemen's work. Lidh, whom he'd met previously, radiated professional security and a humanity besides that was demonstrated in his careful words and actions.

Adrian Palm let out a howl. He had stood up, the bathrobe had slipped open and exposed an upper body in reasonably good shape. It struck Brundin how pale he himself was in comparison with Palm. *He has time to sunbathe in the tropics,* he thought, not without a trace of bitterness.

"Now comes the anger," said Lidh. "First shock, then fury."

Brundin started walking toward the house. Lindell intercepted him. "Ask why the garage," she said.

He stopped. "It's no coincidence that it was ignited, I'm sure of that," she continued.

"A marking, a warning, that goes a long way," said Brundin. Lindell shook her head. "Take a chance," she said, and Brundin understood immediately.

"Think successful multimillionaire with offices in several cities, think money, power." She made a meaningful gesture toward the scene of the fire. "They'll do anything to protect themselves."

"What do you mean?"

"At home with your elderly mother on an island far from everything, there the secrets can be found. Inaccessible to journalists, auditors, and financial-crime investigators."

Brundin smiled. "I've checked him, you should know. He has nothing on him, not a complaint, not a number wrong."

"Exploit the situation," Lindell encouraged him. "Now he's vulnerable. Pressure him, stress him now, soon he'll close up. We know that Cecilia was at his mother's funeral. Maybe she and Adrian made contact. Assume that! Get to it."

Brundin nodded but looked bewildered.

"And one more thing, try to produce something that Adrian has written, anything at all. It would be interesting to see if he's the one who wrote the letters in Cecilia's bookshelf."

Twenty-Seven

"Take your clothes off, quick. Everything!"

He obeyed and in a moment he was standing naked in front of her on the farmyard. She inspected his body as if he were a strange and exciting animal, while she stuffed his clothes and shoes into a garbage bag.

"Take a shower! Scrub yourself! I'm leaving now. Clean your nails!"

That was what they'd agreed on, but even so he felt a little disappointed. He really wanted to talk for a few minutes about what had happened. She threw the bag into the trunk, gave him a quick kiss on the cheek, got into the idling rental car, and drove away.

He went into the house. Showered. Scrubbed himself carefully so that his skin turned red. Went outside again. Waited. Forty minutes later a car showed up. He was actually not surprised that it was the ex–police officer who came.

"Morning coffee," she observed.

He made a gesture toward the chair on the other side of the garden table. "Would you like a cup?" Ann Lindell shook her head.

"What do you want so early?"

"There's been a fire," she said. "A garage."

"Adrian's?"

"What makes you think that?"

"I saw the smoke, black smoke," he said, indicating the direction with
one hand. "And that's probably the only garage that would get you to come
here, isn't it? What about the house?"

"It survived."

"And Adrian?"

"Sad and upset but no injuries."

Blixten nodded. Lindell sat down. "And what have you been up to this
morning?"

"Listen, one thing . . ." said Blixten. He hesitated whether he should humor her or blow up, act really upset. It would be fun to try, but he abandoned the thought.

"I had coffee," he said at last.

"Have you heard anything from Cecilia?"

"Yes, actually," he said. "She came by. We reminisced about old times."

"How old? Not about the necking in the cathedral or high school teach-
ers? Maybe memories from 2015?"

"We talked about life here and in Portugal."

"How bad is it?"

They looked at each other. He could not get angry at this woman. It was
as if she wished him good luck, as if she wanted him and Cecilia to get
together at last.

"Cecilia is a strong lady, she'll manage."

"Could she have set fire to the garage?"

He shook his head.

"She has made threats against Adrian, so Brundin will probably want
to talk with her."

"And the ex–police officer?"

"Her too," said Lindell with a smile. "Do you know that Cecilia inherited a property in Italy? From Stefansson."

"No." He really did not want any more surprises, or to ever again be reminded of Casper.

"I don't believe Cecilia knows about it either. Do you know where she's keeping herself?"

There was no point in lying, but he didn't want to tell where, so he simply nodded. Suddenly he longed to be able to clean up the Man from Skåne's fields, move ahead with the chain saw and brush cutter. He stood up quickly, the table wobbled, he registered for a fraction of a second the worry in Lindell's eyes and stood there as if he was going to give a speech.

"Actually this is crazy," he said. "Maybe I set fire to the garage, so what, in any case I could imagine doing it, but I'm never going to repeat that if anyone else asks."

"Why?"

"To scare that piece of shit away from the island. He only creates distress."

"You want her for yourself."

"I do, without aggravation, without anxiety from the past, all the shit that happened. I like her a lot, I always have, you know that."

They looked at each other. He thought that she understood. "She didn't know anything about the garage. Leave her alone."

"Brundin is going to find her. He knows a lot of people here on the island."

He sighed and sank down on the chair again.

"It's arson," she said and did the opposite, stood up, as if they were caught up in some silly game. "And Brundin won't drop that."

"He knows where to find me," said Blixten.

After Ann Lindell went her way Blixten ate a big bowl of oatmeal, then made and wrapped sandwiches. He'd probably never had so many good toppings to choose from. He put a bottle of water and an apple in his work bag. Maybe the Man from Skåne would provide coffee.

Often he was content to go to a job, even days when he woke up reluctantly with a hangover and morning anxiety. He would use the travel time to think through what had to be done, wave to people he met on the road or saw outside houses and cottages, people he'd known his whole life, that he depended on, but this morning the feeling of unease would not let go. And it was not about the fact that he'd made himself guilty of a serious crime, he couldn't care less about Adrian and his garage. It was a creeping insight that everything would escalate, that he would be drawn into developments where he had few if any possibilities to influence the course of events.

In this matter there were other engines that were working at high speed, and where the energy was generated by widely divergent interests. The fire had escalated the conflict, he understood that now, but perhaps not then, at five o'clock in the morning when Cecilia dropped him off a few hundred meters from Adrian's home. He had walked through the forest with a feeling that he was on his way to carry out a boyish prank. Now he started to suspect what he'd started.

The question was how Cecilia would handle all the information they'd produced the night before. She had worked the whole night in front of the computer while he slept on the kitchen sofa and at a distance heard her muttered comments and satisfied chuckling.

Now it had begun. The cop would get a circus started, of course, Brundin was known as a persistent bastard. Adrian would add to it and certainly think of actions of his own. He was well-enough known on the island that the matter would be widely noticed. There would be talk. People would keep their eyes open.

Highland cattle. Blixten imagined a group of shaggy animals, huddled in a tight group, curious and reserved. Grazing animals. There were few things that made him more content. They all behaved differently, they munched on dainty morsels but rejected other pasturage, moved on separate fields and in that way performed their work with tending the island. Here a combination of cattle breeds and sheep would work. The sheep would take the sections at higher elevation and the boundaries toward the forest where the aspens had sprouted up. That was his idea anyway, how the Man from Skåne would do things no one knew.

Blixten stood there, thoughtful, looking out over the fields, as if it was his own land he was planning for. The scent of bird cherry that the fresh bark and wood gave off still stuck in his nostrils. It wasn't the sweet, stupefying scent of the bird cherry blossoms that made him happy, instead it was the bitterness of the acid that made him breathe in, and out, the Gräsö air.

He looked back at the many stumps. The weeping cut surfaces testified to the loss of mass. The bird cherries were spread out on the ground all around like dark lozenges. The leaves had already started to fall. If nature were to have its way the bird cherries would immediately start initiating new shoots, hundreds of them, and in the underworld the alarm clocks would ring, and root offshoots would be activated.

He smiled to himself, at himself. It was these sights that kept him alive, old pastures, winding overgrown roads that ran between the thickets, a hay barn wandering toward rottenness and death, the outcrops, the juniper trees that like scraggly cypresses shot up like spears. The island of Gräsö. He never got enough.

He started up the chain saw.

From a distance the Man from Skåne came walking across the old meadow. The first impression was that he looked satisfied, but as he came closer Blixten saw that there was something that worried him.

"This will be fine," the landowner began, throwing out his hand, and Blixten understood that this was only an introductory polite phrase. He nodded in response, took off his helmet, visor, and the attached ear protection, dissatisfied at being interrupted.

"I stopped by Hildingstorp," the Man from Skåne continued, "and there's someone there. I'm thinking about calling the police. It's actually a break-in. Maybe it's a drug addict or some criminal gang from the East."

"Not a good idea, and it would take half a day before they arrived," said Blixten. "I can drive down and take a look."

"It might be dangerous," said the Man from Skåne. "No, this is a police matter." He took out his cell phone.

"I know who it is."

"What? Have you seen something?" Suddenly Blixten saw a look on the Man from Skåne's face unseen until now. "Is it a Romanian, one of those Roma as they're called?" he spit out.

"It's a confused woman, completely harmless. Offer me a cup of coffee and I'll tell you."

Twenty-Eight

Maneuvers in a complicated financial landscape filled with pitfalls, dead ends, glitches, and barriers. The art was in knowing in what order everything should happen. She felt rusty but perhaps that was productive, it required a thoughtfulness that kept her from getting overeager.

Before everything could be finalized, a few keyboard strokes on the computer prior to a final command, she was forced to leave the cottage for a walk down to the strait. She needed oxygen but also to identify and analyze all the conflicting emotions that controlled her. It had been an intense twenty-four hours and what was waiting would not be a sinecure, she understood that. The discovery of Adrian's hiding place, the careful arrangements so typical of him, the breadth of his fraud, she could understand and process. She had been mentally prepared, but hadn't thought that carefully about the next step. She was surprised by her own laxness, so unlike her.

As she walked she started to understand how it had happened. It was the island. She had been thrown back to her youth. After the encounter with

Rafaela, in her thoughts she had recalled the games and smells, with Blix-ten the loves of her youth had made themselves known, the feeling of being enclosed at home with her father as supervisor and judge and an evasive mother who in order to bear living seemed to find her bearings outside the home, the intense work together with Adrian, the pride of doing something that led to success, everything had come back, even if in somewhat mutated form. And then Casper, what had he meant? The fact was that the memories faded. Hadn't he betrayed her, came and went as it suited him?

During the years in Portugal the strong emotions had gradually cooled. She didn't like that, she wanted to live with the heat, but the slowness, she could not think of any better word, had also created a quiet satisfaction, as if she was on some kind of sedative. The everyday things and routines in Serpa created new possible paths forward, she'd understood that, even felt it physically.

The strait was breathing heavily, this enormous body of water that was in connection with all the world's seas. She crouched down, let the ripples wash over an outstretched hand. A little aster was clinging in a minimal crack between a few stones. Pieces of reed bobbed lazily at the water's edge. Small things by the edge of a sea. Hers. Casper's.

She stood up and slowly undressed, garment by garment, folded them carefully and set them on the boulder. She saw her own pale nakedness, felt it through the wind on her skin. Took a few steps out in the water. The temperature was around sixteen or seventeen degrees Celsius, but she de-fied the cold and continued on. The bottom stones were replaced by mud and she let herself carefully sink downward and forward, pushed out, made a stroke, two, three, four. The cold water encompassed her, tightened bands over her body. She had actually never been a believer but the feeling she had must still be seen as God-given, and she shivered from the freedom that streamed through her, a pleasure that exceeded most things.

The calm strokes prepared her way. How far would she manage? *Where are you?* She stopped swimming, let her feet sink, treaded water, and looked around. She heard the sound of a boat motor in the distance. For a mo-ment she had the idea that it was Casper who was coming to pick her up.

She closed her eyes, stopped treading water, blew the air out of her lungs, and tried to imagine what it was like to drown.

With her arms extended over her head she disappeared down into the depths until her feet reached bottom, this time stones. The darkness was compact, encompassing, as if she was visiting an alien world. She kicked away and reached the surface, took a gasping breath, closed her eyes, and oxygenated her body. The sound of the motor had come closer.

Would I be able to swim to the skerry? At low tide it was a rock a dozen square meters in size, worn smooth by the waves and the winter ice. In her early teens she had easily crawled there and back. She shot away with a couple of powerful strokes. Breaststroke. Calm strokes. Now, twenty years later, the stretch felt endless. Rune had sometimes swum with her, always right behind. Now she was alone. Perhaps there was a hundred meters left when she seriously started to doubt whether she would manage it. She turned her head as if she was checking that Rune was there. The beach looked distant. It was the skerry that mattered. She counted the strokes, tried to close out the increasing panic. The cold came creeping into her limbs. Fifty-six, fifty-seven, fifty-eight. Her hands suddenly reached an offshoot from the skerry and she pulled herself the last meter, rested a moment before she crawled up on the rock. She had goose bumps and she was shaking from cold. The sun had gone behind a cloud and the sky was dark over the mainland, but she knew that the rain seldom reached the east side of the island. To try to get warmer she did some of the exercises Rune had taught her as a child. He should see her now!

Despite the tiredness and the cold, and a creeping fear that she wouldn't be able to make her way back, she experienced a kind of happiness. She stroked her naked body as if to confirm that it really was naked, or to summon an illusory feeling of warming movement. She breathed deeply, stretched out her arms, and peered over the strait. In the distance a couple of birds of prey were circling, she was sure they were sea eagles. Then she caught sight of a quickly approaching motorboat. It rounded Nässkäret and turned toward the island. She suspected that it was on its way toward the dock where a handful of summer visitors had their mooring.

She got down on her knees, slid carefully backward with her palms over the slick stone, and slowly glided down into the water, all the time with her eyes on the boat, an open fiber boat with an outboard motor. For a moment she saw Casper before her. Here he had gone under.

Now the driver was also visible, a man alone in an orange life jacket. He had evidently not seen her but instead held a steady course toward the dock. The water did not feel as cold. She let her gaze sweep farther toward the horizon. The eagles were still circling seemingly lazily in the sea air.

There were moments and hours from her childhood she happily recalled. Rune had taken her along to a place where sea eagles were fed, pigs and game were placed out on skerries and on the ice. There was a time when the fish were so toxic, so full of mercury, PCBs, or whatever it was, that the shells of the birds' eggs got too thin and cracked. Reproduction of the country's largest bird was threatened.

They would stand in a hiding place and watch. Rune had bought her a little monocular, he himself had an advanced one from Zeiss that he was incredibly proud of and careful about. He was a different person when they were alone out in nature. They had to leave home early, that was part of the excitement and the joy, as if they shared a secret in the darkness. They drove a ways, then had to walk through the forest up to a promontory, where a hiding place was cleverly inserted in nature. The first thing her father did was to light the stove, first birch bark and small sticks, Cecilia followed every step, after that some larger pieces of wood. Sound and movement were something the shy eagles loathed, but a little smoke did not concern them. They had to wait, it was still dark. The first thing they heard were the ravens. After it was light the eagles came, always on guard, with the ravens as their watchmen who warned of danger.

Sometimes there were as many as a dozen, striking with enormous wings, tearing at the desirable meat. The white tail feathers and yellow beaks of the adult birds shone in the morning sun. Rune had a way of giggling quietly when he was content, a habit that fit well in a hiding place. Gunilla despised it but Cecilia loved that sound. There was something magnificent about the simple brush shelter they were squeezed into, close

together, soon warm, with monoculars raised. It was a big deal when people gave all their attention to wild animals. They were on secret ground, on
sacred ground she would think later, few people knew about the carrion
places, and they seldom talked with anyone else about their experiences.

She sank down and let her naked body unresisting bob back and forth.
Then she was reminded of the two thermoses, one with coffee, the other
with hot chocolate, and kicked with her feet, took a stroke with her hands,
and broke the surface. The sun had returned.

Twenty-Nine

"Who is she?" The Man from Skåne's voice sounded normal. The procedure of making coffee and setting the table had a soothing effect, but he was still glassy-eyed. They sat at the kitchen table, each with a mug before him. Blixten considered the alternatives but decided to get right to the point.

"A little over four years ago a woman disappeared from the island. She lived not far from here. No one heard anything from her. It was like she was swallowed up by the earth, but now she's back. She has a few things to think about."

He saw that the Man from Skåne was captured by the introduction. Blixten told the whole story but left out a few things, including the fact that she was the daughter of Rune and Gunilla Karlsson.

"Why Hildingstorp?" was the first question.

"She was there a lot as a child," Blixten said, doctoring reality somewhat. "She wanted to be in a place that she recognized and went down to see if anyone was living there. It was abandoned."

"How'd she get in?"

"There's been a key in the outhouse all these years. She knew that from before."

"Not a Romanian, in other words."

"Not a Romanian. She'll be leaving soon, within a few days."

"You're in contact with her?"

Blixten nodded. He understood that the Man from Skåne was weighing pros and cons, whether he could trust a person who knew about this strange guest but hadn't said a word.

"I want to meet her."

"She's leaving soon."

The Man from Skåne got up, pushed in the chair, felt the outside of his back pants pocket as if to assure himself that his wallet was in place.

"Let's go down there," he said firmly.

Blixten didn't like that. He was uncertain how she would react to an unexpected visit, and said something about her being unpredictable, a bit moody, and that perhaps it was best to leave her in peace. The Man from Skåne listened patiently but he'd made up his mind.

"It's touchy," said Blixten in a final attempt. The Man from Skåne stopped.

"You're in love," he commented. For the island it was such an unusually tender and intrusive statement that in his surprise Blixten nodded.

"I'll do it nicely," the Man from Skåne said when they came out on the yard. The fact that it was an expression that his mother also used had a calming effect on Blixten.

"She's confused," said Blixten, "but a good person."

"Strange times," said the Man from Skåne, and Blixten was prepared to agree.

Blixten could see that Cecilia's car had been left in the thicket well away from Hildingstorp, virtually impossible to discover if you didn't know where to look. He didn't say anything about it. The Man from Skåne drove his SUV ahead on the narrow forest road.

He stopped a short distance from the cabin, smiled quietly to himself, and turned off the ignition. *He likes this,* Blixten thought, to come driving up as the Owner, with the right to correct and reject. That was a new side to him.

"One thing," said the Man from Skåne. "If she makes a fuss then she's out of here immediately." Blixten got out of the car without saying a word.

He felt the door handle, which was locked, knocked carefully on the door. He wanted to be the one she saw first, get a chance to calm her. He walked around the house, tried to look in through the windows. He called her name loudly, and that felt good, it was perhaps fifteen years since the last time. He wanted to do that often in the future.

He's scared, it struck Blixten when he saw that the Man from Skåne was still in the car. He called her name again. The house was silent. A growing feeling of unease slipped up on him.

"She's not here?"

"Doesn't seem like it," said Blixten.

"Does she trust you?"

Blixten nodded. The Man from Skåne got out of the car and looked around. "I lived in Montana for several years, there you could be shot if you trespassed."

"Not here," said Blixten, but the Man from Skåne looked increasingly hesitant.

"We'll leave a message," he said at last.

Blixten went back to the house and pounded on the door again.

"She gets one chance, but tomorrow I'm calling the police!" the Man from Skåne shouted.

Thirty

It wasn't Blixten's car, she could hear that from the sound of the engine. The ancient Simca also rattled in a distinctive way. No, this was a powerful vehicle that made its way at good speed on the road to the cottage. She moved carefully forward, took a detour. The terrain was difficult and the forest had been thinned, with brush piles as effective obstacles that concealed treacherous pits. She slipped once and sank to her knees in a hole filled with water.

She got there just in time to see Blixten walking around the house. "Asshole," she mumbled to herself. She stealthily approached the cabin. A man got out of the car. She was shaking from cold and it was not just a result of the long swim and the wet pants. The man shouted something and she picked up the word "police." Blixten was standing by the house, gesturing, before he hurried to the car. Cecilia saw his worry.

What the hell, she thought, *did he drag an idiot here?* She suspected that it was the new property owner, the one that Blixten called the "Man from Skåne" and about whom he'd spoken well.

Against her better judgment she stepped out from the vegetation, pushing aside some branches. They did not notice her until she started speaking.

"Here I am, scream for the police, then you'll see what happens later." They turned around. She came so close to the man that she could physically sense his fear. Blixten made an effort to force his way in between but she raised her arm.

"It's okay," said Blixten. "He's not going to call the police."

A feeling of great fatigue came over her and she wobbled. It was as if all the accumulated tension from the past week was streaming out in her body, weakening it, putting all her limbs in a state of alarm.

"What have you done, you're completely pale." Blixten put an arm around her waist. "And cold." The property owner had backed away.

"I was in the strait," said Cecilia, feeling an overwhelming need to be taken care of, simply consoled.

"We can't drive to my place," said Blixten. "Maybe later."

Cecilia felt tears running down her face. Her body was shaking.

"I have a blanket," said the Man from Skåne, who had just threatened to call the police but now looked quite moved. He leaned into the backseat, taking out a beautifully patterned plaid.

"Gotland," said Cecilia. "Lamb."

"Yes, a genuine Gotland blanket," Jens Thörn said proudly.

"Get my computer," said Cecilia. "The front door key is under the stone." Blixten looked at her with what she interpreted as gratitude. "And the red folder," she added. They looked at one another for a moment. She understood his unspoken question and shook her head.

"He's still alive," she whispered to Blixten when he returned with the computer and folder. The Man from Skåne had turned his Jeep around and regained some of his self-confidence. They drove to his house in silence. Once there he extended his hand and introduced himself. She mumbled, "Cecilia."

The Man from Skåne listened attentively to what she had to say about her stay in the cabin, asking no questions, making no comments, simply observing her with a cautious smile on his lips. At last she understood why. He did not want to provoke her or make her the slightest bit upset, she would be handled with care. She fell silent, gave Blixten a quick look. He nodded furtively, as if they were conspiring.

"It's lovely in that direction," said the Man from Skåne. "Fine pastures."

"That's Karlsson's on the spit," said Blixten. She thought it seemed strangely laughable that he called her parents "Karlsson," but that was probably the way they were referred to.

"They're the ones who've restored the land. He's careful about such things, Rune." Blixten talked on about what he was an expert in, the Gräsö landscape, about neglect and restoration. The Man from Skåne was no longer smiling but appeared genuinely interested. They had found one another, thought Cecilia. She would also like to be able to talk about reed-choked bays and pollarding of ash trees in the same artless way. There was so much consideration, love really, in his words. It was a separate language where the landscape provided the melody, like when the old archipelago residents talked about the sea and the skerries, the fishing boats and the devious wind gusts.

"Yes, those are fine lands, I'm making an offer," said the Man from Skåne. "That Rune is a man with a somewhat strange sense of humor, that I must say."

"Offer on what?" Blixten asked.

"Karlsson's land. I was thinking it could be divided. The land borders mine of course and I would get direct access to the sea, the beach meadows could be grazed. It would be a coherent unit. They could keep on living in the house."

She didn't understand a thing. Was he going to buy the land that she'd grown up on?

"That's news," said Blixten. He signaled with his hand that she should take it calmly. "And what did Rune say?"

"Go ahead, he said, and raised the price considerably. He demanded eight million."

There was silence around the table. "Thanks for the coffee," Blixten said when the silence became too oppressive, and stood up. "We'll clean out the cabin tomorrow."

"When did you speak with him?" she asked.

"Most recently yesterday. That was when he raised the price."

"Is that why you think he has a strange sense of humor?"

The Man from Skåne laughed. "No, not really. He said something about his wife that I didn't really understand, that she was included with the purchase, or something like that."

They sat silently in the car all the way to the highway. There Blixten pulled over to the side of the road and stopped. "What's happening?" he said. "I'm thinking about your dad."

She sat with the computer and the red folder on her lap. "I don't know, it's been years since I saw him."

"Some people say he's starting to get really batty."

"I'm not angry any longer," she said, so quietly that Blixten was forced to twist his head to hear. "Not like before. They actually don't matter to me, so why get involved, rile myself up?"

She laughed as if to indicate that this was a marked difference from what she had said earlier.

"But if he's serious about piecing off and selling, that's your land too, it's going to be anyway."

"Shall we drive down there?"

"What will become of that, with the documents and Adrian's offshore money?" asked Blixten.

"It's over thirty million, shall we swipe it?"

"What, thirty million? I'll be damned! Can we do that? I mean . . ."

"Give me a few minutes. Everything is prepared."

"I see," said Blixten.

"You don't sound particularly interested."

"I'm starting to get tired of this game."

She opened the laptop, entered passwords, and continued the process she had decided on. Blixten got out, walked around the car, jumped over the ditch, turned his back to her, and positioned himself to stare straight out into the vegetation. During that time kronor, euros, and dollars were swindled and conveyed from account to account, in a long and complicated series across several countries and continents.

When it was done she sat very quietly for a while before she called out. "It's finished," she said. "Adrian is dead. Now let's go to Karlsson's on the spit."

His body was shaking, it looked like he'd been struck by lightning. Rune sank down on his knees and Cecilia associated it with the canonization of the children in Fátima; a picture from the Pope's visit to Portugal a few years earlier fluttered past in her subconscious. She'd been there along with half a million others and seen enough evidence of religious madness for a whole lifetime.

"Do you remember the eagles?"

He looked at her uncomprehendingly.

"Do you remember the thermoses of coffee and hot chocolate?"

He seemed confused, but nodded. Sobbed.

"Where's Mom?"

"Away," he forced out.

"Where is she?"

"She just left."

"Where to?"

"Maybe to Dagny's, I don't know."

Not unreasonable, she thought, and actually didn't care. What was unreasonable about it was that he didn't know for certain where his wife was.

"You've come home," he said, pulling himself up to a standing position. "I have things to tell you. Your mother is a slut."

Blixten let out a sound that in the best case could be called a cackle.

"Always has been," Rune Karlsson resumed. "She . . ."

"We're leaving," Blixten interrupted. "This is not going anywhere. Let's leave and forget about this."

"What do you know about living a false life?"

"A few things," said Blixten, and Cecilia smiled to herself.

"Cecilia has been my great joy in life," said Rune Karlsson, and the sorrow that forced its way out of his tormented voice could not be mistaken. "You said something about thermoses, Cecilia, do you think I've forgotten? Never. Every day, every second, you've been with me."

She was incapable of looking at her father. He was not the same. Oppressed, old, broken.

"I've had time to think."

"You wanted to control everything and everyone. You wanted us to live according to your premises."

He nodded, walked away a few steps, returned.

"I didn't want you to become like her. Faithless."

It slowly occurred to Cecilia how perhaps everything fit together. "Is she dead?"

Thirty-One

"What is this?"

Brundin held a sheet of paper up in front of her. A moment later she understood.

"I don't think it's him," she said, taking out her phone. "But we can check."

They compared the handwriting from the letters Ann had found in Cecilia Karlsson's room with the handwritten lines. Brundin shook his head.

"The style in the letters is refined, that's more than you can say about Adrian's scribbling," he said.

"How did you get him to write this?"

"It was as if he understood that it was bigger than the garage fire. He simply complied, wrote down my dictation without a single comment."

"Strange."

"Not really. He was pressured, nothing seems strange. His thoughts were elsewhere. Then you should take advantage."

Ann understood very well what he meant, that was an old truth.

"Then who wrote the letters?"

"A lover who is very eager," said Brundin, and he made it sound secretive, inviting, and romantic, all at once.

"Right," she said with a smile. "What were Adrian's thoughts?"

"The reason. He's sure he knows who's behind the fire, but he's trying to understand why."

"A first warning, perhaps?"

Brundin looked doubtful. "More than that," he said. "He said one thing that stuck out: 'It was as if she knew,' he repeated several times. When I asked what he meant he kept quiet, but I'm convinced there was something in that garage, other than a motorcycle, a lawnmower, and all the scrap you accumulate."

"Passion or money, or both," said Ann. "That's what this is all about."

"I thought about pornography," said Brundin. "Or something else really shameful and disgusting. Some skeleton in the closet, although it was a garage. Maybe there was a photo collection of a naked Cecilia Karlsson. Maybe she knew about it and wanted to burn it up. And she would never set it on fire as long as Olga Palm was alive. Everyone says that they were close to each other."

She told him about her visit with Blixten, how in principle he admitted that he was behind the fire.

"I've made a few calls," said Brundin. "To get a sense of where Cecilia might be, but so far no bites. I would like to put her on the rack and take a few turns on the crank. I called an old buddy from the hunting party, he's a neighbor of Rune and Gunilla Karlsson and is curious by nature, and he would . . ."

Ann disappeared in her thoughts while Brundin talked on. Who wrote the letters? Who was the recipient? In practice there was only one possibility, but Brundin would not be able to tug on that thread. Should she do it herself?

"I see that you're thinking about something else," Brundin said with a smile. "I'll go to Blixten's place so you can continue brooding. Then I have to go to the mainland. There's a report about a danger to others in connection with hunting. There may be illegal weapons in the picture too."

"Hunting this time of year?"

"Wild boar," Brundin said with a grimace.

"It's probably not a bad thing if a few of them get shot."

"My opinion too," he said, getting in the car.

Ann watched him. *What am I up to?* it struck her. *Playing police again?* Cheese production at home in the village felt distant, unimportant really.

Edvard was at the Gräsö campground. He'd probably given up hope that Ann would be a little more accessible, if he'd had any such idea at all. Ann doubted it. Deep down he was probably glad to get started on the carpentry.

For the third time Ann was standing before Rune Karlsson, and it was obvious that his condition had worsened. If at the previous visit he'd seemed tense, this time he appeared to be in a state of dissolution. Patches of sweat around his armpits and on his chest disfigured the completely out-of-place flowered shirt, his hands moved restlessly over his body as if he was waving away irritating insects, and his face was distorted by tics.

"What is it, has something happened?"

He backed away as if to avoid the questions.

"What do you want?"

"Things are happening," Ann said calmly, careful not to increase his worry. "Adrian Palm has been the victim of a fire. His garage is totally destroyed. But that's not why I'm here, I would like to speak with Cecilia. Has she come back?"

Rune Karlsson stared at her. "Fire?"

She nodded. "Arson, not an electrical defect or anything."

She recognized the Simca that was parked in the yard, there could only be one specimen in that condition, but she chose not to say anything.

"Some say that it was your daughter who set it on fire. Is she here?"

"No."

"But Blixten."

"He's going to help me with the beach meadow."

"You're a lousy liar. I want to talk with her. Before the police bring her in."

"I'm here," a voice sounded from the stoop. Ann turned around. There stood Cecilia Karlsson, no doubt that it was her. She was strikingly straight-backed, perhaps 175 centimeters tall, with a proud but not defiant look, and Ann understood immediately what Robban had meant when he said that she gave an inviting impression. They observed each other, assessed each other like two chess players before an important settling of accounts over the board.

"You're the policewoman who closed up shop but not really, is that so?"

Ann felt relieved by Cecilia's introduction. She could have gone on the attack right from the start.

"Shall we go for a walk?" Ann asked.

Cecilia took the few steps down from the stoop. "Don't say anything that can give you problems," her father said, but his voice was weak and gave no guidance how that would happen. "You haven't done anything illegal."

"Don't say that," said Cecilia. "Yes, let's walk down to the dock. It's been many years since the last time. Do you still have the rowboat?"

Her father looked at her in confusion, as if he didn't understand the question or its meaning at all.

"Maybe we can row out on the strait," she continued, turning her back to him and starting to walk in the direction of the sea. Ann joined her. "Wait here," she said to her father. "Don't follow!"

It did not take long to get to the dock. They walked in silence. Ann mentally recapitulated what she wanted to know, what she must put her finger on, the art was as always to scale away everything irrelevant from an overloaded brain that had to work at too high a speed in an investigation, had too many threads to untangle. Sammy Nilsson was probably the one who was best at that but many times his fiery temperament had sabotaged an effective interrogation. Personally she had often relied on a kind of intuition, together with some notes jotted down on a pad. It often went well. She had been successful in the interview room, but she suspected that Cecilia would be a hard nut to crack. Her disdainful, somewhat teasing attitude, which perhaps attracted men, testified to self-esteem, or considerably more serious, the opposite.

The dock was well constructed. A roughly ten-meter-long stone coffin surrounded by sturdy logs, recently impregnated, and covered with pine boards. Three boats were tied up: an older, apparently unwieldy rowboat and an old-fashioned fishing boat, plus more surprisingly an aluminum boat with an outboard motor.

They looked out over the strait. Neither of them had yet said a word.

"You probably missed this," said Ann.

"I had the Atlantic," said Cecilia.

"You were in Portugal the whole time?"

"Almost. And you, future Gräsö resident?"

"No, but I like being here. Both Edvard, the man I see, and I have a need for . . ."

"Solitude," Cecilia filled in. "Blixten has talked about you. Otherwise he often has a hard time with folks from the mainland."

Ann didn't think that the word "solitude" sounded oppressive. So the introduction was over. She took a breath, as if bracing herself. "Did you set the fire?"

"No."

"What was in the garage?"

The question disturbed Cecilia's self-confident expression a little. She turned her head, peered toward the horizon in the south.

"He died there."

"Casper quarreled with Adrian, you know that, right before he disappeared overboard?"

"They quarreled pretty often," said Cecilia.

"Has anyone told you that you've inherited a house in Italy?"

Cecilia turned around. For the second time Ann had succeeded in disturbing her equilibrium. She told her what Brundin had said. "I think it's south of Turin or something like that, I don't have any details but the house is there."

"We were going to move there," said Cecilia barely audibly.

"But death came in between," Ann said, smiling to herself at her dramatic words.

"It's in a little village called La Morra, I remember the name, I thought it sounded funny. Casper showed me pictures from there, it's beautiful, set in between vineyards. Wine and hazelnuts. And now it's my house, is that what you mean?"

"Wine and hazelnuts," Ann repeated. "That would be something." She told Cecilia that the only thing she had inherited was a water-damaged ninety-five-square-meter house with Eternit facade in Ödeshög.

Cecilia smiled as if she understood very well.

"Go there," Ann resumed. "Forget about this. Reconcile with your parents and then leave."

"He wants to sell the land," said Cecilia. "He wants eight million. That's a shameless price."

Ann grimaced, she'd always had a hard time with large sums.

"The Man from Skåne wants to buy it. I broke into his cabin. A dismal place with a deathwatch beetle that rattles in the wall. All the time! I was there as a girl, then it was nice. I remember that I wanted to have it like that. I wanted to have Rafaela's parents, do you understand? Now the deathwatch beetle is crawling in the wall."

"Who was Rafaela?"

Cecilia told Ann about her playmate, the family from Chile.

"So what were they like?"

"Free, maybe, I don't know, but they wanted . . . maybe refugees can never be free. I played with Rafaela for days on end."

"Is that a fishing boat?"

"Yes, my grandfather's originally."

"I looked in your room," said Ann. "It was like a museum. They've been waiting for you to come back."

"Can you imagine that I lived at home?"

"No, it seems very unlikely," Ann said honestly.

"I must have saved ten thousand a month." She laughed as if she'd suddenly discovered what was funny in that a thirty-year-old, otherwise so independent woman was still living at home with Mom and Dad to save money. "No rent and I didn't even have to pay for food. I set aside money to be able to build a life of my own."

"If I say Hotel Knaust, what do you think of?"

At the same moment she regretted the question. Maybe she was in the process of sabotaging a police investigation.

"Sundsvall," said Cecilia without needing any time to think.

"Have you stayed there?"

"As a child. I remember that I played on a big staircase."

"Why Sundsvall, was it sports competitions?"

"Why do you ask?"

"Rune talked about Sundsvall and Knaust."

Cecilia laughed. "Did he show you pictures? He loves browsing in old albums."

Ann smiled as if to confirm her theory. She did not feel a bit duplicitous. The strange thing was that Cecilia so nonchalantly talked about things that Ann did not have anything to do with, or any reason to be interested in.

"We had an old aunt and a few others, must have been cousins, on Mom's side in Norrland. Those were the only relatives we had contact with. Really boring, and with a hideous dialect, but I remember that I thought it was okay. Dad was good at one thing: organizing competitions, but it was never a game. You met to compete, not to socialize. But up there we did things that other people did, played mahjong, went on outings, played Kubb, and swam in the sea. It was even colder than here, but as a child you didn't care."

"What was Gunilla good at?"

"Hitting the bull's-eye," said Cecilia after thinking about it. "And baking rolls with vanilla cream."

"Do you have any contact with the relatives up there?"

Cecilia shook her head.

"I don't see my relatives anymore either."

"Do you have children?"

"A teenage son."

Cecilia went and stood farthest out on the dock with her back toward Ann, as if to mark that the conversation was over, or at least that she wanted to take a break. There was a ladder mounted. Everything looked neat. There was even a life buoy hanging on a stand, as if it were a public swimming place.

Ann waited. It struck her that she had passed the dock many times at a distance together with Edvard when they crossed the strait on their way to go fishing. She tried to imagine Casper Stefansson's body as it slowly descended to the bottom of the sea. Or how was it, was a weight required so that a person's body would sink? Sad to say she wasn't certain. She would have to ask Brundin, maybe Edvard. Regardless, she and Edvard had set out nets in the strait, caught fish that knew where Stefansson's remains were.

Cecilia had turned around. "Where are you?"

"I'm setting out nets," said Ann, taking a few steps closer.

"I'll talk with Brundin, I know who he is, every Gräsö resident probably does. Do you have his number? Then I'm leaving."

"Where to?"

"I don't know . . . maybe Italy. Or else I'll get lost. Sometimes I want that."

"In the forest? Here on the island it's hard, you always come to the sea at last."

"Then it's just a matter of continuing straight ahead, straight out, straight down," said Cecilia, and Ann glimpsed something mournful in the woman's face, as if she was recalling something painful.

Ann rattled off Brundin's number from memory. Nothing more was said. Just like on the way down to the dock, they walked wordlessly back. Ann remembered other paths, while she observed Cecilia's back and legs. She moved ahead gracefully as she glided over worn roots and stones embedded in the trampled-down ground, avoided the prickly branches of the rose hips and the sharp junipers along the path that wound its way up toward the house. She gave a self-aware and physically fit impression.

That's what made it unreliable. The fragile and pale were easy to identify, and through their frailty signaled something deformed, perhaps a lack, a suffering, something to be on your guard against.

Suddenly Cecilia stopped. "Look," she said, pointing at a butterfly that was resting on a leaf by the edge of the path. It flapped its wings, which were white with black streaks. "Black-veined white," Cecilia continued, and it was as if her attitude was changed in one stroke. Even her voice lost its harshness, the sarcastic streak that otherwise marked her comments changed to a warm tone.

Ann happened to think about Erik's talk of wanting to learn the names of plants, and the irritation at Cecilia's unpredictability was reinforced, but she said nothing more than a few words that it was beautiful.

"You see them mostly early in the summer." Cecilia looked around. "Rowan and blackthorn," she noted, as if to verify her species designation. "We don't have that much hawthorn here."

"Are you good at butterflies?" Ann felt compelled to ask, having noticed that Cecilia used the word "we."

"It was Rune who dragged me along," said Cecilia, once again with the sarcastic tone, as if she diminished the significance of her own words.

"Post office box 339," said Ann.

"Uh, what do you mean?"

"You don't know about it?"

"What do you mean?" Cecilia asked again.

They looked at each other. Another black-veined white came flying, but neither of them noticed. Ann saw how the insight slowly sank in, that there were happenings and relationships here that Cecilia didn't know about, even though she was her father's daughter who wanted to keep track.

Ann took out her phone, tapped up "Images." "This is an extract from a letter," she said. Her hands felt unsteady, likewise her voice as she read a few lines out loud: "Can we meet next week? I'm going to Sundsvall. We can stay at Knaust, you know the hotel with the stairs. Don't you have some relative up there in the Lapp country that you can pretend to visit?"

"What post office box? What is this about?"

"I have no idea," said Ann in a tone that suggested the opposite.

"What do you want, what do you want from me?"

"I was a police officer for many years and sense when things don't add up, when it's doubtful."

"Who got the letter?"

"I really don't know," said Ann, feeling the other woman's intense gaze, and hesitated a few seconds before she continued. "Maybe your mother."

The word "mother" sounded strange in that context. It was obvious that Cecilia had a similar feeling. "My mother?" she said, and it sounded as if she was tasting the word and found it bitter. Ann nodded. She really wanted to have a discussion with Cecilia. She was the key, she was the one who despite everything stood the most free from this tangle. A little crazy or not didn't matter, for who isn't when all is said and done.

Cecilia started to walk. Ann did not want to let her go yet. "One thing," said Ann. "Do you recognize the handwriting?" Cecilia stopped. Ann held out the phone, which Cecilia gave a quick glance before she looked out over the strait, which was visible between the trees.

"No, I don't know who wrote that," she said, turning on her heels and continuing her march toward her parental home.

Ann observed the restlessly fluttering butterflies before she joined her. Now she could identify four species: black-veined white, common brimstone, peacock butterfly, and mourning cloak. That felt both good and completely worthless.

She picked up the pace, anxious not to let Cecilia out of sight. Anything at all could happen. Cecilia's anger could not be mistaken, there was no longer anything beautiful in her progress, and the fact was that Ann felt a certain satisfaction over having managed to shake her up.

Blixten and Rune Karlsson were sitting on the porch having coffee as if everything was just fine. On a plate was a pile of rolls with vanilla cream. Ann reached over and took one. Blixten stood up and followed Cecilia, who without a word had disappeared into the house. Rune sat as if paralyzed, back straight and with arms and hands neatly extended on the arm support. It reminded Ann of an electric chair.

"Call your wife," said Ann. "Tell her to come home."

Rune turned his head. "She's never coming back again," he said.

Thirty-Two

"Three police reports on one and the same day. Gräsö is getting to be a lot of work, a no-go zone," said Brundin, and Ann thought that for the first time he sounded a little stressed. "One from Rune Karlsson that his wife Gunilla is missing. Adrian Palm has reported Cecilia for unlawful threat and arson, and as the cherry on the cake one Jens Thörn has reported a break-in at one of his houses. He bought . . ."

"I know who he is," said Ann. "That's the least important. Cecilia has been staying there a few days. A trifle."

"Trifle," Brundin repeated, and he sounded depressed. Ann could imagine how the hard-pressed policeman tossed aside the printout of Thörn's complaint and immediately forgot the whole thing.

She was standing in the kitchen staring down at a saucepan where potatoes were boiling intensely. She turned down the heat. Edvard would be coming soon. Ann had promised to fix dinner. He was traditional, wanted to sit down at the table right away if possible. He had never said anything but Ann sensed the expectations and couldn't really get worked up. There were other things that were more important. And when he was at home then food was always on the table when Ann arrived, so it evened out.

"What do you think about Mrs. Karlsson?" Ann asked.

"What did Mr. Karlsson say?"

"That she'd gone to Timrå to visit a relative, but then hadn't been in touch and didn't answer the phone. He called the cousin or whoever it was, but she was quite perplexed, she hadn't seen Gunilla Karlsson in a long time and wasn't expecting a visit.

"Maybe she's staying at Hotel Knaust," said Ann.

"With who?"

"Joking aside, I'm a little worried. Rune seems completely out of sorts."

"Has she left for good?" Brundin asked.

"It's leaning that way," said Ann.

"You mean she's been sunk in the strait," said Brundin, making it sound like a reasonable alternative.

"You don't like her?"

"Never have." Ann waited in vain for the motivation. She was struck by the thought that Brundin was perhaps too deeply involved in life on Gräsö. He seemed to know most everyone and have opinions about most everything.

"The cell phone," said Ann.

"I've requested a search. She must have been in the vicinity of a cell tower somewhere. It seems to be a trend in the Karlsson family to disappear. It's getting tiresome."

"You want something solid, like a group of dead wild boar in the forests by Ånö or an assault in Långalma."

Brundin chuckled but turned serious again at once. "We have Cecilia in an interview," he said unexpectedly. "We got a tip that she was driving on board the ferry and had a stroke of luck that there were colleagues in Öregrund. They drove down and when she drove off the ferry they could bring her in directly."

"Any protests?"

"Not at all. We explained that we simply wanted to question her for informational purposes. She is friendliness itself, but hasn't let out anything of real value. She repeats what she told you."

"The garage," said Ann. "Go back to Adrian's garage, was there anything exciting there or was the fire simply malicious? Pretend like you know more than you do."

"I always do," said Brundin, who already seemed to be in a better mood.

"Who called in the tip? One of the ferry guys?"

"No, Blixten called," Brundin said. "He said something to the effect that it was just as well that we talked with Cecilia, get it out of the way, as he put it. He was probably tired of the cat-and-mouse game."

"Did he say anything else?"

"No, just that he was worried about Rune Karlsson, that his old lady was capable of anything."

"What did he mean by that?"

"Gunilla Karlsson is a tough dame, everyone knows that. She has lived on the island most of her life but has never really been accepted." He didn't say more, provided no details. Ann had to try to imagine and it was not particularly hard. The mentality on the island could sometimes be cranky and dismissive if not exactly judgmental, but she had also experienced that a few years ago when she moved from Uppsala to the village outside Gimo. It was probably like that everywhere in the Swedish countryside.

They talked back and forth for a few minutes but in the absence of more facts there was mostly speculation. They both understood however that the situation was not hopeless. The dynamics were there. People prepared to tell what they suspected or knew were there too. Ann said something along those lines in order to encourage Brundin a little before they ended the call.

Ann checked the smoked sausage, which was sweating in a cheese and tomato sauce in the oven. Suddenly she was taken back in time, became someone else, she became her mother who always made that dish when she wanted to show off. Ann's father had loved smoked sausage. The sight and smell always changed his mood for the better, and the funny thing was that he never understood that it was a simple, calculated trick from his wife's side and not an expression of consideration or affection.

She grinned and turned down the temperature. The contemplation made her both slow and increasingly restless. She felt that she was missing something essential, or something trivial and meaningless. The feeling was the same, she knew that from experience, but equally annoying. With complicated investigations during her time as a police officer she had felt it purely physically, the pinpricks in her arms and the sweat gathering on her lower back and between her breasts.

She turned off the oven and cracked open the lid on the potatoes before she went out and sat on the sun porch, indecisive, uneasy. In her old life she would have had wine, now she drummed impatiently with her fingers on the table. There was an open bottle of Vinho Verde in the refrigerator, and in the living room there was a bottle with a little red wine from Priorat in Catalonia, a new wine district she had discovered. The clock in the living room struck and Edvard was surely on his way.

Slowly the insight crept up on her, she straightened her back, stopped the nervous drumming, laced her hands as if in prayer, and fixed her gaze on a point in the garden, but in reality it was the living room and the cupboard with the bottles she saw before her. In her eagerness to get up she bumped the table and a vase with flowers fell over. She picked it up quickly and observed for a moment the water that had run out on the tabletop before she hurried into the living room. It was as if the reverberation from Viola's old wall clock was still hanging there with the six strokes vibrating in the air. She opened the cupboard door. Five bottles, two of which were wine. The others contained vodka, cognac, and tequila. The same kinds as always with Edvard. The person was a creature of habit, smoked sausage or vodka didn't matter, you returned to your favorites.

She took out her phone and pressed redial. Brundin answered immediately with a "Now what?"

"I seem to recall that there was alcohol in the boat that Casper Stefansson fell out of."

Brundin hummed in response.

"What kind?"

He answered immediately. "There was a bottle of Captain Morgan in the boat. Half empty."

"What's that? Rum?"

"From Jamaica," said Brundin, and Ann heard in his voice that his curiosity was aroused, but she said thanks, promised to get back to him, and clicked off the call.

Edvard had come home without her having noticed anything. He was standing in the doorway when she turned around. She picked up on his look, understood that he was wondering over the fact that she had opened the liquor cabinet.

"I think I've thought of something," she said. "Have you ever had Captain Morgan?"

"It's probably happened."

The relief in his eyes was obvious.

"Is it good?"

He jerked his head as if to show that the taste was probably okay.

"Smoked sausage," said Ann. "There's smoked sausage in the oven. Shall we eat?" They went to the kitchen. She quickly wiped off the table, Edvard took out the baking dish, and Ann tipped the potatoes into a bowl, set out grated cheese and ketchup.

"I thought about mashing the potatoes with a little chopped onion . . . but it doesn't work with new potatoes."

"It's fine," said Edvard, helping himself to the food. He ate in silence, looked at Ann and smiled. "Captain Morgan," he said.

"Does the bottle have a pirate on the label?"

Edvard chuckled and before he answered he took a substantial portion of sausage with threads of cheese hanging and chewed carefully, with his gaze steadily fixed on her. In its ordinariness it was a striking sight. She wanted to get up, round the table and hug him, tell him that she wanted to live with a man who ate smoked sausage with melted cheese so pleasurably, but sometimes the best evidence of love is silence and quiet. In Edvard's case that was a truism.

"That it is," he said at last. "A pirate."

"When we were at the Karlssons' I saw a bottle like that," she said, and told him that Brundin had mentioned just that sort in connection with Casper Stefansson's death.

"Yes, I saw too that they had lots of alcohol at home, but I didn't know what kinds," said Edvard. "I'm no connoisseur."

It was a line that could be perceived as a reminder of her previous habits, but he only looked good-natured when he continued.

"Do you mean that the bottle in the boat came from Karlsson?"

"Maybe."

"I think that rum is pretty popular."

They continued eating in silence. "There's only one way to find out about that," said Lindell.

"It was more than four years ago," said Edvard.

"The Karlssons seem unstable," said Ann, "and their relationship is on the skids, and then perhaps one wants to injure the other."

Edvard gave her a quick look.

"I've seen it before. It's terrible to exploit division between a couple, but effective." Ann talked on about a couple of cases from before but she felt increasingly uncertain about what she actually wanted to have said, and above all whether it was worth it. Edvard, the smoked sausage, and an existence liberated from crime and investigations stood out more and more as the most essential in her life.

It was as if Edvard was reading her thoughts, took the lingering and uncertain voice as a sign that it was time to change track. "Erik seemed both nervous and harmonious," he said, starting to clear the table, piled the two plates and the dishes, snapped up the last slice of sausage with his fingers, and arranged everything on the kitchen counter.

"It's obvious that it affects a young guy to meet his biological father for the first time," said Ann. The rattling from the porcelain stopped.

"He was happy but also afraid of what I would think," she continued, and the old worry came back.

"And what did you think?"

"It's okay with me," Ann said.

If he wants to know more he can either ask me or, less likely, Erik, she thought. He liked her son but he was also the obvious evidence of her infidelity and betrayal, a constant reminder, if you chose to drill down into the story. Edvard had a tendency to do that. He returned more and more often to his childhood and upbringing, his parents and the work they did on the farm where Edvard and his father and grandfather had all been hired farmworkers, brief bits of information that testified to more extensive musings. He seldom if ever mentioned his two sons. Their lives, and the lack of contact with their father, and not least their crazy view of society, their unconcealed racism and hatefulness, was Edvard's wound that would never heal. Ann knew that without having to talk about it.

"That's good," said Edvard, and so the matter was apparently off the table. Ann leaned her head back, closed her eyes, took a breath, neutralized in her thoughts and for a moment liberated.

Edvard started doing the dishes. He did not miss having a dishwasher and would probably never acquire one.

"Do you want to see him, Erik's father I mean?"

"No," said Ann without hesitating a second, but it was a lie.

"Tomorrow we'll go out on the water," said Edvard as they sat on the porch, each with a cup of coffee.

"Don't you have to work?"

He shook his head. "It's important to take the opportunity, autumn will soon be here."

"We can pack a lunch," said Ann, happy but nonetheless split. She would really like to talk with Rune Karlsson again.

Thirty-Three

Was it a biblical expression? He had a faint memory from his earliest years, when his grandmother used the words "brute beasts" and that they are born to be taken and destroyed. Then he didn't understand, became afraid of the irascible old woman with the chapped hands. From her sharp nose a clear fluid was constantly dripping as if she was being drained of all the sap to slowly dry up, be mummified. Of all her Christianity and seeming piety nothing remained other than condemnation and caustic quotations from the Bible that was placed on a white cloth in the unheated parlor. It was ancient, bound in leather which over the years had become stained and faded and dominated the room through its weight. He was forbidden to browse the brittle pages, a thought that had never occurred to him.

Now he knew what the words stood for and was just as afraid, no, more afraid than in childhood. Experience and common sense did not govern what had been etched in sixty years ago. He hated his grandmother, the memory of her. He had burned the Bible up in the ceramic stove as soon as his father was dead. When one of his brothers wondered where it had gone, he claimed to be quite puzzled about the fate of the holy scripture.

Brute beast, he had thought as he closed the door to the timbered shed where nets, buoys, and everything else that had to do with fishing were stored. It was perhaps her whimpering and the rattling from the chain around her one foot that made him think of hunt, catch, and butcher. The chain had been hand-forged by his great-grandfather Karl a hundred years ago. Rune Karlsson liked the thought of sinking down through the centuries. He had imprisoned her by means of rusty links, laboriously joined by hands he sensed behind so much on the farm. The smithy still endured, from the shore it was possible to glimpse its roof. But he had also imprisoned her by means of the Bible's condemnatory words thrown out by his grandmother, a witch with stinking breath through loose-fitting dentures.

She had been taken, now she would be destroyed. He had worked in silence. There was no point in saying anything. The words had lost all meaning. There was no rhyme or reason any longer, probably hadn't been for many years. She was morally corroded, that was the word that came closest. She had screamed, threatened, pleaded, and prayed, scared to death of course. He hadn't cared, didn't try to calm her, didn't give any motives, hadn't said a single word, and that had surely increased her fear. That amused him.

He stopped halfway between the shed and the dock. Some stately loosestrife rocked by the south wind shone fiery between the stones on the shore, like a final greeting. It was a good time of year. Nature slowed down, flower turned into seed, fruit, and nut, surrendering slowly and languidly, dripping a touch of sorrow from worn leaves and broken stalks, aware that there was no eternal summer, in jest changing their colors indecently, dressing up before they finally undressed.

Had it gone too far? Had he gone too far? It wasn't possible to rewind the tape. There was a lot that argued that Gunilla must die. Tomorrow she planned to go to Stockholm. A conference. For him that was the breaking point. She comes home just to repack. She hadn't understood a bit of what he talked about in the cellar, that she would get one more chance. Perhaps understood, but didn't care. Now she intended to take off again!

She had dropped the expensive leather suitcase he'd bought for her in Milan nonchalantly on the hall floor, pretended to be tired and worn out, put on water for tea and bustled in the kitchen, cleaned up crumbs from the kitchen table, sighed, studied the contents of the refrigerator, sighed again. The dissatisfaction seemed to enclose her entire appearance and being. More sighs. It was as if he didn't exist. Not even when he picked her up in Öregrund had she expressed anything that could be interpreted positively, aiming ahead. She had complained about delayed trains and grumpy bus drivers.

"Tomorrow I'm going away for a few days. It's a conference about the special association's calculations for 2020. As usual it's chaos and the good Eriksson needs a little assistance. If you drive me to Öregrund I've arranged a ride from there. I'm sorry, but I have to be at this conference."

She didn't look a bit sorry. Wouldn't be at some hotel in Stockholm either, he was convinced of that. *Arranged a ride*, he thought, and could not understand what that might mean, but he didn't care to ask.

"The milk has gone bad," she said. Then he struck her on the back of her head. Not a hard blow but enough that she would fall forward and strike her head on the faucet in the sink. He pressed her down. The milk she had poured out was mixed with the blood from a gaping wound between her eyes and disappeared bubbling down the drain. He held her arms together, hissed something that he didn't recall other than that the word "whore" recurred. She screamed, but to what use? She resisted, and vigorously too, tried to kick backward to hit his crotch. But the resistance was in vain. He exploited his fury, his strength, and not least the element of surprise, dragged her down on the floor, reached and pulled the open ironing board to him. She screamed and now in a more desperate tone, perhaps convinced that he would kill her with the iron. He used the cord to tie her wrists behind her back. It was not an easy maneuver and he was forced to press one knee down between her shoulder blades. "I'm suffocating," she gasped. He pulled on the cord, quickly turned her on her back and gave her a frightful punch across the jaw with a clenched fist. Her head jerked to the side and she lost consciousness. The feeling of triumph when her eyes fluttered and closed was immediately replaced by fear that the blow had been fatal. He had never struck anyone before, neither man nor woman.

A few white birds were screeching over the sea. He went out on the dock. The boat was bobbing pleasantly. The waves lapped against the planking. A lovely day with a light breeze. *I'll wrap the chain around her body*, he thought, looking out over the strait.

When did things change? Hadn't he always provided for her and Cecilia? For thirty-five years they had been together. He had truly exerted himself to give her a good life.

The gulls were squabbling on Lillskäret, all screeching at the same time, agitated emotions. Was it about territory, partners, or food? That was probably the sort of thing gulls fought about. Then it struck Rune that perhaps they were playacting, or more likely it was their way of conversing, quite simply a high-volume discussion, nothing more, because birds can't dissemble like people do, can they? A lying gull would not be long-lived. Was it that animals probably told the truth? Rhapsodic segments from some of the many nature programs he'd seen on TV showed up, but he could not recall a single example of bluffing and disinformation in the animal world.

To break his idiotic train of thought he pulled the fishing boat to him with the mooring line and jumped on board, parried expertly when the boat rocked. He sat down in the stern, placed his right hand like always on the worn railing, stretched out his legs, and decided to stay until he had figured out how to proceed from here. There were probably only three alternatives: release her, keep her imprisoned in the net shed, or drown her using the chain.

He left the boat without making any decision. It was getting to be evening. The night would be clear but not especially chilly. No sound came from the shed.

Thirty-Four

There is only one explanation. *There is only one person in the whole world who could have staged it all. There is only one answer.*

For the past few hours Adrian Palm had been drinking steadily and deliberately. He was getting more and more drunk but still considered his mind completely clear. In front of him on the table was the computer, as well as a few binders, a heap of folders, computer printouts, and other loose papers. There was no doubt: He had been robbed of millions of kronor. From what he could see several of his accounts were drained. There was one on the Cayman Islands that was intact, likewise two that concerned the "Mediterranean money," as he always called the assets in Malta and Cyprus. Common to those three accounts was that they had been opened in the past year. The money in the Philippines also seemed to have survived. There he had received a warning about an attempt at hostile intrusion, so the account was blocked by the bank for "further investigation," they had reported.

He had called Bengaluru, Manila, and Singapore. There he had long-term acquaintances and business contacts that worked with the expanding "digital banking" and monitoring of global money movement. None of them sounded especially surprised when he described, albeit in vague terms, what had happened. One Mr. Michael Sinha, with a base in Kuala Lumpur, but who seemed to live a life in constant movement between the countries in Southeast Asia, had explained how the whole thing had probably been done. Adrian heard clear criticism in the Indian's voice, with an element of sarcasm that was reinforced by Sinha's whistling and verbose speaking style. He had even used the word "amateur" when he somewhat scornfully criticized the gullible Swede.

"Fucking pidgin idiot," Adrian Palm mumbled.

He tried to understand and summarize. Combined, over five million were left. That wasn't small change, but over six times as much was gone. Yes, he was an amateur, a clueless amateur. He was forced to accept it all, he understood that. Getting at and trying to retrieve the assets was pointless. He would have to live with the loss. The certainty that he ought to kill someone was growing stronger and stronger. Courage rose in pace with his drinking, more and more greedily, no sipping, no finesse. There was no consolation in the fact that someone must die, simply a kind of primitive desire for vengeance.

The bottle with the familiar label was half empty. It was on the floor, next to the nearest table leg. It was a habit he'd inherited from his father, Verner. He raised the glass, but hesitated, stared unseeing at the row of his mother's books in the overfilled shelf and transported himself to another island. A tropical paradise, completely different from the cramped Gräsö. He didn't need his childhood island any longer. He shook his head, in this way resumed a here and now, saw the familiar book spines by working-class authors, with titles like *Flowering Nettles*; *Goodnight, Earth*; and *Mother Gets Married*. He had read several of them but did not remember much of the depictions of misery Olga Palm praised and insisted that he must work his way through.

"Stop it now," he said out loud, but brought the glass to his mouth. He knew very well what would happen if he kept on drinking. The initial anger would slowly be transformed to tearfulness. It was already on its way. The image of Cecilia would not budge from his inner eye. He could not drop the thought of her, of her grip on his dick when they met outside Gräsö Inn. The memories from before stepped out mercilessly, they'd had it good, wildly good.

There was no doubt that she was the one behind the attack and the draining of his assets. She was the only one who knew about the extent of his multi-year swindle and the entryways for sneaking into the system. What was amateurish, Mr. Sinha was right, was that he had not changed many of the procedures and search paths where the electronic assets were concerned since she disappeared four years ago. The table had been set for Cecilia Karlsson to devour millions.

But, there was always a "but," could he win her back? He did not see Blixten as a threat. He was the local patriot with the appearance of a fool. It wasn't enough to buy a bottle of expensive wine to steadily conquer Cecilia, strength and refinement were required. Vision was required. The insular Blixten lacked all this, the kind-in-his-soul-but-ever-so-limited Blixten.

Could the theft of the money be seen as a provocation? A demonstration of power? She liked the feeling of dominance and the exercise of power, he'd known that a long time, but also the interplay between the weak and the strong. That was certainly one of the reasons she had succeeded so well in the company. She had exploited her beauty and femininity and combined it with smarts and ruthlessness, a worn cliché of course, but this dangerous cocktail had attracted him and benefited him. She was one of the reasons that the company got a considerable push forward in those early years, and the first under-the-table money could be transferred abroad.

"Go to it, win her back!" he said out loud and got up from the armchair. Something invigorating. He laughed, once again one of his father Verner's words, who the hell used that word any longer? He aimed a pretend golf stroke, a big swing from the tee at the sixth hole at Sentosa in

Singapore. A tricky challenge with three strategically placed bunkers. The movement put him off balance and he had to support himself against the bookshelf.

"Fuck her!" he shouted, with the conviction that the performance at Gräsö Inn contained something more than a simple threat. In her grip like so often he had found a mixed message. Behind the loathing the promise of a kind of joint victory was hidden. They had actually worked together for ten years. He had seen her capacity, hired her with good terms, actually made her, and naturally she was aware of that. If he hadn't existed she would be sitting at a boring accounting firm forced to work with the minor leaguers. He and his company had represented the big leagues.

"Drink water," he mumbled, staggering out to the kitchen, aware that he needed to hold back on the alcohol.

Her swindling was a test, he decided, as he filled a pitcher with water. She had used Blixten as an instrument, because purely logically she needed a base to proceed from, but also at least just as much to weaken him, even ridicule him, when she'd chosen a borderline alcoholic forest fool as an ally. Now she awaited his move. He gulped down another glass of water.

He left the house. The smell of smoke still lingered. The sooty remains of the garage underscored the decline of the farm. Verner's at one time so carefully laid gravel paths were spotted with grass, the lawns a swatch of all kinds of weeds and moss, and the once so inviting lilac arbor was one big brushy thicket that expanded beyond its boundaries. He'd seen it before but it was only now that the extent of the negligence stood out clearly. Couldn't Blixten have fixed it? Hadn't he been paid? He took out his phone. Now he would damn well hear a few home truths!

Half an hour later the Simca came rattling. Blixten got out but remained standing by the car with the door open, forcing Adrian to get up from the bench by the flagpole.

"It looks just terrible," he began.

"Yes, you said that on the phone," Blixten said calmly. "But if you mean that I should have taken care of it you're mistaken."

"You got paid!"

"A hundred bucks a year," Blixten said flatly. "How far does that go in your world? I cut the grass and removed trash and brush. Besides that I voluntarily fixed the fence and cleaned up the flower beds in the spring. A hundred bucks."

The figure spoke for itself, Adrian understood that too. That was what he might pay for lunch for two.

"Where is she?"

"With the police in Östhammar."

He forced Blixten to tell him what had happened, that they had brought her in to talk.

"Do they have anything on her?"

"Nope, not a thing," Blixten said with a laugh.

He was astounded that Blixten could maintain his calm, but it was as if his old friend from antiquity was unapproachable. What could put him off balance? Adrian could not think of a single tool from the kit that he normally used to force through his will. It wasn't possible to negotiate with Blixten, no threats or sanctions took hold; he owned his own house, and evidently had plenty of work.

"And my fucking garage?!"

"Yes, it burned down, but what are the cops going to do about that? Maybe it was a short circuit. You probably monkeyed with the electricity."

"Arson, the firemen said. Someone set it." He observed Blixten, who almost looked bored, or maybe he was just tired. "What do you want with Cissi? She's playing with you, you get that, huh? Exploiting you. Then she'll leave."

Blixten lowered his eyes. He had never seen him so contemplative. Blixten would get worked up if he was provoked. Now he stood there calm as a cow, avoiding confrontation.

"She's a thief. She has stolen lots from me."

"You don't want for anything, I would think."

"Help me," said Adrian. "Help me put her in jail. You'll get a reward, a substantial wad of money. Cash." He came right up, forcing the other man to look at him.

Blixten shook his head.

"A million in your hand."

The response was a smile.

"The alternative is that your house burns."

The blow came quite unexpectedly and hit him on the left cheek. A hook with restricted force but which nonetheless made him stumble backward, lose his balance and fall down flat.

"Don't threaten me," said Blixten. "Ever." They observed one another before Blixten got in the car and drove away. Adrian remained sitting on the ground, touching his face, testing his jaw by gaping widely. The pain was manageable but the disgrace was considerable.

He got up with some difficulty, looked around as if to check that no one had seen the fracas. If it had all played out in the little settlement in the Philippines where he lived, and Blixten had been a cheeky underling who resorted to violence, well, then Adrian could have arranged a brutal reprisal within half an hour. Money and commercial success didn't help much to improve your appearance on the island. That had been clear during Olga's funeral. Most had gone around him and headed for his mother, naturally of course as she was the one they were saying goodbye to, but it was as if the funeral attendees hadn't seen him, no one had mentioned any of the many things that made him proud. Quite a bit had also been written about the company and its fairy tale–like expansion in the press, the talk and the gossip had surely been passed around the island. They could have spared a few words about his successes, but no! Did they understand his grief at all? Now it was over, it had slowly but surely become clear to him, the bonds were broken.

"I am Adrian Palm, son of Verner and Olga," he said out loud. "Their only son who they had such hopes for." He'd become someone else. That was clear to everyone.

He looked toward the house. Should he sell it? That was probably the only right thing, but it still felt strange. Would other people move into his childhood home, fill it with hope and expectations? Would children run around and romp on the grass, swing on the Åkerö apple tree, pick raspberries and gooseberries, bushes that Olga cared for so tenderly? *I'll burn down the shack,* he thought. *Everything will be wiped out.*

Thirty-Five

Edvard sheered in toward land. Ann stood prepared with the mooring line. The anchor splashed into the drink aft. The boat slowed down and glided ahead the last stretch. She jumped over to the dock, tied up. The engine was choked. The silence was immediate. No white birds, no people in sight, the bobbing and lapping of waves receded. It was truly a lovely day, even if the easterly wind had picked up somewhat, but it was silent as in the grave.

Sometimes Ann felt it, that terror of being left alone in a world emptied of human presence, coexistence, where only mute nature surrounded you, where wind and waves were the only signs of movement, for some a meditative silence but for her a kind of torture. She said something simple and meaningless that Edvard didn't find worth commenting on, he didn't even give her a glance. He only had eyes for the orderliness on the bottom, that it looked good if someone were to come by and cast an eye down into the boat.

They came from the sea, previously probably as common as landing on a road or path, but Ann felt like an intruder. When she visited the family earlier, Rune Karlsson had met her on the stoop. He had heard and identified the visitor. Now perhaps he would be taken by surprise. The dock was a good distance from the house and concealed by trees and bushes, which also caught and perhaps distorted the engine sound from boats that tied up.

They left the shoreline and passed the boathouse, which was now some distance from the water. Ann heard a hollow thumping sound, unclear from where. She stopped and Edvard almost ran into her.

She went up to the boathouse and opened the door, peeked in, but discovered nothing interesting or unusual. She closed the door again. Then the sound came again, a faint thumping.

"What was that?"

"I didn't hear anything," said Edvard, and that was not surprising, his hearing was steadily getting worse. He always blamed a lifetime of noise from machinery and tools, and carelessness with ear protection besides, when he didn't hear or didn't want to hear.

"Something's making a sound, tapping."

Edvard looked around. On the wall of a shed a short distance away old oars were attached and a pair of orange buoys of a modern design were also hanging there.

"The buoys," he said. The buoys were rocking in the wind and striking against the red-painted timbers, as if to confirm his theory. "It's an old shed for nets and tools, maybe from the nineteenth century. There's a similar one by Victor's dock too. A beautiful structure. Maybe the same old man built it. They knew their stuff back then."

They resumed the walk toward the house. *Thump, thump*, but this time she didn't care. They passed the place where Ann and Cecilia had stopped. "Black-veined white," Ann said as if in passing, turning her head and pointing. "Black-veined white," she repeated, louder. Edvard laughed but showed no visible surprise even though Ann and entomology were an unlikely combination.

The farmyard was deserted. The flagpole was still stretched out on the ground, cut up and partly chopped apart with what had probably been an

ax, as if an overactive beaver had let off steam. The crushed pieces from
the ball were still by its top. "Strange," said Edvard, stopping to observe
the destruction. Ann understood that it all went against his sense of order.
He could have a messy kitchen table or an unmade bed day after day, but
a boat deck or bottom without style or tools and gear scattered around
violated his world order. That made him an untypical Gräsö resident. He
had pointed that out himself and Ann could see it with her own eyes: an
islander's farmyard could often be compared to an extended and diversi-
fied junk pile, especially if there were EU subsidies involved.

Rune Karlsson willingly told that he happily drank Captain Morgan, but
that unfortunately it happened all too rarely.

"I don't want to drink alone," he explained. "And Gunilla, she . . . why
are you asking?"

They were sitting on the porch toward the west. The temperature was
still pleasant, but Ann felt a little cold anyway, as always after an outing
on the water.

"Stefansson," she said, uncertain how she should present this. Her ten-
tative conversational style perhaps did not hit home in all situations. It was
different when she was with the police, then she had a kind of mandate
and not least a psychological advantage, it could be a little convoluted, no
one could actually have an opinion about that. When it came to an ordi-
nary conversation in civilian life it was different. People expected a certain
logic and stringency.

"He drank rum," she resumed, but stopped there, and she sensed more
than registered Rune Karlsson's worry. "Up to the last."

"You can't understand how it feels to lose your only child," said Rune.

"What do you mean?"

"Now I will actually have a Captain Morgan. Would you like some?"

Ann shook her head. Rune got up, unexpectedly lithely, it was the athlete she was seeing for a moment, and he disappeared through the open
French doors. *Should I be worried?* she thought. She stared at the frosted
doors where the late afternoon sun glistened in the panes. *Have a rum,*

you're not driving. Don't do it, there will be more. She struggled with herself in the old way, back when good sense usually lost. Rune Karlsson returned with a lovely crystal glass in his hand.

"You drink it straight?"

He nodded and raised the glass, which also cast a reflection toward her, flashed as if to say, *Everything is housed in me,* before with a theatrical gesture he sipped the pirate drink. Did he enjoy it? Or was it a shiver of displeasure? She understood that it was not the first drink he'd had this afternoon.

"What did you mean by losing your only child? Cecilia exists, right now even on the island."

"She was going to go to Italy," said Rune. He still had the glass in his hand, weighing it back and forth. "Disappear out of my life with that Stefansson. Why? Why not be content with what's here?"

She realized that there was no point in having that discussion, but instead said something general and flat. Rune took another sip.

"You have children yourself, right?"

Ann nodded, but did not want to draw Erik into the argument. "The police found rum in Casper Stefansson's boat, which was drifting around in the strait. Did the bottle come from here?"

"I have a hard time imagining that," he said, and then repeated almost word for word what Edvard had said. "And this rum is pretty popular. I'm sure they sell it at the state liquor store in Öregrund." He finished the rest of the liquor and set the glass down on the table with a thud.

"Your wife, is she still away?"

"She's missing," he stated factually. "Just like that."

"Have you separated?"

Rune Karlsson gave her a look that was filled with equal parts surprise and guilt, as if he'd been surprised with something indecent. "You get right to the point."

"You're a person who surely can take that."

"No, we haven't separated. Sometimes she disappears, but this time I can't get hold of her."

"Are you worried, more than usual I mean?"

"She sleeps with other men," he said quietly, as if in passing. "I've known that a long time."

The strange thing was that the deceived man said that in such an everyday, albeit somewhat distressed, tone, as if he was stating that he suffered from diabetes or some other disease, which admittedly could be treated but stayed with you throughout your life.

Edvard sauntered up. "I've taken away the remains of the flagpole," he said, placing his hand on the railing that surrounded the porch.

"Thanks," said Rune Karlsson, smiling. "Would you like one?" He held up the glass.

"I placed the wheelbarrow by the garage. Maybe a beer would be good," said Edvard.

Ann observed Rune Karlsson, who now got up with some difficulty. He was visibly intoxicated and stumbled by the door into the house.

"There's something sick about this. In this family the women leave."

"Is his wife gone?" Edvard asked. Ann simply nodded, because at the same moment the host returned with two cans of beer. One he gave to Edvard, the other he opened with a genteel gesture. "When I was active I didn't drink at all. Not even light beer."

They raised the cans toward each other. During the time it took for Edvard to finish his beer the two men made small talk with each other. Ann observed Rune Karlsson. She had a hard time believing that he was the one who shoved Stefansson into the water. Rune's love for, not to say fixation on, his daughter was strong and tangible, and that he opposed her plans for a move to Italy was obvious, but was that a motive for murder?

"I don't know how it will be," said Rune Karlsson suddenly. "Maybe I'll sell the dump. I've got an offer on the land. This new guy, the professor from Skåne, wants to buy it all. It's wrong, but what the hell, nothing will be like before anyway. You can't go back. We should have kept the old ferry that took twelve cars. Now those yellow monsters go back and forth and unload a lot of shit from the mainland."

"I'm not a native," said Edvard, "and I came with the big ferry."

Rune Karlsson ignored the objection and continued. "When I grew up there were only a few summer visitors and they were quiet. They fit in."

"What does Cecilia say about selling?" Ann asked in order to interrupt the complaining. It reminded her a little of the talk at home in her village about the immigrants, that they were both fewer and better before.

"She doesn't know anything yet." He looked at Ann. "Do you want to talk with her?"

"Do that yourself," she said. "You probably have to work out a few things. It's actually her childhood home too."

"She doesn't care about such things. In that respect she's like Gunilla."

"Does she know that her mother is missing?"

"I think we need to get going," said Edvard. Ann knew that there was no point in making objections, he had things to get ready before tomorrow. "I have to pack the trailer," he added. She had nothing either against leaving Rune Karlsson. The fact was that the feeling of discomfort was growing stronger and stronger.

"I'll go down with you," said Rune.

"We'll find our way ourselves," Edvard said, which Rune did not comment on.

They traipsed single file down toward the dock with Rune in the lead. No one said anything. At one point Edvard turned his head and gave her a quick look. She understood immediately that he had something on his mind.

The wind had died down somewhat but some pennants attached to the roof of the boathouse were still flapping. The strait looked inviting. Ann thought it was strange that both she and Edvard, who originally had been such pronounced landlubbers, had become attached to Gräsö and its archipelago, its straits and bays, islets and skerries.

This time there was no thumping sound. The buoys on the net shed were not moving.

Edvard got the boat ready, Ann thanked Rune for the visit, got an incoherent mumbling in response, where the names "Gunilla" and "Cecilia" recurred a couple of times. He looked tired and sad standing there on the dock. All in all he gave an awkward impression and seemed to have aged quickly just in the past week. Ann got the sense that he thought it was gloomy to be left alone after a period of company and talk, now the brooding about his missing wife would surely return with full force. She could sense the breadth of his indecision. Suddenly he was an abandoned old man.

Edvard accelerated and sheered toward open water. When they had come out a few hundred meters he turned toward her and throttled the motor. "I carted away pieces of the flagpole and I think there were specks of blood in the wheelbarrow and on one handle."

Thirty-Six

The chain at her feet had scraped away the skin above her ankle. The window, covered for years by dust and debris, only let a minimal amount of light through but she could still see how inadequately it was arranged. He'd wrapped the chain around her right calf and anchored the two links at the ends with a padlock that required a combination to be opened. Rune would buy those kinds of locks. Numbers pleased him and keys could so easily disappear.

It was not an effective way to snare a person, the chain did not close tightly around her leg. Why he simply wrapped the chain around her one leg she didn't understand, but probably he'd decided that he couldn't anchor her well with a chain, and for that reason left it all half-done, to instead bind her arms to a wooden post in the center of the shed, put there by himself many years ago to support the roof that sagged noticeably in the middle.

With her free left foot she had tried to push the chain over her right foot

but gave up, it hurt too much. She felt more than saw how blood was dripping on the worn wooden floor. If she only had her arms and hands free
then perhaps it would work, but they were locked behind her back with a
rope. She thought she'd seen that he took a line from a buoy they used for
the nets. It was a short distance away, orange in color like the fruit, the size
of a small soccer ball. She had reached it and it had slowly rolled away a
meter or so. She was lying on her side and stared at the buoy, an everyday
thing in a boathouse that got a new significance. The fatigue in her body
surprised her. She was a competitive person, always had been, but chained
and caught like an animal she had sunk down into a quagmire of apathy.
The muzzle reinforced the sense of hopelessness.

For a short time she had even dozed off, but was wakened by a motor
starting up. It was the same boat that she'd heard berthing earlier. It wasn't
one of theirs, she could tell from the sound. Then despite the pain, with the
links that chafed, she had pounded her feet on the floor to attract attention,
but in vain. She had heard voices. One of them was probably Edvard. The
other was certainly the former police officer that he hung around with. Now
they were gone and she cursed herself for falling asleep.

Someone coughed. It must be Rune. He had probably gone with them
to the dock. Maybe he was standing outside the boathouse? She listened
intently but could not hear anything.

It was not a sturdy rope, but it was tightened hard and cut into her
wrists. She understood that she couldn't count on any help from outside,
how often did strangers berth at their dock? The net shed was isolated
from everything, she was alone. Outside there was a man who showed all
the signs of a raging insanity that at any time could unleash more brutal-
ity. She had heard him talking to himself as he tied her to the post, something about "sinking her." That could only mean one thing.

She looked around from her low perspective, her gaze scanning the
smoothly worn floor. Well-cleaned. Rune's specialty. Everything in its
place. In one corner were several wooden crates. The printed Norwegian
text on their sides suggested that at one time they contained sugar. Rune's
father had been in Norway a lot, she knew that. It had something to do with

the last war, he'd done his military service in Töcksfors, he had carried on about that in the autumn of his old age. She had no idea how the crates ended up on the other side of Sweden, but she knew that they contained fishing gear for herring, long poles, hooks, cans with floats and sinkers for bait fishing, all in good order.

Would she be able to reach them and give the stacked crates a shove with her feet? Maybe it was possible if she managed to slide around a half turn. It would put strain on her legs but above all on her wrists, she understood that, but there was no other alternative. The chance was that one of the crates contained a knife or some other sharp object.

For a few minutes she gathered strength, tried to use the breathing technique she had developed before competitions, but it wasn't possible because of the rag reeking of oil over her mouth. She only got dizzy. Better to lie still, breathe through her nose, and close her eyes.

Then she was ready, raised her buttocks and pushed off with her left foot. It went well. She moved a few centimeters in the right direction. A new attempt. Her right leg dragged, weighed down by the chain, it surely meant an extra ten kilos. Once again she moved a few centimeters but this time it hurt seriously when the rope tightened around her wrists behind her back.

Sweat was beading on her forehead. She steeled herself before a third round, tried to move her arms a little in order to reduce the pain that would come. She braced with her feet, raised her body, and pushed off to the right in the direction of the crates. She was gasping from pain. *I'm not going to make it* was her immediate thought. She lay completely still, breathing heavily through her nose before finding a kind of balance after a few minutes. She glanced at the Norwegian crates and repeated nonsense rhymes of words that she used in decisive stages during archery competitions.

What was his plan? Would he throw her in the water with the chain around her leg? She closed her eyes, tried to think rationally, but the only conclusion she could come to was that he was a crazy man who was capable of anything. It was that bad. It had gotten that bad. He had gradually given up his own life and taking hers would only be a consistent action.

Did she regret it? No. Living with him had been a prison for a long time. She had met others, she'd betrayed him, that was true, but it had been necessary.

She gasped for breath before she once again braced herself, raised her body, and pushed away. Screamed behind the muzzle over her mouth. Besides the unbearable pain around her wrists it felt as if her arms and shoulders would break apart. Without hesitating she repeated the procedure, one time, two times. Fainted. Came back to life.

This is my punishment, take it, she thought. That was a lie, a kind of flirtation with fate, she understood that very well. If she was going to die she wanted to take Karl Rune Karlsson with her.

Thirty-Seven

"You're sure that there was blood in the wheelbarrow?"

Edvard nodded. "I've cut and injured myself enough times to recognize bloodstains," he said.

"Maybe it was Blixten's blood," said Ann. "Rune said something about that, I don't remember exactly, but the ball had broken apart when Blixten cut down the flagpole." She took a sip of wine. For the moment she had abandoned the Alentejo in Portugal. "You should drink wine from Piedmont," Blixten had suggested. "It spices up existence."

"The ball had broken apart," Edvard repeated with a smirk. "You can safely say that. My God, what a mess. Let's forget about them."

"We can't, you know that."

"I know," Edvard said good-naturedly. "I'm thinking about what he said about his brother, that he devoted a whole life to Nepal."

"Without being Nepalese!" Ann said.

"Yes, can someone be more narrow-minded, not to have the imagination to understand what this is about."

"What is it about?"

"I don't know," Edvard said after taking a moment to think. "To be honest I don't know, not in his case."

"In other words you have no imagination."

Edvard smiled but directed the smile inward, he didn't look at her. "It's probably the longing," he said. "He comes from this flat island and then settles in the mountains thousands of miles away, the highest mountains you can find, far from the sea, and searches for frozen mountain climbers."

"He gets married and has three children too," she interjected. "But the fact that he ended up there was perhaps by chance."

"Maybe so, but not that he went away from the island and Sweden. *All* the siblings did just that, except Rune."

"Someone has to take care of old Mom," said Ann. "But yes, it's exciting."

"He must ask himself what he missed."

"I think you know," said Ann. "Isn't he a typical man who just trudges on, refusing to see beyond the horizon? He doesn't think he's missed anything by being faithful to the island."

"The bad thing is that he's lost. The life he wanted to live is no longer possible. It's gotten to a point where it's not even possible to get a proper catch of herring, much less cod! The fields are overgrown, the barns collapse, the paths get covered with brush, the old roads aren't navigable. People from Stockholm buy acre upon acre. Blixten trims and trims. Landscape care? Nonsense! It's a manicure for summer visitors and rich people from Stockholm."

"And now Rune wants to sell," said Ann.

"He'll never sell! He's just toying with that guy from Skåne. You'll see. And then his daughter was going to move to Italy with Casper Stefansson. Maybe Rune sank him in the sea. I think he's capable of that."

"Imagine how happy he must have been anyway during those years Cecilia lived at home on the farm." Ann recalled how moved Rune Karlsson was when he talked about his smart, successful daughter.

"And how unhappy he must have been when she left for Portugal."

"Bah, how sad, how soiled," said Ann. She didn't like it. Nothing in this tangle spoke to her. She would like to forget the whole thing.

"I'll stop rooting in this manure pile," she said, "and devote myself to—"

She was interrupted by the cell phone vibrating on the table. Edvard chuckled. "I'll have another beer." Ann followed him with her gaze as he disappeared, waited a couple of ringtones to answer, as if she was pretending that there was any doubt.

"Hi there, it's Brundin!"

"I see that," said Ann, trying to sound somewhat dismissive.

"Listen," her former colleague continued. "Östhammar's answer to Columbo" as he was sometimes called. He was the right age, likewise the rumpled style and unbiased dress code. "I got a call . . ."

Edvard returned with a beer, opened the tab with a pop quite close to Ann's head. As the analytical detective Brundin was he had no difficulty interpreting the sound. "I'm coming over," he said and laughed.

"A certain man from Skåne, Jens Thörn, called," Brundin resumed. "He'd gone to see Rune Karlsson with a proposal for a contract. Can you imagine what an audacious bastard? The reaction was violent. Rune was sitting on a garden chair, cleaning a gun."

"When it's raining?"

"This is an hour ago, there were surely clear skies then."

"Is he dead?" Ann asked, mostly to scare Edvard a little.

"Who?"

"Any of them."

"I need help," Brundin said without any elaboration. "Can you and Edvard go to Karlsson's, but go by boat? It's a tricky channel in, lots of reefs."

"Edvard will manage it, he's chugged into that dock many times with Victor in his old boat. And we were just there."

Edvard looked up.

"But don't tie up at the dock. You have to keep out of sight. Is he there? Maybe better that I speak with him directly."

She handed over the phone. Brundin gave a speech. Based on Edvard's facial expressions Ann tried to figure out what was being said. It wasn't possible. Edvard nodded and hummed before he made a comment.

"Maybe I'm not really absolutely sure that I can do it in a tidy way, so that it looks good I mean."

Brundin's response was curt. "Okay," Edvard said with a smile. "He probably knows, but if he asks what I'm up to? We'll take the aluminum boat, it will take twenty-five minutes at most. One problem: We've been drinking."

Ann heard how Brundin laughed heartily before they ended the call.

"We're going on another outing to Karlsson. We're leaving right away. I just need to fetch a toolbox. Some warm clothes and rain gear too."

He got up immediately without explaining more. That was his style and nowadays she wasn't offended. Soon enough he would tell what it was all about. He loathed unnecessary talk that involved a loss of tempo.

She went upstairs, changed, put on a pair of warm pants and pulled on a sweater she normally only used during early spring. She felt possessed by something familiar and at the same time unfamiliar. *Should I be armed?* she thought. She had a license for the pistol she always took with her when she left the house in Tilltorp, afraid that it would be stolen even though it was stored in a gun cabinet. It was like a remnant from her time with the police and she'd always been hesitant about keeping it. It felt a little strange, especially when she wasn't a practiced pistol shooter. "May be good to shoot rabbits with," Sammy Nilsson had said. "Or arsonists." He knew nothing about rabbits.

Boots and rain gear were downstairs, she looked around, nothing was lacking. The pistol had to remain at the bottom of the closet under all the shoes.

On the way down to the dock Edvard filled her in on what she'd missed. Brundin wanted them to put the boats at Karlsson's dock out of commission.

"Thus the tools," said Ann.

"If I don't succeed we should call the One and Only, he's a whiz at motors, but I think I'll manage it. We'll lay to north of Karlsson's, on the far side of the promontory."

Edvard talked on, unusually verbose for him. Ann understood that he was nervous. She herself felt calm. How many times had she been part of a raid? This seemed to be a simple assignment, and besides it was Edvard who would have to figure out how to arrange the sabotage of the boats.

They came up to the dock, jumped on board, Ann untied at the bow and Edvard pulled the boat with the aft line, untied and started the motor, a fifty-horsepower Yamaha. It was all done in half a minute.

The showers had ceased. As so often the wind came from the northeast, a choppy sea that would have been uncomfortable in a smaller boat, but the new boat took the sea well. He'd bought it last fall, a transaction of almost two hundred thousand with the motor. "I coughed up cash," he'd told her, unexpectedly and in passing, and she understood that there was a lot of pride in that disclosure. Edvard would very much like to be one in the line of diligent tradesmen and a "substantial" person. That was his inheritance, about which there could sometimes be a bit too much of the respectable boy, but obviously it was good to have a calm man at the helm. Ann was never afraid at sea when she was out with Edvard. He had it in him, it was another one of his splendid sides, that thing with routines, safety details, distance, and everything he talked about or simply demonstrated as a natural part of life. It was about his background as a machinery operator and tractor driver and in the winter it was forestry work. Strong forces were in play and it simply could not go wrong.

It could be tiresome but Ann had come to the conclusion that it also made their relationship stable. He left nothing to chance, everything should be anchored and secured with double strokes and mental straps. That was probably why her one-night stand with an unknown accountant, her foolish infidelity that resulted in her beloved Erik, in many ways was unfathomable for Edvard. Such a macabre breach of order, at the very least a foolhardy gamble, sleeping with a strange man when everything had argued for Ann and Edvard, had made him irreconcilable for years. He later told her that he'd never been unfaithful to his wife; the thought had never occurred to him.

She glanced at his dogged profile. He was moved by the seriousness of the moment, that was clear, pulled into something dark and unusual for him. As a confirmation of his thoughts he asked whether she'd brought the pistol with her, something she had mentioned as a possibility. She shook her head.

"No, and it would be a little strange to bring it," she simply said. He could draw whatever conclusions he wanted.

During the rest of the ride they sat quietly. As they got close he throttled the gas to a fraction, sheered starboard instead of aiming for the dock, glided in through the cramped passage the last ten or fifteen meters toward land while he turned off and pulled up the motor. Ann stood prepared, jumped to land, and started mooring around a boulder. Completely unprompted she got the improbable image that her son, Erik, was standing there waiting. It was such a strong feeling that she was compelled to search the section of shore with her eyes, but not a living soul was there. Everything was quiet except for the water lapping at the stones on the shore.

"We'll split up," Edvard whispered. He took a small toolbox with him. In it was everything needed to put three motors out of commission. "You keep watch on the boathouse while I tinker. Okay?"

She didn't like it even though she realized the wisdom of a scout, and nodded. Edvard put on a headlamp. It might be needed where the old boat was concerned as he would have to work in the dark in cramped spaces with an old Albin motor that perhaps was new sometime in the 1940s. They walked carefully along the shore together before Ann would turn off toward land and the boathouse. "Now is when a pistol would be good to have," Edvard said before he disappeared in the dusk, and she didn't know if that was an attempt at a joke or not.

Ann was cold. That was uncommon. She zipped up the fleece sweater, pulled up the hood, and wrapped her arms around her body. It was quiet as always at the end of summer. The bird serenades were over. She felt melancholy. *I have Edvard,* she thought, and her lower lip quivered from emotion or from cold.

The task was to keep watch and she peered at the path toward the house. Everything was calm and quiet. She happened to think that she ought to communicate with Brundin, took out her phone and texted that they were on the scene, everything calm. She waited but did not get an immediate reply. Brundin had never been that quick to respond.

Soundlessly Edvard sneaked up along the wall of the boathouse. "Fixed," he said, and a visible piece of evidence was an oil stain on his forehead. *Bindi,* she recalled that it was called, but wasn't it only women who wore such a mark? *India,* she thought, and from there the step was not far to *Erik.* She smiled to herself, how he would have loved such a secretive evening adventure.

"I'll check the sheds," Edvard whispered, and carefully opened one half of the door. Latches and hinges were all hand-forged and certainly very old. He came back after half a minute, shaking his head, and continued to the net shed, which was a bit farther up on the rise, placed on a rock with plinths of rough-hewn stone. The whole thing resembled a homestead museum. The door was cracked open. He disappeared into the shed, and stuck his head out a few seconds later and waved her to him. Despite the darkness she could see the worry on his face, how he glanced into the shed as if to assure himself that he'd seen right, and she hurried over.

Edvard turned the headlamp on and let its beam sweep across the floor. "Blood," Ann said immediately. "Stand still! Don't move at all." She looked around, didn't believe it was a serious shooting injury, which many times resulted in more considerable pools, bloodstains on walls and dragging marks with blood when the victim tried to move, get away. Here the wooden floor was stained, no more than that.

"No Mauser," she simply said. "Probably not a knife either." She crouched down, extending her hand toward Edvard, and he understood immediately, taking off the headlamp and giving it to her. She shone it on two overturned crates where the contents had partly spilled out on the floor. Fishing gear, in brief. Around one post in the middle of the shed there were remnants of rope, mangled and worn away. There was also a fishing knife with a toothed blade, a model of which there were many in Gräsö homes. Edvard probably had half a dozen, most of them inherited from Viola. Ann had no difficulty imagining what had happened in the shed. Someone had been bound but managed to get loose.

"Who?" said Edvard.

"Gunilla Karlsson," said Ann. "Who else?"

"Cecilia?"

"No, she's with Blixten."

"Maybe the Man from Skåne."

That was a possibility, she realized. Had Rune and the neighbor quarreled? She called Brundin, who answered. He sounded out of breath. She heard voices at a distance.

"Where are you?" Ann asked.

"We just came up to Jens Thörn's to get updated. We must get a picture of what had happened, maybe it's only talk from his side. Professors are sensitive."

"I can add a bit to the picture," said Ann and told him about their find. Brundin was silent and for once stayed quiet for perhaps five seconds.

"Are you still there?"

"Oh yes, I'm listening a little to Jens Thörn. He just came out."

"Not the Man from Skåne," Ann said in a stage whisper to Edvard.

"Yes, you know how . . ." Brundin said, and Ann understood that he meant just what she had ordered Edvard: *Don't touch anything.*

"Yes, we'll back out of the shed and make our way up to the house." She clicked off the call before Brundin had time to offer opinions or protests. She looked around one last time, let the light from the headlamp play over the floor, walls, and ceiling. In black sacks were stored what she thought were nets, all supplied with a neat label. There were stacks of pots, buoys hanging like gigantic Christmas tree decorations from the ceiling beams, grapnels and anchors of all kinds of ages and types, antique round cans stood in a long parade, similar to ones she remembered from her father's garage where he drove the beverage truck in every day, mooring buoys, lines, and much else that had to do with archipelago fishing. What had taken years, decades to buy and produce, organize, took her half a minute to survey. *So much history,* she thought, *who will take care of all this in the future, Cecilia?*

They followed the path up to the house. It was almost eight o'clock in the evening but the sun had not yet gone down. Edvard looked around as if to confirm that they should continue. Ann nodded, that amused her, seldom if ever did she have command on the island.

They again passed the thicket where Cecilia had stopped and pointed out the butterflies. *It's surely too late for butterflies,* she thought, but peeked in among the bushes and grass anyway. Under a broad, flourishing bush she spotted a hand.

"Edvard!" He stopped immediately and instinctively tensed up. "A body," she added, pointing. When he made an effort to leave the path she raised a hand. She looked around. "Get a long stick or something." He seemed to understand immediately, leaned into the vegetation and broke off a branch, bare for the first few meters but with leaves at the top.

Ann had seen countless homicide victims and dead bodies during her twenty-five-year career with the police. The first body was a drowning victim who had gotten stuck in a sluice. Nothing could really be worse than that. With the stick she pushed aside the branches that concealed arms and parts of the body. What she saw reinforced the feeling that it was a corpse, and she also thought she knew who it was. She had studied Rune Karlsson's hands as they grasped the hand railing, the whitened knuckles and the hair on top of the hand.

"Is he dead?"

"Think so," said Ann, setting the branch down on the ground and pushing it in under the bushes. "I have to check," she said, balancing on the stick as if it were a gangway, all so as not to trample around too much. She leaned forward. The corpse was alive. The little trickle of blood that worked its way in spurts down the throat was evidence enough that his heart was still pumping. "Call for an ambulance!" she said.

Rune Karlsson had been struck by two arrows. One was sitting right in the throat, the other in his abdomen. There the loss of blood was considerably greater, his clothes were drenched. She crouched down, set a couple of fingers against his neck. A weak but still clearly identifiable pulse. His breathing was choppy. He was in shock. His eyes were closed but the lids fluttered now and then.

"Should we pull out the arrows?" she said, and realized at once how sick that question must sound.

"Don't think so," Edvard said calmly. "First responders are on their way and the ambulance will get here as quickly as possible."

Once she had tried to string a competition-style bow. No matter how hard she tried, she couldn't do it, and she understood then what strength and technique were required to shoot an arrow, but also with what force the arrow flew away and penetrated the target.

Rune Karlsson opened his mouth with a smacking sound. Blood ran from the corners of his mouth, not great quantities, the shot in the throat must not have hit the carotid artery, otherwise he would have been dead. Ann leaned forward as far as she was able. There was already a raw stench of blood and excrement around the injured man, perhaps he had emptied his bowels. Dying people are never beautiful, only on film when a sad, tearful epilogue to the accompaniment of a string orchestra is being marketed. Rune's struggle would not be sold. He would die under some bushes on the island that had seen him born and within an hour or two he would be stuffed into a body bag and taken away.

It didn't take a Sherlock Holmes to guess who'd shot the arrow, and for that reason she simply asked, "Why?"

He opened his eyes and suddenly looked considerably more alive. Maybe he would survive? Rune Karlsson braced himself, he really wanted to get something out. It wasn't much. Besides, it was virtually impossible to understand what he was saying. The injury to the throat was surely the cause. His speech was wheezing and mushy by turns.

"The whore," Ann thought she heard in any event. It was nothing new, he'd called his wife that before. Rune forced out more sounds that turned into sentences, as if he was arguing in an unknown language with a deformed intonation.

"What's he saying?" Edvard asked.

"Wait," she said. Her legs were shaking, squatting while she had to lean her upper body forward was not her strong suit, but she didn't want to set her knees down on the ground considering that this was probably a crime scene.

Rune's face was distorted. He was in serious pain.

"Did you argue? We found bloodstains in the net shed."

He nodded, as if he realized there was no point in trying to talk. "Is that her blood?" Another nod. "Did you tie her up?" The anxiety shone from his eyes, and he forced out a few words. "Escape," she thought she heard.

"Murdered Casper" then came quite suddenly, clearly, and audibly. "Fucked, then murder. Black widow." That was a peculiar turn, but it turned out not to last. The convulsions returned even stronger. All color had vanished from his face. Ann had her right hand around the arrow in his abdomen the whole time and with her fingers tried to press as hard as possible on the entry point. The question was whether the arrow had penetrated right through the body and was sticking out his back.

"Edvard," she said. "Come here. I can't keep on." She gave up the thought of not contaminating the scene. In the back of her mind there was also the thought that Edvard should be held back, protected, he was not a sensitive child but why should he have to see the misery? Why should he have to experience what she had worked with all those years? As if it were shameful.

"Press," she said.

"Goddam mosquitoes" was the only comment he made, and she gave him a quick look. How could he be so calm? Or was it the opposite, was he terrified?

Ann placed a couple of fingers against Rune's throat again. The uninjured side. His pulse had weakened. "Gunilla murdered Casper, what evidence do you have?"

Rune nodded.

"Evidence! Where is the evidence?"

He looked at her almost triumphantly and hissed out a word that she could not possibly understand. It almost sounded like the name of a Bulgarian seaside resort: "*ballga*" or something like that.

"I don't understand," said Ann. He made a new attempt but now the life force was irrevocably in decline and there was only rattling from a wounded throat. She stroked her hand across his cheek, cold and stubbly, it was an instinctive movement, as if she wanted to convey something human, a last expression of . . . what? Trust perhaps, that despite his somewhat sad peculiarities he had been a living, vital being. She remembered Cecilia's words when they were walking on the same path.

"You took your daughter with you out in nature. She loved that. And you taught her about the butterflies, all the names."

He looked almost terrified, fumbled with his hand across her leg, pinched her thigh with a surprising strength. "*Ballga*," he repeated, and stared in desperation at Edvard as if he could solve the whole thing. "Found. The *vrang*," he forced out.

Edvard gave her a quick look. "He found something in the boat, he's saying. It must mean that. Long ago it was called a *vrang*, I think. That's the boat frame."

Now Ann wasn't even sure what that meant. She felt how the grip on her thigh got stronger again and understood that Edvard was on the trail of something. "Which boat?" she said. They both looked at the dying man who was stretched out before them.

With an ominous croak he cleared his throat. Ann had heard that sound before. That was at her father's deathbed and it had been the last thing that she heard from him. But Rune surprised again by heaving himself up a few centimeters with the help of his left elbow and in a flat voice whispered short sentences, however completely audible and lucid. "She swam to the dock. Blue bathing suit. Hedwig." He sank down again.

"It's the fishing boat," said Edvard. Rune looked at him and they thought they saw confirmation in his eyes. "A bag. Tossed it, I said. Trash." He shook his head. "Hid," he got out, and Ann thought she saw how he smiled, as if he was still satisfied about his lie.

"Where?" asked Ann.

"Ballga," he said, and the unintelligible word was the last thing he managed to get out. In the end Rune Karlsson met death. He struggled all the way to the finish line but had to see himself conquered. There the story of Rune Karlsson came to an end.

Thirty-Eight

She crawled backward out of the thicket. The evening chill made her shake. "Edvard," she said. "Let's go up to the house."

"I'm coming. I just want to . . ."

What he wanted never came out. She thought she heard some words. The phone in her pocket vibrated. It was Brundin.

"The doctor is here," he said. "Where are you?"

"It's over. Rune Karlsson is dead. We're coming."

"His wife is here. Roughed up but okay. The doctor is looking at her now."

"How does she seem?"

"Shaky. She's mostly crying."

"She shot Rune with an arrow."

"I'll be damned. Yes, there was a bow on the porch."

"We're coming," she said and clicked off. "Come on now!" She was eager to have a look at Gunilla Karlsson. Edvard came out of the bushes, hunched over and a little shaky. He still had the headlamp on. She reached over and turned it off. "You're blinding me," she said, and there was a reason why she resented his appearance. It reminded her a little too much of the face her old colleague Ola Haver used to put on at murder scenes. He was the one at Homicide that had the hardest time with dead bodies.

"Can we leave him here?"

"Maybe it's best if you stay. Don't touch anything else. I'll send down one of Brundin's constables. Come up later." She made it sound as if she was still a police officer on duty.

He looked at her with great seriousness and reached out his hand. What was it he was experiencing? It was obvious that Rune Karlsson's death struggle and last words in life meant something different to Edvard than they did to her. She had experienced it before, victims of violence, shot or knifed, assaulted and led to the borderland between life and death, the stench of death and blood, the electrifying feeling that ultimate things were being aired. No detail could be missed. Every murder's triviality, the meaninglessness of every death, but also the mystery. She took his hand. "I'm going. Come later."

She set off at a fast pace toward the house, not least to work off the stiffness in her joints and the cold inside. To the right she soon had the dark silhouette of the smithy, whose chimney leaned to the north. She stopped there for a few seconds, wondering how to continue. She had taken command and that amused her a little. *Just so I don't continue in this style,* she thought, *it's Brundin who is the policeman on the scene. You're the civilian.* Happy that the insight came to her in time she jogged the last stretch up toward the house. The various buildings were outlined against the evening sky, robbed of their original functions. She passed a couple of old timbered sheds. A little farther ahead was a barn and at last the garage. She remembered Edvard's words about the wheelbarrow soiled with blood. Was that where he'd placed it?

Brundin was standing outside the entry where a few days ago Rune Karlsson had met her. He was smoking. She could not recall having seen him do that previously but chose not to say anything. Smokers had the most peculiar excuses when they were going to explain their behavior; clandestine smokers were the worst, of course.

"How is she?"

"Okay," said Brundin, taking a puff before he flicked the butt away over the railing in the direction of Ann. "Step on it, if you don't mind," he said with a smile. "Rune had tied her up in the net shed, but she managed to wriggle loose."

Ann crushed the cigarette with her foot. "And then?"

"She shot him. Self-defense, she says."

"Where was that?"

"Down by the boathouse, then she ran up to the house. Or not exactly ran, she had a chain around her leg. That lady is something else."

Ann told where they had found Rune. "Then he took a shortcut, it's a shorter stretch than the path, it goes in a curve as you know," Brundin observed, and it struck her how well informed he was about Karlsson's property.

"What about the chain?"

"We managed to get it off," said Brundin.

"Can she hear what we're saying?" Ann asked.

Brundin stepped down from the entry. "Let's go over here," he said. "The doctor is still working."

"Can you send someone down on the path to relieve Edvard?"

"Sure," said Brundin, taking out his phone. "Wiberg, you can go down toward the shore, we have a body that needs to be kept company." He clicked off and grinned. "A trainee." Ann understood that Brundin liked the situation. A young policeman, who appeared to have recently left middle school, was suddenly standing before them, and Brundin gave him some brief instructions.

"Are you Lindell from Uppsala?" the young policeman asked.

She nodded. He disappeared down toward the shore, certainly to his first corpse. "Lindell the legend," Brundin said with a wry smile. Ann smiled in return. She could grant him that. It was actually not at all uncomfortable.

"Why did he lock her up? Has she said anything?"

"Madness and unmotivated jealousy. When she told him that she was going away to a conference tomorrow, he struck her down."

"Down by the shore?"

"No," said Brundin. "In the kitchen, there's blood."

"And then he took her down to the shed in the wheelbarrow?"

"What do you know about it? Did he say that before he died?"

"No," said Lindell, and then she told him what Edvard had seen. "Confiscate the wheelbarrow," she said. Brundin only grinned in response.

"Was there a bow down by the shore?"

"She says so, two or three of them even, hanging in the boathouse, and then arrows in a quiver."

"Why?"

"I think she used to do target practice at seabirds. I've heard that talk before. Not everyone was happy. Karlssons have always done what they want. A complaint actually came in a few years ago, but it was retracted. But it was clear that she probably did practice target shooting at gulls and terns."

"Okay, she shot him, went up to the house, and called you, is that how it went?"

Brundin took out a pack of Marlboros and lit a new cigarette. That made him a kind of chain-smoker in her eyes. "Damn how you smoke, I didn't know that," she said.

"That's her version, but in some way it seems probable."

"What is 'vragg,' or maybe 'vrang'?"

"What do you mean?"

"Rune mentioned it before he died."

"My old man used that word. It's the rib on a boat. But no reasonable person says that today."

At the same moment Edvard came up to them. He greeted Brundin with a nod. "That scout you sent down seems afraid of the dark," he said.

"He needs a little practice away from the desk," said Brundin.

" 'Ballga' then, what does that mean in the Gräsö dialect?"

"Not a clue." Brundin suddenly looked stressed, and she understood why. He didn't have the full picture.

"There you have the solution to Casper Stefansson," said Ann. "Shall I step on that butt too? I want to see her."

Brundin took a puff on the cigarette. "Then Edvard and I will leave, but it would be exciting to see Gunilla," she added when she felt the gaze of the Östhammar policeman. "We came by boat, as you know, and it will soon be pitch dark." Brundin needed to be reminded that he was actually the one who had summoned them there.

"You can get a ride home," said Brundin.

"That would really be nice," said Ann. "What do you say, Edvard?"

He nodded. "I set a piece of plywood over the wheelbarrow, it's going to rain tonight." Ann smiled to herself. This was the man she loved.

They walked toward the house together. "Who will tell Cecilia?" Ann asked.

"We have a car on the way to Blixten's," said Brundin. "There's a retired minister in Öregrund that I know she trusts. They picked him up. It will be fine. I called the minister and told him what had happened, and he didn't hesitate at all. He lives near the ferry and came over immediately. A good minister."

It will be fine, he's good, Ann repeated silently to herself. The tension between her and Brundin had eased up, not least after the news that she and Edvard would go home.

"Good," she said. "Well done."

"I'm going down to the body," said Brundin. "I want to see something while it's still possible."

Gunilla Karlsson was mangled, that was the word that came to Ann. The doctor, whom she recognized from some other investigation, was working with a nasty wound on Gunilla's forehead. He had just loosened a temporary bandage and carefully cleaned the wound. She sat stiffly upright on a kitchen chair and grimaced, but gave Ann a glance anyway and made a face that could be interpreted in different ways. There was perhaps a touch of triumph, as if she wanted to point out that she actually was right: Her husband had gone crazy.

"Two shots," said Ann Lindell. "Two arrows that hit a little randomly." The doctor looked up. "Hi there," he said. "That was a critical judge's voice that . . ."

"I was in terrible pain," Gunilla Karlsson interrupted, "and I was a little shaky."

"I can't even string a bow," said Ann, "much less hit a bull's-eye. He died down by the path, do you understand that?" Gunilla nodded.

"It wasn't possible to stop the blood flow," Ann continued, now turned toward the doctor. Albinsson was his name, he was called Albin, she remembered at the same moment. "We did what we could."

"I believe that," said Albinsson. But had she and Edvard done everything, hadn't she been more interested in pressing information out of Rune Karlsson than in placing an effective pressure bandage?

"Where were the arrows?"

"One in the throat, not that bad other than that he had difficulty talking. But the one in the abdomen was worse," she said, pointing at her own stomach to indicate where the arrow had gone in.

"Maybe the liver," said Albinsson.

"Did he say anything?" Gunilla asked.

"He did, quite a bit actually, even if some of it was hard to understand."

Gunilla looked at her unexpectedly as if to force her to tell, but Ann had decided to keep her mouth shut. "Albin, does she need to be hospitalized?"

"A night of observation would probably be good, and more information may emerge," he said somewhat evasively, and Ann noticed that he was fishing a little.

"I'm no longer a police officer, so you'll have to take that up with Brundin," said Ann.

"I know that you've retired," the doctor said.

"What do you mean," said Gunilla Karlsson, "that part about information?"

"Take that up with Brundin, Gunilla. That was just a general reflection. When the shock has settled there can be various reactions. Some become quite calm, for a while anyway, others become terrified and anxious. It's so different, but it's good that you'll be under observation. And then we can look at the injuries first thing tomorrow."

"I want to stay at home," said Gunilla. "Now I'm no longer afraid."

"Take that up with Brundin," said the doctor.

They took off ten minutes later. Wiberg had been relieved and seemed content to leave the farm. Ann and Edvard got in the marked police car, an environment, an arrangement that she recognized well. Even the smell in the car was reminiscent of her former life. Despite that she had a feeling of taking a taxi, largely because Wiberg drove so gently and carefully. That was to be expected, he wasn't a man who compensated for his own shyness with horsepower, Ann had soon figured that out.

"I've never seen a dead person before," he said. He turned toward Edvard, who unexpectedly got in the front seat on the passenger side. Was that because men usually did that, for some reason always take a seat next to the driver, if it was a man that is, or had he noticed the young policeman's hesitation and understood that he needed to talk a little?

"Creepy," said Edvard. "And then the twilight down there. I understand. It was a little spooky with all the shrubbery."

"And the sound from the sea," Wiberg added. "There were birds screeching."

"They can do that, the white birds, a last call before bedtime. Maybe they felt Rune Karlsson's death, what do I know? Wise animals, who surely knew who he was, saw him crawl from the shore and finally end up there in the bushes."

"As if he was hiding to surprise them later, is that what you mean?"

"Maybe so, but I don't think they thought he was any threat, they've seen him for so many years, followed him with their gaze, gotten scrap fish when Rune cleaned the nets."

"Maybe it was his wife they were screeching about. The one with the bow."

"There's a lot to that," said Edvard, nodding and giving Wiberg an appreciative look. That strengthened the young policeman to continue.

"I've thought about that, encountering all the awfulness. A colleague said that suicides, especially the ones that jump in front of trains, are the worst. There are only scraps left, he said."

He won't last long, thought Ann. She chose not to say anything, but instead leaned back and closed her eyes.

"Why did you become a policeman?" Edvard asked.

"I don't know. My grandfather was a detective."

"And was he good?"

"The best," Wiberg said with warmth in his voice. "They called him 'the Knuckle.'"

"Why is that?"

"It was a thing he said to the crooks at the time when he patrolled in town: 'Settle down, otherwise you're getting a knuckle sandwich.'"

"And did they?"

Wiberg nodded and told about Söderhamn where he came from, about his grandfather who had been a classic feature of the street scene, about his dad who'd worked with everything imaginable but never as a policeman. The trainee's voice was changed, the local dialect that he had no doubt made an effort to suppress deepened the more he talked.

"The old man's in Gävle now. They're going to expand the container port and he's there to do planning. Mom isn't exactly happy, he stays over in Gävle quite a few nights. But he's that way."

Ann smiled to herself in the dark privacy of the backseat. She wanted him to continue, mostly to hear the young man's voice and get images from other lives and places. That was one of the things she appreciated about police work, because even if the background could be violent and tragic, the stories were there. She wanted the ride to last longer but knew that it would soon be over, and sure enough Wiberg slowed down and turned up toward Edvard's.

When they arrived they got out and stood quietly a moment in the absolute last gasp of daylight. "You two have a nice place. The sea so near."

"This is Edvard's house. I live outside Gimo."

"Yes, Brundin told me. You work with cheese, right?"

Edvard said goodbye to the chauffeur and went in, immediately turned on lights in the various rooms. He liked having a lot of lights on. The sun porch was lit up with discreet sconces on the wall. It occurred to Ann that they hadn't had crayfish yet, a tradition with obstacles during the long time they'd been separated but which they had resumed last year.

"Brundin thought it was a shame that you quit, but he understood. I don't think he's all that content either. If he can fix this maybe it will be better. He's talked a lot about that guy who drowned a few years ago, that there was something shady."

This was news. Ann had always thought Brundin was satisfied at the agency in Östhammar, where he had some of the old-timer's laid-back style and perhaps authority, and she had probably never suspected that the Casper Stefansson case had been an unhealed wound for him.

"It can work out now," she said, but said nothing more. "And you're right, people on the train tracks are never good, a lot to clean up, but children subjected to violence and assaults are the most awful. They come back later, when you start thinking. At home."

Wiberg nodded seriously. They shook hands, Ann thanked him for the ride, and he drove away. The silence took her, literally. The air, saturated with oxygen and the smell of the sea, made her take a deep breath. "It's going to be fine," she said. She could see Edvard in the kitchen. She understood that he was making something to eat.

When she came in he was standing in front of the stove. He had showered, there was an aroma of lemon around him. A frying pan sizzled and it smelled of fish. "I'm making something light," he said with his back to her. She went straight to the refrigerator, took out a bottle of white wine and got two glasses. She set everything on the table. That was her contribution. "I'll take a quick shower," she said.

When she came back everything was ready, a couple of flounder filets were on the table along with a bowl of fresh pasta, the wine bottle opened and the glasses filled.

"Good kid," said Edvard, and she understood that he meant Wiberg. He said nothing more about the evening's experiences, did not say a word about Rune's dramatic death, as long as they were at the table. Ann followed his example even though it was rather painful. She was used to quickly summarizing, comparing impressions and drawing conclusions, all to lead an investigation further. Now she had no case, but that didn't matter, it was in her blood. She was convinced that a special enzyme regulated this in every serious police body, and what she felt was a seriously elevated level. She poked at the food.

She cleared the table, rinsed off the worst but let the plates and everything else sit in the sink for the time being. "Tomorrow will be another day," she said to Edvard, who was on his way out. He simply smiled in response. *He's worried,* she thought, *he's brooding about what Rune had tried to say.* She watched him in the yard, going up to the pile of building materials, things that should have already been packed on the trailer and the pickup, but did nothing to uncover the tarp. He would surely arrange that in the morning, long before Ann had any thought of leaving the bed.

She saw him take out his phone and make a call. The call was not long. It was almost nine thirty, long after the time Edvard would usually call anyone. Was this about work? Was there some ex who had texted and asked him to be in touch?

When he returned she tried not to show her curiosity or worry. "We have cold beer, right?"

"There is some," said Ann, who had taken it as her task when she was with him on Gräsö to refill the refrigerator. If she needed wine, and he accepted that, then beer refills was the least one could ask as a return service.

"I called the One and Only Robban. He's coming over."

"Now?"

"In ten minutes."

"Why the rush?"

"I don't like the idea that Rune is seen as a violent idiot."

That was the explanation she had to be content with for now, she understood that from his thoughtful expression.

Thirty-Nine

Einar Nygren had passed eighty and then some. Cecilia Karlsson studied him as he got out of the car with some difficulty. He resembled the archetype of a patriarch, with a white, unruly mane of hair; wrinkled, rickety, and skinny, and somewhat stooped, as if he had set aside his own needs in his calling to bear the burdens of others. *It's time for him to crawl into bed soon,* she thought, but he'd insisted on coming even though the evening threatened to be a late one before he could make his way back to Öregrund. He was the one who had informed her about Olga's final days and when she would be buried. They had never met before but she recognized him from the funeral.

They shook hands. "I'm sorry," the minister said. "You've lost your father. Your sorrow can't be measured." There was something extremely professional in his appearance and in the way he delivered his lines, but she could not dislike him for that. He was only performing his task as a man of God, without her knowing how much he had meant for the atheistic Olga

Palm. They had been friends for decades, unclear how and why. The minister was doing a service for Olga as he took Cecilia to him, that was how she perceived it all.

The tears came quite unexpectedly. He let her cry in peace, before he put an arm around her shoulders. He smelled of aftershave which he must have patted on his cheeks right before the departure from Öregrund, which made her sob even more.

"Olga talked about you," he said and released his grip, but took her under the arm and started walking, as if he thought that movement could loosen up some of the sorrow, and forced her along. "She was a remarkable woman. I know that you were close to each other."

He got her to talk about Olga. They walked down the road a bit. "Did you know her husband, Verner, too?" She did, but only as a girl in her early teens knows a kind, harmless old man who liked to sit leaning against the wall of the house or in a plastic chair at the edge of the forest. In that way it was done. He had skillfully built a bridge between them, before he started talking about Rune Karlsson. He knew surprisingly much about her father.

"I was a very young minister when he was confirmed, that must be half a century ago, but I remember him extremely well from a church camp we had."

"What was he like?"

"Unbending," Einar Nygren said and smiled. "He gave a fresh impression, one of those boys that you knew you didn't have to worry about. I was not a bit surprised that he developed his talents and became an elite athlete. Later we happened to meet in various connections, he did a lot for the youth on the island, but you probably know that."

He did not tell her more than that, but instead asked a question: "Did he do a lot for you too? Did he have time to take care of his daughter?"

She stopped. The memories of her father had changed character and significance over time. For a long time the image of the controlling paterfamilias dominated, and that would never fade completely, but it was as if the recent experiences injected new recollections, no doubt because she hadn't been staying in her childhood home but instead saw everything from outside. The time in the dilapidated cabin, the encounter with her childhood friend Rafaela, and the discussions with Blixten had changed her. Likewise the experience of the island landscape, Gräsö, whose mixture of lushness and scarcity was in contrast to her life in Portugal, and brought up experiences from her childhood and youth.

"He taught me a lot," she said at last and told Nygren about their outings in nature, where the crisp chill of early morning during the eagle-watching expeditions and the hot drinks from the thermoses had reinforced the togetherness, just as much as the running during sunny summer days on the meadows, each with a butterfly net in hand.

The minister listened without asking questions or commenting, as if he knew all about it but would really like to hear it from her mouth. She realized that this was news to him, she and Rune never talked with others about their nature adventures together. Gunilla was completely outside of it all. Rune had a kind of integrity that could sometimes be mistaken for defensive bullheadedness, she had experienced that so many times, but in this case it had brought them together, it was their experience and theirs alone.

"Then it was as if he disappeared from the world," she said. "And I don't really know why. It was as if he went into a great solitude. He stopped socializing, lost friends. It was as if he lost his trust in other people."

She cut off the line of reasoning as if she had said slanderous things about her father. "But mostly he lost trust in himself, as if he didn't mean anything to anyone. As if it didn't matter. Sometimes I thought that he became almost worthless in his own eyes."

"I know that he loved only one person. In any case that was what he said to Olga on several occasions."

"Why did he talk with her so much?"

"Do you know that Rune spent a whole summer and winter with Verner and his parents?"

"What do you mean? Did he live with them?"

The minister nodded and resumed their walk. "It was a little difficult for a time at home with the Karlssons, they were a big family, that was when your great-grandmother and great-grandfather were still alive and both were bedridden, and Rune's mother had cancer," Nygren continued.

"Why just Dad?"

"Perhaps he was the most sensitive, what do I know? But it wasn't just him, another one of the sons lived at Norrboda for a time to provide relief. Folks did that back then. Olga was often there, she and Verner became a couple already in their teens, and she mothered Rune."

"That was why Dad always spoke well about Olga and Verner," she said.

"Yes, he had a good time there. There was a calmness and security that perhaps he had lacked. And that was why Rune later came to dislike Olga's son," Nygren added. "He thought that Adrian was a charlatan who was sailing under a false flag. It took a while before Olga and Verner realized that, so there was no competition to put it like that, Rune was of course so much older, but he could never stand Adrian. Do you know that it was Verner who got Rune to start running?"

Pastor Nygren smiled. "Verner loved sitting down, you've probably seen some of the many stools and benches he set out. If you saw an old kitchen chair in the forest you knew that it was Verner who had placed it there. He would sit down and philosophize, but he also liked to run, and he took Rune with him. That was how it started. They ran up to Norrboda and back, to Svartbäck and Vargskär, everywhere on the back roads and paths. They became friends in the process. One time, it was at Larslagärdet, do you know where that is?"

Cecilia stopped, nodded. "We were there," she said, and it felt as if she was revealing a military secret.

"Verner picked Rune up in his arms, you know back then that wasn't so common, people didn't touch each other, and said something to the effect that Rune was always welcome at Solhem, that he saw him as his own son. Rune told me about that incident many years later and I understood that obviously it was an important memory for him. Hard to take in, surely, but important, decisive."

"We were often there, Dad and I," said Cecilia, "with the nets. At Larsla. And then at Lökäng, those were his two favorite places for butterflies."

"It was good for Rune to hear Verner's words, but at the same time hard. He truly loved his parents but life wasn't so easy with the Karlssons. Everything had to be done in a particular way."

"Why are you telling me all this?"

The minister looked at her. "People are so dependent on love," he said. "And not just that, but also faithfulness. Rune was an insecure boy and young man, but he grew into himself, if you understand, in many ways became unbending, principled. But all through life he was also dependent on faithfulness."

Cecilia suspected that the minister's words concealed things that he was keeping to himself. Perhaps it would come out later, Nygren seemed to be a cautious man.

"He loved you above everything on earth," he resumed. "More than the God he believed in."

"Dad believed in God?!"

Nygren nodded. "In his own way, as if he had invented a separate deity. He never went to church, never sang along in the choir if one may say so, but we talked many times. I considered him a very good man. He reached out his hands, not toward God, but to you."

"I didn't know," she whispered.

"I think you knew," said the minister. "The problem was that he didn't know how."

They stood quietly a long time, side by side. The twilight came creeping in from the edges of the forest and across the meadows on either side of the road. A sweet aroma of herbs lingered as a trace of scent that glided past in a sudden gust of wind.

"I understand that there's a lot to take in, but I wanted to tell you about your father, who met such a terrible fate. It wasn't easy for him, but I can tell you that Olga kept him informed about what you were doing. He knew that you were managing, where you were. I know that he searched on the internet for names and pictures of places, buildings, and rivers to try to create an image of your life. He kept Gunilla in the dark about all this. 'This is between Cissi and me,' he said."

The tears ran down her cheeks. The minister had taken a few steps back and she appreciated that. Heaviness and lightness were mixed. Sorrow, absence, and warmth likewise. The feeling of guilt was there too, and she understood that she would have to struggle not to let it crush her.

"There you have your father," said Pastor Nygren. "A person is not just one thing. But now you have to go back. We have to talk more, I have things to tell you. Nice things. But first we have to pray together."

"I . . ." Cecilia stammered, before the minister raised his hand. "It doesn't matter what you believe, just lower your eyes. We will pray for Rune Karlsson and I want us to stand here united. Think about your father, take Rune to you, that will go a long way. We will help him along the way."

The minister prayed silently, she only saw his lips moving, how the prayer sounded she would never know, and that didn't matter. She closed her eyes and created her own images. When she opened her eyes she looked out over the meadow by the side of the road. There he stood with the net in hand and his happiest smile.

They said goodbye on the farmyard. The minister squeezed into the car, a fairly new Volvo. From what she'd understood Brundin had arranged for an old acquaintance who offered transport. The chauffeur raised his hand in greeting. He had not left his place but instead stayed in the car, listening to the radio or an audiobook on his earphones.

The car bumped away on the poorly maintained road. Cecilia took a few hesitant steps before she started walking faster and then finally ran. The back end of the Volvo was still visible, the driver drove carefully, avoiding the worst potholes. Cecilia kept running. Perhaps she could catch up. Perhaps a glance in the rearview mirror would get him to stop. The feeling that she must hear the minister's voice again was growing ever stronger, she was unsure why, but it was like a nightmare, not getting there. Everything was threatened, lost. He must stay here awhile! After a hundred meters she understood that this would not happen and she stopped, leaned forward, panting.

The mosquitoes swarmed around her sweaty face. The emptiness inside her was pulsing. Her childhood was over. Her father was dead. There was nothing to say, she hadn't said everything in time, now it was too late. Olga was gone. The minister had done his part, he was now headed to his home and his bed. He had truly looked tired.

But despite all the emotions that had been stirred up, Cecilia was happy about the visit. Pastor Nygren had proved himself as good as Olga had said. Perhaps he should bury Rune? She regretted that she hadn't asked. When she had collected herself a little the phone rang. Unknown number, the display said. She answered. Perhaps it was the minister who wanted to add something.

"Hi, I'm so sorry. So damned awful."

"How did you know?"

"Rumors spread quickly on the island," said Adrian, but without the customary nonchalance. "I wanted to be in touch, I understand that you're sad. You probably think that I'm mad as hell?"

She let the question hang in the air, unclear about what it meant, what he wanted.

"Let's wipe the slate clean on all this."

I've tricked him out of a fortune and he wants to wipe the slate clean, she thought, perplexed and speechless.

"I understand," Adrian continued, but did not explain what he understood. "I have enough to get by, and the only thing I want is for us to be friends. We've learned a lesson, haven't we? Taken a few hits but now it's time to move on. Can we meet?"

"Not a good idea," she managed to say.

"Maybe tomorrow, then I have to fly to Hamburg for a couple of days. I want to see you."

"Why?"

"We haven't exhausted all the possibilities," he said, making it sound like a negotiation about a deal where despite great opposition it might still be possible to come to an agreement.

"I don't think there's any point," she said, and the wimpy response annoyed her, but it tallied with the state of mind she found herself in. Adrian had been there since childhood. Now he called. It felt as if, even though he'd often been an asshole, he had always been near her.

"Come over tomorrow morning," he said.

"I don't think so," she said again.

"We have to move on."

In a way she agreed mostly because there was no other alternative, stopping and staying in the same spot had never been her thing. Not his either.

"Come about ten, okay?" He clicked off the call without awaiting her response.

She was met by the vacuum cleaner in the hall. Blixten had cleaned in the kitchen, put things away and wiped down the counter. It smelled of cleanser.

"Therapy," he said, taking the word from her mouth. "How are you? You look completely wiped out. What was he like, the preacher?"

"Good," she said, sitting down at the kitchen table.

"Have you talked with your mother?"

She shook her head, it hadn't struck her at all that she, or Gunilla, should have been in touch with each other.

"Adrian wants to see me tomorrow," she said.

"Forget about him, he just wants to mess with you, exploit that your father is gone," said Blixten, and a streak of worry in his voice reflected what she herself felt. She did not have control over herself, others were determining the course.

"I'll have to see," she said, unwilling to tell him what Adrian had said about wiping the slate clean. That was such an abnormal reaction for a resentful person like Adrian, and the fact was of course that she had stolen millions and burned down his garage. "I'll have a glass of your whiskey and then I'm going to bed," she said, and was grateful that he kept what he was thinking and feeling to himself.

"Rune is dead," she said, as if to soften what Blixten must fear, that she was going away.

Forty

"Talk," said Edvard, giving Ann a glance, as if to say *Keep your mouth shut.* "You said you had something to present, something about Stefansson."

The One and Only Robban nodded twice, heavy and meditatively, as if he had meticulously thought about a complicated question and come to a result. Or else it was simply the seriousness in Edvard's voice that made him apparently compliant. *Willing to cooperate,* thought Ann, who was sitting away from them, leaning against the wall in the sun porch, a distanced presence that was designated as a compromise. Edvard and Robban sat at the table with the mosaic top that Edvard had bought at an auction in Österbybruk. They each had a beer in front of them, anything else would have been unthinkable. The dramaturgy in Robban's life required a grip on a bottle or can when important issues were to be discussed. When Edvard set down the bottle, Robban suspiciously studied the label, as the beer was a nondescript English IPA, and made a face to mark that it was okay, but preferably shouldn't be repeated.

"Blixten came to me, it must have been a fortnight after Stefansson disappeared. He was loaded and it was a marvel that he missed the base of the sundial when he drove up on the yard. Then he had an old Audi that he wrecked later. Seriously tanked, if I may say so."

Robban raised the bottle to his mouth and drank.

"Blixten is maybe my best friend. He *is* my best friend."

How many can there be? thought Ann, and it was as if Robban heard her unexpressed question. "I don't have many," he said, finishing the beer in one drag. Edvard got up immediately and returned with a can of Norrlands, God knows where he found it.

"He was drunk and crying, blubbering about Cissi. He'd seen her with Stefansson in the boat that day, but didn't want to say anything to the police, that Brundin. We know him. We're a little . . ."

"What did he see?" Edvard's question cut through the room. Robban popped open the beer. Smiled broadly.

"He saw them go ashore on an island north of Gällfjärden. It was quite a while before he saw the plastic rowboat again and then there was only one person in the boat."

"How drunk was Blixten?" Edvard asked.

"Tanked, like I said, but he wasn't lying, I know that. We know each other that well."

"And you're only telling this now?"

The One and Only turned his head and observed Ann. "I had nothing against Stefansson actually, even though he was one of those rich bastards who sail along in life, never have to worry about putting food on the table."

"But you didn't want to send Cecilia to prison," Ann observed.

They looked at each other. "This is an island," he said at last.

"Another thing," said Edvard, and Ann understood that now he would squeeze out the actual purpose for Robban's late visit. "Rune talked on a bit before he died, a lot of it was hard to hear or understand, but there was one word that I've wondered about." He raised his beer can to feel if there was any left.

"What is that?" said Robban.

" '*Ballga*,' " said Edvard, drinking up the last of it.

"*Ballga*," Robban repeated.

"What I understood is he wanted to tell that he'd hidden something, a bag maybe, and that was in a '*ballga*.' "

Ann nodded. "I understood it that way too. Something that had to do with Stefansson. He also called his wife a black widow."

"A female who after impregnation eats up the male," said Robban. "*Ballga*," he said a second time, savoring the word.

"Do you recognize it?" Edvard asked. "It sounds like dialect, and I thought that you . . ."

"No, not directly," said Robban. "He hid something. What was it?"

Forty-One

He was bewilderingly like his father, Verner, sitting there by the raspberry patch. There was a bowl by his feet. The plastic chair which had once
been white was now more a shade of gray. The greeting he condescended
to give her was also Verner-like, a good-natured nod.

Cecilia got out of the car, but then just stood there. She took a quick
look at what had once been the garage. The remnants of fire had been removed, only a black patch remained.

"It's European red," he said.

She smiled in response, unsure of what he meant. He liked that: being
ambiguous.

"The raspberry variety is called that. Mother told me. She knew about
that sort of thing. This year there are more than enough."

"Are you going to make jam?"

He laughed heartily, aware of the absurdity of him making raspberry jam. "I eat them with cultured milk. You can take some. There's enough and to spare."

He tossed a few berries in the bowl by his feet, looked at her, suddenly serious. "How are you doing? How is Gunilla doing?"

"She's grieving, of course," said Cecilia, and the sarcasm certainly didn't escape him.

"She killed him, huh?"

"Self-defense, she says, and that may well be right."

"In cold blood," he said, seeming to savor the words.

Why am I standing here talking with a man that I despise? Did she say that out loud?

"You don't despise me. I want you," said Adrian. "Like before, but better."

Her tongue felt as if she had gorged herself on mayonnaise. *Now he'll say that he's changed,* she thought, and discovered yet another little plastic pail filled to the brim with raspberries.

"I'm a different person," he said.

She went up to the pail of raspberries, took a handful and stuffed it in her mouth. There was a time when she was terrified of raspberry worms, but no longer. "Take the whole thing," he said. "Mother would have wanted that. But I want to keep a few."

"Five million," she said, letting the raspberries work. "You can keep five million."

He laughed, looking at her as if he appreciated her sense of humor, but she didn't let herself be fooled. He was clever about such things. Make conversation, spin nets.

"Last night, when the rain and the thunder came, I was afraid. Really fucking afraid, do you understand? That has probably never happened before. You know in the Philippines it can thunder so the house shakes. And the lightning."

He got up but remained standing with arms hanging, giving a powerless expression.

"It probably wasn't the thunder you were afraid of, right?"

She looked around for a chair. There was a stool over by the currant bush. She went there, sat down. It felt good. The rain had released the aromas.

"I think it's time to take off," he said. "I've packed what I want to keep, there are half a dozen boxes. That will fit in the car."

He took out a pack of Winstons and matches, but made no show of lighting a cigarette.

"And a couple of boxes for you too, the sort of thing Mother talked about. Then you can take the books you want. You do read, or have you stopped doing that?"

"I like to read," she said. She pulled off a couple of wrinkly currants and put them in her mouth, uncertain how she should take his considerate words. He wasn't even looking at her, otherwise it had always been an attack from his side. Now he was talking to the sky, turned toward the house, looked at the cigarette pack as if he had a hard time deciding, to smoke or not.

"So you're going to sell?"

"No," he said, tapping out a cigarette and lighting it. "I didn't smoke as much when you were gone. No, I'm not going to sell. There are so many people on the island anyway."

He took a pleasurable puff. "Here," he said, tossing the box of matches in a wide arc to her. She caught it with her left hand, which made him smile. "Fifteen points," he said.

"Once you've taken away the books and such, set fire to the piece of shit."

"The house?"

He nodded. "I don't want to see it anymore. I think they'll understand." She understood that he meant Olga and Verner. "I didn't become what they believed, whatever that was, they didn't say, never a suggestion of what I should study or anything."

"How nice," said Cecilia. "I see, you're packing a few boxes in the car, and then what?"

"We'll drive to Italy. You have to check on the house you've inherited. There I'll drop off the boxes, go to London, Singapore, or Manila, arrange a few things, come back. Then we can drink wine."

She couldn't laugh, not even smile at his talk.

"I know that you want to get away from here again. You hate your mother, don't you?"

It was typical of Adrian to overlook Blixten. He wasn't part of the calculations and that annoyed her but also involved a temptation. And not only Blixten was counted out, the whole island with all its connections could fade away. Like herself Adrian had the capacity to rationalize, "walk over dead bodies," as some would perhaps put it. He was so sure of himself, convinced that his analysis of what she wanted or didn't want was correct. He formatted his surroundings, she'd seen that, it was that ability that made him successful, and made her a competent teammate in his eyes.

They were sitting a few meters from each other, separated by the berry bushes. There was August heat, horseflies in the air, and she would not be surprised if he had fresh crayfish in the refrigerator, purchased for a last meal at Solhem before everything would be set on fire.

"I can't go anywhere," she said. "Travel ban according to the police."

"Is it Brundin?"

She nodded. "He's sure that I murdered Casper."

"He should forget about that. Who cares now?"

"Not everyone has such a lighthearted view of justice," she said.

They looked at one another, assessed what had been said, how much had real substance or was simply loose talk that concealed something else.

Forty-Two

He felt dirty in a way that he never had before. Dirty inside. What were his words worth? Nothing. There was no other conclusion to draw.

"What do you think?" said Jens Thörn, but Blixten understood that it was not really a question, more an attempt to break through the massive wall of reluctance and bitterness that he must be projecting.

He took a few steps away, looking out over the parcel closest to the Man from Skåne's residence. It was cleared, beautiful in a way that perhaps only he was capable of seeing. Beautiful for a few days. Like the lawn there at home when it was freshly cut and before the tufts of various weeds started to sprawl.

"Let sheep loose here," he repeated for the third time, even though he knew that it was meaningless. Thörn had decided. "A lot of aspen is going to come up. For that reason sheep are best."

"Highland cattle would be beautiful here," Thörn said. "Then you could see them from the house. I like the view of those shaggy animals, they look like prehistoric creatures, you can get the illusion of . . ." He swallowed the rest of the sentence, but now braced himself. "The sheep can go down toward the meadows."

"It's not about your fucking view, but instead about what view the animals like. It's too damp on the meadows, Highland tolerate that, but sheep don't like it at all," Blixten argued. "And tall grass grows on the meadows, better for cattle."

"I think we'll move ahead as planned," the landowner said, smiling.

Perhaps it was the smile that caused Blixten's outburst. "Are you blind?! Don't you see what grows here? It's blackthorn and rose-hip thickets." He threw out his hand toward the parcel before them. For the first time he let out the growing fury.

"What do you mean? I love the blackthorn when it blossoms, like a white sea."

"Don't you understand, those are different types of grazing! And the blackthorn is going to take over everything."

Thörn smiled. "I think you take it personally."

"Personally?" Blixten shook his head. He took a few steps, turned around toward Thörn. "You can take your fields and stuff them," he said, quietly and calmly as if he had proposed a household cold remedy. "Personally? Are you completely nuts?"

For the first time he truly observed Thörn. Before he had hardly registered him, listened, nodded, and continued working. Now he saw the tight facial features in the oblong face, the bushy eyebrows and the narrow lips around an overly large mouth. The mask of forced folksiness, which only tolerably concealed the smugly superior manner, perhaps a result of the years at some academic department in Lund, struck him completely. Thörn quite simply looked mean. The teeth discolored by smoking seemed to want to chomp down on Blixten's throat.

The transformation made it easier for Blixten, who without another word turned on his heels and walked away. "Hello!" Thörn shouted, but Blixten trudged on, got in the car, and drove away. Even though it was tempting he did not look back. He didn't even give the cleared fields a glance, but instead stared straight ahead, firmly resolved never to return again.

This of course would be the end of their cooperation. That morning Blixten had calculated and added up how much Thörn owed him. The bill he submitted would probably be paid, but there was a lot of work that remained, a good bit into autumn he had counted on. He would lose tens of thousands of kronor, he understood that.

It was not surprising that Cecilia had left the house; her car was gone. She had mentioned something about a visit to the bank, papers that weren't in order, signatures that were needed. It sounded a little strange, she could manage her bank errands by computer, couldn't she? Maybe she was on a visit to her parental home, but hadn't wanted to say that considering her previous sullen attitude? No, Blixten continued reasoning with himself, that wasn't likely. From what he could understand she didn't want to see her mother. "Never again," she'd said, and he had taken that for what it was, an emotion for the moment, in due time perhaps things would change. She had changed her opinion many times during the short time they'd been in contact. Her father, who had been an object of hatred, she now presented in another light. She had talked about their outings together in nature as one of her best memories from childhood. Blixten also believed the talk with the minister from Öregrund had changed her mindset.

"Fuck that," he exclaimed, getting out of the car. It felt as if everything was swaying. What would he do now when the work with Thörn was no longer relevant? Never before had he left a job in that way. Thörn would surely spread the word that Blixten was unreliable and moody, but such rumors didn't worry him. Thörn was an outsider, with a dialect besides that stood out as a parody. Blixten was born on the island, a known entity, admittedly a little unsteady sometimes, but when it came to clearing pastures, forest, and coastal meadows he had a solid reputation, he knew that. That was what he lived on, both economically and mentally. There was also, despite hard words and sometimes scorn, a widespread tolerance among Gräsö residents when it came to the natives' behavior and life choices. They all had a history, many times interlaced with other local residents, they all had problems to varying degrees, they all had a relative or good friend who over time had been a "little shaky," as Blixten's mother used to put it. Blixten didn't deviate, he blended in.

Thörn on the other hand would not find any mercy in the general opinion, Blixten was convinced of that. An intruder who didn't understand to let the right animals out on the right pastures.

Blixten sat down on the garden chair. His chain-saw pants smelled of fuel, chain oil, and sawdust. The worry, and even a touch of shame, about having left a job he'd promised to perform had subsided, and was replaced by a feeling of righteousness and pride. He was a professional who could speak up. He viewed the powerful fists that passively lay on the table before him, turned them, observed the palms where the lines that ran a little back and forth could show a person's future fate and longevity, according to what was said anyway.

He waited for Cecilia. She was his future fate. The decisions she made would provide the direction. Where could she be? He hoped that she'd taken the ferry to Öregrund, opened a bank account, or done something else forward-looking. Had she really embezzled twenty million while he was half asleep? He tried to imagine what a fraction of that sum would mean for himself. A few hundred thousand, maybe half a million, that would go a long way.

Maybe she'd gone to the mainland to shop for food and wine? He wondered whether he should call, but was reluctant to be so intrusive. He must learn not to be so clingy. She needed freedom of movement, he'd understood that already when they were in their teens. Wait, he told himself.

The phone vibrated on the table. It was the One and Only Robban. Blixten answered after a moment's hesitation.

"How the hell are you? Are you working?"

Blixten laughed. He could talk about Thörn, grazing lands, and sheep to someone who understood.

"Are you drunk?"

"Maybe that would be a good idea," said Blixten.

"Forget about that," said Robban. "I'm on my way. Want to check on something. Your grandfather was a blacksmith, wasn't he? Is he still alive?"

"How's that?"

"I know that he was an asshole and not that nice to . . ."

"Why are you asking?"

"Can we go there? Does he still live above the harbor somewhere? I checked on the internet but he wasn't there, and the hell if I remember where he lived."

"I think he still lives there," said Blixten. It was many years since he'd seen the old man. He had no desire to do that again. He'd seen him in Öregrund, outside the liquor store or on a bench down in the harbor, but he always avoided his grandfather.

"He was a pretty capable blacksmith, wasn't he?"

A capable blacksmith, sure, but a drunk and a tyrant too.

"He must be in his eighties," said Robban. "I'll pick you up, if you're drinking, then we'll drive over." The eagerness in his voice revealed that he would not accept a "no."

"My old lady is going to murder me," said Blixten.

"I know that it was hell for her but she doesn't need to find out," said Robban, and his voice suddenly sounded tender. "I mean, who would tell her?"

"I hate him."

"I know," said Robban. "But you haven't just inherited the thirst for liquor from him but also the touch. Do you understand? The touch. It's what . . ."

"I understand," said Blixten.

Nils Oskar Lindberg hated life, but himself even more; that was how he summarized his existence. The self-hatred was unquenchable. On the sideboard in the old parlor were three portrait photos depicting his children in their early teens. All dressed up, with serious gazes directed right into the camera lens, perhaps taken in connection with confirmation or, even more likely, graduation from primary school.

He hadn't seen them in many years. The pictures stared toward him as a reminder of the hatred. He stood before the sideboard like a shame-filled defendant before a courtroom railing. Daily he put himself on trial. Before his eightieth birthday he had written letters to them. In similar terms. The invitation for coffee and cake, envelopes addressed and stamped, but they never reached the mailbox. When he was dead they would be found in a drawer where over the years a good deal of scrap had been collected. There was no self-pity left, that had disappeared decades ago. There was no pride left. What remained was a physical machinery that refused to give up, which struck back all attempts at decomposition and death. Nils Oskar had always been a prime specimen, and despite smoking for seventy years, dark spirits for almost as long, and long periods of heavy, repetitive work.

There were those who considered him an eccentric, a bit of an attraction, that they could point out in the summer throng down by the square and the harbor. "One of the last," they said, and it was often uncertain what that might mean, but summer residents and temporary visitors happily soaked up the legends.

He rarely spoke, he never raised his voice, but instead managed his chores and contacts with the outside world, which primarily concerned visits to the supermarket and the state liquor store, with balanced movements and a stoic calm. Some thought that he was senile, or in any event brought into disorder somewhat by age when it came to the ability to understand and express himself. Nothing could be more incorrect. Like his body, his intellect had avoided the abrasive tooth of time. In reality he felt all the wiser and more lucid, the longer the years passed. That was why many times he chose silence in his sparse contacts with others. Once there had been a neighbor who had enticed him to talk and even laughter, but that time was over. The neighbor had been dead for several years. Nils Oskar took care of the grave, the only urgent chore he had, besides feeding himself and raising the flag on flag days.

The One and Only Robban and Blixten Lindberg left the car in the parking lot right by the state liquor store. Robban went inside and bought a few bottles before they walked the short stretch to the old man's house. Blixten took the lead but soon it was Robban who took command. "Now I remember," he said. "I was here many years ago." The house was idyllic, low, covered with brick and adorned with a stubby chimney, a green-painted door, and small windows toward the alley. *It was a fisherman's residence,* thought Blixten. Back then poverty, now a motif for a postcard and attractive for a summer visitor.

Robban knocked on the door; there did not appear to be a doorbell. Blixten waited by the gate. No response. Blixten felt almost relieved, even though against his will he was a little curious about how his grandfather would behave.

"Let's look around a little," said Robban. "He probably doesn't go far."

"I think I know where he is," said Blixten. "He used to sit outside the small boat harbor and the Strand Hotel."

They found him on a bench. He was looking out over the water toward Gräsö, the island that had seen him born almost exactly ninety years ago. He would not be writing any invitations before that anniversary.

The old man was wearing a hat, not a silly light summer hat, one of those that the swimmers strutted around in, no, it was a dingy, gray worn thing. Blixten thought he recognized it from far away.

"That's him," said Blixten, pointing. He stopped, it was still not too late to back out. "Here," said Robban, giving him the bag with the bottles. "I'll go up and talk, then you can follow after a while. I can say that you've been at the liquor store."

Blixten shook his head, even though he would really like to have a moment to himself, not least to be on the lookout for Cecilia, but the clinking from the bottles in the bag made him worried. He didn't trust himself. Maybe he would be tempted to step away to take a sip or two.

"I'll come along," he said.

"Nils Oskar," said Robban. The old man turned around. He was the same, as if sculpted by the landscape and the work he'd done for all that time, the powerful features of his face were unaffected by the passage of the years, the bushy mustache was even more walrus-like than Blixten recalled, the smith's hands rested laced on his lap as if they had surprised him in prayer.

"Do you recognize me?" said Robban. "Edvin Olsson in Svartbäck was my grandfather. We met at his house. The two of you socialized quite a bit."

Nils Oskar nodded but maintained the dismissive facial expression which for decades confirmed his lack of popularity. "Quite a bit? A whole life. He was my only friend. And who are you?"

"I'm your grandson," said Blixten. He had a hard time putting the word "grandfather" in his mouth, much less saying the name of the blacksmith's daughter.

Another nod and a barely noticeable quiver at the corner of his mouth which could be interpreted as a smile. "They ought to ban those sea mopeds," he said. His voice too had preserved its resonance. Blixten understood immediately what Nils Oskar meant. The noise from the water was noticeable.

"Have you come to bring me to justice?"

"What are you talking about?" said Blixten, who understood perfectly well what the old man meant.

"We've come because you were a blacksmith," said Robban.

Nils Oskar turned his head with an incredulous expression.

"I am a blacksmith," the old man said. "The occupation of blacksmith isn't something you put on and take off as it suits you."

Robban started talking about some childhood memories, how he and his grandfather visited Nils Oskar when he was still living on the island. It was about the smithy and forging, how as a child he'd been impressed by the fire and the weight of the materials, but also the force in Nils Oskar's arms when seemingly unaffected he swung his tools. Blixten understood that this was a warm-up, he wanted to get the old man in a good mood, guide his thoughts to the past. Whether that had an effect was hard to say, but Nils Oskar did not tell them to go to hell anyway.

"There's a word that I've been wondering about," Robban continued. "I think it has to do with blacksmithing."

"I see," said Nils Oskar, unexpectedly docile.

"It's Gräsö dialect."

"I see, that kind of shit," the old man said. "I'm on a tape recording, an old geezer and an old lady drove around and recorded. They were probably at Svartbäck-Edvin's place too, but he said flat-out no and drove the riffraff away. They probably came from some museum. That's where I belong. I'm turning ninety next week."

He looked at Blixten as if he was expecting a comment from his only grandchild, an exclamation of surprise. Or even expectation, unclear about what. That they should celebrate something together, an anniversary, stood out as macabre considering the family history.

"If I say *ballga,* what do you think about?"

Nils Oskar grinned, his mustache bobbed and his otherwise dull eyes glistened. "So much shit," he said. "Have you been reading a book?"

Robban didn't say anything. Blixten thought that was a good tactic. The old man had always loved to jawbone.

"Ninety," he said. "Nineteen twenty-nine. Then there was a depression. But there was herring. And work for my old man. I grew up in a smithy."

"That's why I'm asking you," said Robban.

"I got black as soot. Sometimes glowing red, but most often black." He pulled his cheeks together in a grin, like a poorly executed smile. "I'm aiming for a hundred. The doctor said that it would surely work out if I just stopped with the strong stuff. And I've done that, take a clear shot every morning but then nothing more. I can feel it."

He struck the stone pavement with his cane.

"I recognized you so clearly. You're called Blixten now, I know that, people talk, and that's probably good," said Nils Oskar. He took in air through the compressed lips, as if he lacked oxygen, and then forced the air out with his lips formed as if for a kiss. It was a peculiarity, a kind of tic Blixten recognized so well from his childhood, how his grandfather, using words less and less, instead produced sounds and expressions that astounded his surroundings, to then explode in unpredictable tirades of oaths and curses.

"You clear up on the fields, I've understood," he continued. "That damned sedge is the worst, isn't it? Have you seen the smithy I'm talking about? It's still there, they say. Equipped, rescued for the outside world, they say."

Blixten nodded, against his will moved by the seriousness in his grandfather's eyes. Who "they" were he didn't know, but it was obvious that Nils Oskar kept himself informed about what was happening on the island. "But it doesn't matter," the old man concluded. "All shit has to fall apart in the end."

Yes, Blixten had seen the smithy as recently as a couple of months before. It was sure enough equipped. He had the idea that Rune Karlsson had been involved in the work. It was perhaps the island's oldest farm smithy, as a sign maintained. The historical society was visiting and Blixten had taken the opportunity to tag along on the group's visit. He hadn't said a word about having hung out there as a child, that he knew the history of the smithy very well, and that he had learned to despise the last blacksmith. A few in the society knew of course that he was related to the last blacksmith, but kept that to themselves.

"*Ballga*," Robban repeated.

"You need air," said the old blacksmith.

Suddenly Blixten understood. He'd heard the word, of course he'd heard it!

"You ought to know that," said Nils Oskar, as if he'd read Blixten's thoughts. "You got to work it."

"The bellows," said Robban. The old man smiled. They were all in agreement.

One question remained, a very reasonable one, but Nils Oskar never asked why Robban was so interested in that particular word in the Gräsö dialect.

They left him sitting on the bench with a view of the island. It was difficult to figure everything out, Blixten thought, and he suspected that Robban felt the same.

"That was maybe the last time," said Blixten.

"Are you going to tell your mother that we've been here?"

"I don't know." Blixten knew very well that he would never utter a word about their visit.

On the ferry crossing they sat silently to start with, but then started talking at the same time, as if they had to get something urgent out before they reached the island. Robban was the one who took priority to continue.

"I wonder what that old cop woman has on her mind? She used Edvard to bring me over late last night simply to ask about an old Gräsö word. There's something shady about this. Do you know what she's thinking?"

"Not a clue," said Blixten.

"I have to ask," said Robban. "You're my buddy, my comrade on the journey. Did you really see Cissi on the strait that day? I mean, did she kill Stefansson? I don't really care about that, I mean, really, a guy from Djursholm. We have other things to think about. I won't say a word to anyone."

"Of course you will, you love to jabber, especially with the cop. But, but, maybe I saw her, maybe I was dreaming."

"You want her, you always have," Robban observed. "Stefansson will have to cough up."

"He's dead."

"Did Cissi say that?"

"Shut up now," said Blixten, who wanted to tell Robban about Italy but had lost the thread.

Forty-Three

Ann Lindell could not keep from smiling to herself when she saw the two men get out of the car. It was an ambiguous smile, however. She felt it in her body as an absence, that thing with context and common memories she'd always had so much trouble with. It was as if life has to start over, again and again, and where the painful thing was to leave places, people, and relationships, often for good.

That was the one side, staggering ahead in life, but if you flipped the coin there was an inner warmth, which passed like a shiver through the body, admittedly far from what it once was, but still: We belong together, I exist here and now, for me and for others. There's still life. Still hope. A few steps more to let loose a little of the hope that after all there was a spark of light to brighten the future. A view over a future landscape.

She had often needed help; there was her old boss Ottosson, her colleagues Berglund and Sammy Nilsson, invaluable for supporting her, sometimes literally getting her on her feet. There was Edvard, and Viola too, the old Gräsö woman whose upstairs he came to rent and then inherit, and who meant so much for Ann and her self-esteem. Like no one else Viola had filled the fifty-years-younger Ann with knowledge and wisdom. Erik was there obviously, perhaps not as often as when he was little, but she saw that as a healthy sign. Her wise son, whose understanding she also feared, that one day when the loyalty broke he would step aside, say what he really felt and thought. She didn't want to think that way, but she didn't believe she had given him everything he needed, was afraid that the insignificant crack between them today would expand to an abyss.

The move from Uppsala to the little village outside Gimo, away from toiling as a police detective to the job at the creamery, Erik's natural and apparently good-natured adaptation to new circumstances, and not least the increasingly stable relationship with Edvard, everything had worked together to a new life, organized life, loving life. She was grateful to those around her, but also to herself. She patted herself on the back more and more often. That was new.

Added to this was the island of Gräsö, a new landscape but above all new acquaintances. Two of them were now standing in the farmyard, talking intently with each other over the roof of the car, taking a few steps, then stopping as if they'd forgotten where they were, that they had an errand. The One and Only Robban was the one who had the initiative, while Blixten Lindberg ducked and countered, that was how she understood the shadowboxing. Why had they come? Curiosity got the upper hand and she revealed her position by knocking on the kitchen window. They looked up. Robban caught sight of her first.

"The new Viola," he said as she stepped out on the front stoop in front of the porch. "She used to stand there, hidden behind the geraniums. I remember when I came here as a boy to buy eggs."

Blixten nodded. "I remember too," he said. "She could be stern, but sometimes you got juice and rolls, always cardamom rolls, do you remember?"

I have to get chickens, thought Ann, and it was as if the tears threatened to come from that thought. She turned on her heels. "I'll make some coffee," she said with her back to the men and disappeared inside.

Robban and Blixten told her about their visit in Öregrund, and Ann Lindell got a little family history along with it. She didn't know about Blixten's family, other than that his mother lived a little farther north on the island. His grandfather was unknown to her.

"He was sure of himself, and he ought to know," said Robban. " 'Ballga' means 'bellows.' Rune Karlsson probably fell back on his childhood dialect, I'm sure his father and grandfather would have used that word."

"We have to call Brundin," said Ann.

"Shouldn't we go up to Karlsson's and check?" said Blixten. "The smithy is located so that we can get there without the car being seen. If Gunilla is even home."

"No, this is a police matter," Ann decided. They probably heard in her voice that there was nothing to discuss, because both men nodded.

"Where's Cecilia?"

"I don't really know," said Blixten.

"Has she split?" asked Robban, who wasn't known for his tact.

Blixten shook his head. "I don't think so, she's going to stay on the island." His depressed appearance suggested something else.

Maybe just as well if she disappeared, thought Ann, but said something else. "No, she's going to bury her father first."

"Yes, it's strange how that can go," said Blixten, but didn't explain further. Was it Rune's fate to be shot by his own wife he meant, or was it the fact that Cecilia developed a conciliatory side with respect to her previously so despised father?

"It's easy to love someone who's on the skids or even dead," said Robban.

"She knows something that we don't know," said Blixten.

"Yes, what happened when Stefansson disappeared," said Robban. "And she's never going to reveal that."

Ann wanted to tell them what Cecilia had said about the butterflies but perhaps that was known to the two of them. She didn't want to seem sentimental either, act as a kind of spokeswoman or advocate, and not for anyone in the Karlsson family. She knew that the events of life were more complicated than that. Absolute judgments were meaningless.

Instead she took out her phone and called Brundin. Robban got up and went to stand by the window and looked out. Blixten on the other hand watched her intensely, as if it were his future destiny that was being determined.

"*Ballga*," she said after the call. "Can you hide something in a bellows?" She had no concept of what it all looked like.

"It's possible," said Blixten.

"I've never been in a smithy," she said.

"Sooty and massive," said Robban. "And then the clang of metal."

"Hot," Blixten added. "I got to help my grandfather sometimes."

The two men started talking about incidents back in time, most of them associated with forging and blacksmiths, not necessarily what they themselves had experienced, sometimes it was episodes from decades ago, retold through generations of Gräsö islanders.

"Then he died," said Blixten. Robban shook his head. "He ran away from the old lady, yes, but he's alive. Lennart saw him at the auction."

"Is Lennart alive?"

"Brundin is coming," Ann interrupted the folkloristic tales. "He's in Snesslinge, so it won't take long. He should probably bring a colleague with him from Östhammar, so that may delay him."

Robban grinned. "I know who Uncle Brundin is visiting," he said, and Ann was uncertain whether he meant a known old customer of the police or a lover of Brundin. Blixten gave him a look as if to say: *Keep your mouth shut.* Ann was once again reminded of how ignorant she was about people's lives and doings in the area.

It was just past four before Brundin showed up together with Wiberg, the young trainee, and another uniformed colleague that Ann didn't recognize. They came in two cars. Good, thought Ann. Brundin looked almost embarrassed when she greeted Wiberg. His youth and innocent appearance stood out even clearer in comparison with his uniformed colleague, Ljung, at least thirty years older, who was burly and a bit on the fat side, and who smiled at Lindell.

"He'll learn," Brundin mumbled in passing, and Lindell understood that he meant Wiberg. "You have the chance to teach him," she said, and the previous sense of loss she'd felt returned. She would really have liked to be a police officer in these parts. What she missed was the collegiality and the excitement. Making cheese was one thing, and good enough, but a murder investigation excited her more.

They stood assembled on the farmyard. Ljung was the one who talked. He was evidently acquainted with Robban. Brundin took Ann aside.

"Gunilla Karlsson is at home. I called to check, said that we'd be coming over. I don't know if we actually have the right to snoop."

"Of course we do," said Ann. "A man was shot to death. Consider it a crime scene for the time being."

"Self-defense," said Brundin.

"We know so little about it," said Ann. "Can I . . . it would be nice to . . ."

He shook his head. "For me it's no problem, but for Gunilla Karlsson it surely would be. And for Wiberg it's important to show how it should work. We'll do it by the book. Only police officers, no posse from the area."

"It was Edvard and I who were there when Rune Karlsson died, we were the ones who heard him say the words."

"And we're grateful for that," said Brundin with a bland smile.

They took off after Blixten and Robban repeated what the old blacksmith had said. Lindell and the two connoisseurs of forging stayed behind.

"Damned exciting," said Robban.

"Keep quiet about this," said Lindell. "Don't spread it around." Robban simply smiled.

Blixten walked away a few steps, turned, and came back, as if he had a hard time deciding in what direction he should go.

"Let's go," he said.

"She's coming back, or maybe not," said the One and Only Robban. "You know how Cissi is. Maybe it's not meant that . . . I mean . . . look at it this way: You had some amazing days and nights with an amazing woman, awesome, isn't it? But we know that the good and the fine take to flight. Then you sit there on a damned stool in the kitchen and feed logs into the woodstove, confused as hell, as if it hadn't happened. Am I right?"

"That's just it," said Blixten. His face expressed a mixture of despair and surprise, as if he only fully realized in that moment how fragile his relationship to Cecilia Karlsson was. "And then there will be no letters, nothing. This time definitely not. Everything has been said."

"Letters? Who the hell sends letters?"

"Cissi did that a few times," said Blixten, "right after she went away. Then."

Lindell thought it was a dialogue worthy of a couple of country-western verses at home with Robban.

Forty-Four

Brundin was a little worried. He always was where women were concerned, approaching women, whether suspects, guilty or innocent didn't
matter. Alone probably went okay, but now he was coming with two colleagues in tow, as if he wasn't sufficient. A handshake perhaps. Wiberg
would surely be of no great help if anything were to flare up but Ljung was
experienced and sturdy. He rarely let himself be worried or impressed. An
ideal constable if he just didn't smile so damned much.

He was doing that now too. Quite unexpectedly he took command.

"I'm sorry about your loss," he said, seeming to overlook the fact that it
was the woman before him who had shot her own husband to death with
two arrows. He extended his hand and Gunilla Karlsson took it instinctively, but immediately appeared to have regretted it.

"Åke Ljung, from the police station in Östhammar," said Ljung. "And
this is Wiberg, a trainee, but you probably recognize him, such a charming
little lad, and Brundin needs no introduction, notorious everywhere."

Why is he talking so much? Brundin wondered, and realized at the same moment that his colleague was nervous, someone who otherwise never let himself be perturbed was trying to handle his own worry with empty talk. Gunilla Karlsson had that effect on many people, Brundin knew that from before, and it made him calm that Ljung was shaking somewhat.

"We have a few questions," said Brundin, "and we'd like to take a look around."

"I see," Gunilla Karlsson said evasively.

"It concerns the buildings around the farm," said Brundin, deliberately ambiguous. "But that's okay, right?"

"Why?"

"There may be connections that we've overlooked," Brundin continued. "There almost always are, and Ljung here, even though he's not especially charming, has a special talent."

What that talent consisted of he didn't say, but he was content with the formulation. *The archery lady can just as well wonder about that,* he thought.

They looked at each other for a few seconds before she granted her acceptance, surely aware that she didn't have any valid reason to deny them entry.

"I assume that all the sheds and outbuildings are unlocked," said Brundin.

"I'll be in the house if there's anything," Gunilla Karlsson said and left them. Wiberg looked jumpy, surely because of the tone in the conversation, while Ljung grinned. "Special talent," he said.

They immediately headed for the smithy, with Brundin in the lead. He knew very well where it was. There weren't many buildings on the island that he didn't know about.

It was a traditional smithy, if perhaps somewhat larger than most of the old farm smithies. It was in good condition, the tarp covering the roof seemed of recent vintage, windowsills and mullions were painted white and the windows newly caulked. Rune Karlsson had done his job.

The door was wooden and sturdy, barred with an iron hasp, anything else would have been strange. "*Ballga*," said Brundin. He and Ljung stared at the bellows while Wiberg's gaze wandered over the smithy's furnishings.

"It was powerful," said Ljung. They stood quietly, not to say solemnly, and observed the hearth and the bellows, which was mounted on the one side with a channel in toward the hearth. It still looked completely functional, with the mechanical arrangement intact, and was larger than he remembered. From what Brundin could tell the leather was not that old. "*Ballga*," he said again, as if it were a magic spell. He grasped the wooden rod that ran from the bellows and pumped. The wood creaked, a few sooty flakes flew up. He repeated the procedure. The bellows went to the bottom without any problem.

"What could that doohickey conceal?" said Ljung. He got down on his knees and inspected the bottom, a framework of sturdy timber. A year, 1892, was carved on the bottom plank, and a pair of letters.

"Maybe Rune's great-grandfather," said Brundin.

Ljung stuck his hand between the wooden frame and the brick foundation for the hearth, a space of perhaps ten centimeters. "There's something here," he said, turning his head and nodding at Brundin. "Plastic."

"Be careful," Brundin ordered quite unnecessarily. They both knew that was necessary if it was the case that the bellows concealed the answer to a person's disappearance and probable death.

"Shall we tear the whole thing apart?" Ljung asked. "We can disassemble the bellows itself, then we'll get at it better."

"No, go ahead," said Brundin. "If Rune did set something in there it should be possible to take it out."

"She's coming," said Wiberg. "The archer, I mean."

Brundin turned around. Sure enough, Gunilla Karlsson came walking across the brown-scorched grass. It struck him how youthful she still looked, even though one leg was obviously injured.

"What are you doing?" Her face was neutral, expressed no surprise, anger, or any other emotion.

A competitive person, Brundin thought. "We don't know," he said. "But Ljung thinks he's found something."

"The smithy," she said, with a kind of smile on her lips. "This was where Rune liked to be. It was probably here he hid his secrets."

"Wait," said Brundin, turned toward Ljung, who was still on his knees, or rather half lying down with his arm thrust behind the understructure of the bellows. His face was red from the exertion.

Brundin took out a camera, a handy little Japanese device. "I'm going to film," he said, giving Gunilla Karlsson an apologetic smile. "There are these kinds of regulations," he continued, giving the young Wiberg a look that meant he should hold back the comment he was about to make.

Brundin guided the camera in a wide arc around the smithy, capturing everything on video, stopped by Ljung and signaled with his free hand that it was time to take out whatever it might be.

Ljung was panting. "Damn but it's cramped," he said, sliding even closer.

"Maybe Wiberg," said Brundin.

Ljung adjusted the angle of his body; his face shiny with sweat testified to excitement. This was the treasure hunt of youth but for real, that was how Brundin interpreted it all, and he too felt the excitement. He gave Gunilla Karlsson a quick look. She looked just as neutral, but her body was tense, as if prepared to run. He would not be surprised if she conjured forth a bow and put an arrow in policeman Ljung's fat-furrowed neck.

The policeman carefully backed out of his position. In his hand he was holding a plastic bag. Brundin saw that it came from the grocery store in Öregrund. Gunilla took a breath and then let the air seep out through her nostrils. Brundin zoomed in and immortalized the foolishly smiling Ljung and his find.

"We'll stop here," said Brundin and completed the filming. "We'll take whatever it is to Östhammar."

"What's in the bag?" Gunilla asked.

"I'm sure you can guess better than I can," said Brundin.

She shrugged her shoulders and left the smithy. "Wait," said Brundin, now was when a decision must be made, he had understood that ever since

Ljung signaled a find under the bellows. She stopped. Brundin understood that she too was ready for a decision. One that would deprive her of liberty.

"You have to go with us," he said.

"Why?"

"So that we can look in the bag together."

Forty-Five

The knife blade told a few things: the sharp edge had torn apart a living organism, Casper Stefansson. How that happened in more detail was impossible to know but the remnants of blood spoke for themselves.

"It's undeniably his," said Friman, an otherwise truly incompetent crime technician, but who in this case could support himself on the statement from colleagues in the National Forensic Center in Linköping. Of the thousands of DNA profiles from unsolved crimes that were archived, there was no problem in establishing that it was Stefansson who had lost blood on that spring day four years ago.

The shaft told the rest: Gunilla Karlsson had been the one who performed the deed. Exactly when and where could not immediately be established, but in time the course of events had emerged. The investigating police and the prosecutor who was the leader of the preliminary investigation had not exactly been surprised by her story, they had heard and seen too much of it, but Gunilla Karlsson's exact account down to the slightest detail of what happened on that day in May had stood out as inhuman in its clinical coldness.

After Stefansson bled to death she dragged him down to the boat ("he'd put on a few kilos"), took a bathing suit out of a small backpack ("he probably thought I'd brought champagne"), and changed. In a couple of burlap bags she gathered stones from the shore. They would later serve as weights. "It takes surprisingly few stones to sink a person."

Once the corpse had been tipped overboard ("I actually read a verse"), with the sacks tied firmly around the body, she followed him down in the water. The backpack she had with her, there was the knife in a plastic bag and her clothes. "It took me thirty minutes to swim home to the dock."

Once there she had set the backpack on the dock and taken out the bag with the knife, uncertain where she should hide it. Just then her husband had come walking on the path from the house. She'd tossed the bag in the fishing boat, pushing it in under a thwart between a grapnel and a few other things that always littered the boat bottom.

When Rune Karlsson stepped out on the dock he looked completely perplexed.

"I took a long walk, but decided to swim home," she had said. "I tested the new bathing suit." She walked up the path, took the backpack, and left him, aware that he was watching her, and that he liked what he saw, that he so much still wanted to caress that body, but that he was completely defenseless before the woman he had loved for decades. She knew all this and that granted her a certain satisfaction, but also a fair amount of irritation and impatience.

"What do you mean?" Brundin had asked. "Impatience?" He had to guess at the answer.

"Why?" the policeman continued.

"Casper betrayed me. We were doing fine, but he chose Cecilia. She was the one he was going away with."

Blixten Lindberg had also contributed. As the only witness, albeit at a long distance, he had contributed to a reconstruction. Under guard Gunilla

Karlsson got to drive the motorboat and step ashore. Blixten had observed it all from the position where he'd stood four years earlier when he peered over Gällfjärden, always curious about who was approaching.

"They're alike," he simply said. "Like berries. Frightening."

Brundin, who was standing closest, understood immediately what he meant.

"Do you draw any conclusions for your own account?"

Blixten laughed. Didn't he smell a little of alcohol, Brundin?

"You sound like a fucking book," he said. "Yes, maybe it was Gunilla I saw. It probably was."

"She's coming home from Italy for the trial. She's no doubt comfortable in Stefansson's house," said Brundin. "It's located high up with a view of the vineyards. I've talked with her a bit. She sounds calm, but hasn't asked a single thing about her mother. Cecilia is truly unfeeling."

"Home," said Blixten.